I0635472

The Book of Lost Spirits

By

Yun Johnson

A Peacock Manor Mystery

Dedication

To daydreamers,
to those who have ever felt lonely,
to the pets we must outlive,
to tiny cakes and owls and piano nocturnes and
campfires
and all who love creepy-cozy—
this book is dedicated to you.

Praise for The Book of Lost Spirits

"Beautiful, textured, and addictive...the novel makes for a stunner. Un-put-downable."—Prairies Book Review

"Evocative, compelling, and thought-provoking."—Midwest Book Review

"Johnson crafts a sweet, yet spooky story that allows the characters to complexly explore grief and trauma. By building on the conventions of the horror genre, the novel follows unique twists and turns that keep readers guessing. *The Book of Lost Spirits* offers a fresh take on a haunted house story, adding warmth and love to a classically scary genre."—Publisher's Weekly BookLife Prize

"Johnson's narrative adeptly intertwines the human condition with the inexplicable, crafting a beguiling prose that irresistibly ensnares the reader."—Literary Titan

"Powered by the lure of supernatural encounters and adventures, *The Book of Lost Spirits* thus introduces psychological encounters and growth opportunities rarely seen in an action-packed adventure such as this."—Diane Donovan, Senior Reviewer at The Midwest Book Review

"*The Book of Lost Spirits* is a fascinating and haunting tale that stays with you long after the final page."—Reader's Favorite

Acknowledgements

Infinite thanks to The Wild Rose Press, Lea Schizas, and Rhonda Penders for working so hard to make my dream come true. Your magic changed my story's life.

My deepest gratitude to Peter Senftleben, Andy Ross, Anna Bowles, and Nicola Hodgson. Your insight and inspiration shaped this manuscript to where it is today. Thank you for your guidance and encouragement starting from the very first cringe-worthy drafts.

At its heart, this story is about friendship. Thank you to Shari, Meghan, Kristen, Keri, Stef, Patty, Katie, and Alicia who always make me feel like I belong— ever since we met in elementary school. I am lucky you are all still in my life. May our text chain and girls' weekends that I always have to cancel on never end. Thank you for sticking by me.

Thank you, dear parents, parents-in-law, and siblings. You are there for me in ways no one else can.

Finally, to my husband, Kit, who makes me laugh all the way until the end of the day when we're trying to fall asleep, who believes in me more than I deserve, and who never wavers in his support, especially when I shrivel up in doubt—I love you with all my heart and soul and hope we can return together as ghosts to haunt each other for eternity.

Introduction

Day 146,600

At the beginning of every summer, a new family moves in, and at the end of every summer, a family moves out. Not everyone returns home.

I've been here for a very long time—hundreds of years. I slumber and I awaken, but all the while, I'm alone, learning about life and death. There is not much else for me to do.

Sometimes I terrify people. But mostly, I am trapped, and useless.

There are rumors about me in town. People whisper and gossip about darkness, lost souls, and hauntings. There are more truths than lies in the stories.

The engraved plaque at the top of the stairs says:
Peacock Manor.

I am a haunted house, named after the family who built me atop this grassy hill on this mountain of ghostly mist, cypress, and cedar.

I watch people come and go. Mostly, they go, and I am lonely, but I cannot change my destiny.

I will always be haunted and will carry on watching everyone I know turn to dust. This is my eternal fate.

As for the fate of those here for the summer—

There will be one who does not return.
There is always one who remains behind.

Chapter 1

Impossible Things

Rose has her reasons for wanting to find a ghost, even though the last time she saw one, someone *died*.

She leafs through the crumpled brochure about Peacock Manor, hoping the rumors are true. In more ways than one, she needs them to be. After all, the tourists are drawn to the house for the history, the local lore, the whispers.

Whispers of impossible things.

Of *The Book of Lost Spirits*.

Of disappearances.

The mountain road writhes and narrows, as if she were traveling up a dark river. A fingernail moon casts shadows on the craggy rocks, forming faces that stare back at her. She exhales onto the window and traces her name with a single finger: R-O-S-E. Rose Green. She may as well be named Tulip Blue. Or Daffodil Red. Yuck.

"Is this place really haunted? Are we close?" Rose asks as her mom steers into a hairpin turn.

Everyone in the car slants right, and she tips her head into her palm, having run out of daydreams hours ago: she already won the hearts of all the boys she could think of—real life and celebrity, then gave her thank-you speech accepting a prize for a talent she doesn't have, cheered on by all the friends a sixteen-year-old could want.

Reality check. She's never been in love and friends are lacking, but she intends to change all that this summer.

Anyone can take charge of their fate, right? She flutters her lips, blowing her milk-tea-colored hair out of her face. For years, it's been in a pixie cut, short and jagged. It suits her angled chin and cheekbones, and emphasizes her dainty lips that naturally frown.

Her mom's eyes flick to the rearview mirror.

"We're almost there. Right, Obsidian?" Mom asks, calling Dad by his ridiculous pen name. "Do you think the plumbing is modern?" she adds, taking one hand off the steering wheel to nervously twirl the small gold cross around her neck.

"Right. I'm sure they've updated it since the 17th century, darling," Dad reassures her.

Rose glances askew at him in the passenger seat reading *Wild Mushroom Foraging*, his latest whimsical hobby. His whimsy is why—every summer—the Greens rent a vacation home somewhere quirky and remote.

Remote, as in, she can scream her head off and nobody would hear her for miles.

June. July. August. That's a lot of screaming.

Dad bookmarks the page of poisonous toadstools. "Did you know that the original owners—the Peacocks—were famous ocean explorers? Treasure hunters who found half of the Pearl of Phoenix, *The Book of Lost Spirits*, the Abyss of Kiyama…"

"No learning on vacation, Dad. Plus, everyone and their grandpa knows that," Rose reminds him, keen to avoid being trapped in his road trip "did-you-knows." Dad loves details. He's hoping to be inspired by Peacock Manor's real-life details for his new book, a horror story about a supernatural child haunting an ancient property.

The next bumpy turn over a red, arched garden bridge deposits the Greens at the base of a grassy hill. Perched at the top is their magnificent house for the summer.

"Can you believe this place was still available?" Dad marvels.

Rose snorts. "Famous last words in every horror movie ever." She tilts forward for a look, nearly colliding with a gray spider that has hitched a ride with them. It's given up on weaving a web in the back dash and now dangles in front of her, hanging by an invisible thread, swaying as the car stops.

"You're not going to find any food in here, little guy," she tells it kindly, sweeping the spider up by its webbing even as it tries to scramble back up.

It reaches the scoop of her palm and—*ouch!*—it bites her. She resists shaking it off even as the welt stings. *I'd probably do the same if I were attacked by a giant.* With her free hand, she drags out her book-filled duffel bag, dumping it onto the driveway, and swings her half-asleep legs over it.

Rose stoops, bowing at the waist, and transfers her spider friend to a row of black petunias lining the base of the hill.

"May you have a better fate than being trapped in a car, sir. Good luck here," she says to it, and to herself. The arachnid scuttles into the small yellow dot where the ebony petals meet.

She examines the red bump near her thumb. The bite itches, but the spider isn't poisonous.

She hopes.

The edges of her shirt ripple in the night winds as she rights herself and inhales the unmistakable scent of alpine evergreens. Woodsy and minty. The tiny hairs on her arms stand on end, so she rubs off the chill and tilts her head as far back as it will go, mouth agog.

Peacock Manor.

The majestic mansion rises from its foundation of stone, set against jagged rocky peaks and a star-speckled sky.

Dad stands beside her and Mom, pointing out details their less-informed eyes miss.

"Curved roofs were built to repel evil spirits, who were thought to hate curves and only travel in straight lines. They'd slide right off those steep angles there," he says of the sloping green pagoda roof guarded by a golden sea dragon coiled on one of the curly eaves. "And did you know—red garden bridges like the one we crossed represent passageways between worlds, earthly and spiritual?"

His voice fades away as Rose collects her duffel and marches up the walking path carved into the hill, her sights fixed on the stained-glass windows—their brilliant jewel tones muddying at night into mustard and blood, olive and cobalt.

If the house is haunted, what will she find in the darkness? She yearns for the one thing only her wildest, most treacherous imaginings will allow: her sister.

But that's impossible. She's tried.

She folds over at the top of the hill, breathless. Her knuckles brush against a tulip-shaped urn brimming with pale moonflower, unfurled like white umbrellas. She tips forward, flaring her nostrils at the honeyed scent, and deciphers the dates etched in several languages on its pedestal:

1620.

"Whoa," she whispers. She loves old. Old has character. Old has *secrets*.

Secrets, born of denial and longing and shame. The longer they fester, the more they want to be discovered. She's counting on it.

The thought occurs to her briefly that everybody is a prisoner of their own secrets.

But Rose isn't thinking about what she's hiding, though. Her eyes are locked on a high upstairs window.

A window, where a luminous figure,
hazy like a moon behind clouds,
is gazing down
at *her*.

****

What—?! Rose inhales sharply.

She doesn't dare blink. She stumbles backward for a better view, but the mystery figure fades away near the highest pavilion, in a tower with an ocular window—a window with an infinite number of sides. Oops, Dad's lecture accidentally absorbed.

"Up there! Did you see?" She spins toward her parents, but they're deep in the back of the car unloading luggage, their backsides jutting out at her.

When she whips her head around again, the inexplicable light is gone. Vanished as abruptly as it appeared. She swallows her heart back down her throat, even as it continues to flutter like a captured bird.

Peacock Manor whispers to her, promising

tremendous possibilities, promising the change she seeks this summer. If any place hosts spirits from beyond, it would be a place like this.

Rose has her reasons for needing to find a ghost, even though the last time she saw one, her sister died.

Chapter 2

Twins and an Octopus Fountain

Grandma is a twin, Mom has a twin, and I had a twin, Rose suddenly thinks. Had.

Her chest heaves, unbearably tight. She slings her duffel bag over her shoulder and climbs the front steps, taking two at a time in hopes of catching the source of light if it still lingers in the house. Two, four, six…twenty-two steps later, she's at the monstrous front door of Peacock Manor.

Amber was her name. It's hard to believe it's been a year since she died, and still, no one knows what really happened.

She glances back at her parents. They're contentedly rolling the biggest suitcase ever up the hillside. Dad pulls from the front, bumping over the uneven ground, while Mom steadies the suitcase from the side. *B.o.r.i.n.g,* Amber would have said.

Amber. I would do anything to bring her back.

There is a slight delay as her dad jostles his pockets and bags for the key. *Hurry up, Dad.*

Rose presses both palms into the wooden door and peers into the grand hall. Turquoise marble floors. Cypress pillars and beams. A large firepit in the entryway wafts traces of burnt timber from winters past. When it snows, there's skiing nearby. Her mind leaps to *The Shining*: a writer dad in an empty mansion, driven mad by sinister spirits. Her own dad is too much of a goofball—as in, worst dad-jokes in the world kind of goofball—to ever be murderous.

One day, Amber and I laughed together for the very last time and didn't know it.

She winces. Her shoes slap against the shiny floor, echoing off the floral-painted ceilings that rise much higher than she imagined from the outside. The soul of such bygone places fills her stomach with tremors of curious excitement—*there have got to be secret passageways in here.*

Rose peers to her left into a gold, mirrored ballroom.

She turns to ask Dad if he's ever been to a ball, and why people don't have them anymore, but finds herself alone. Her parents are outside again, collecting luggage.

"Welcome to my summer, my life," Rose says to a bronze bust of a Captain Peacock. She vows that this summer will be different—that she is in charge of her own destiny.

Rose has her choice of bedrooms from the twelve upstairs (she knows the brochure by heart) accessed via two S-shaped staircases wrapped around an inner courtyard.

East Wing, West Wing, six bedrooms aside. Which way to the strange light?

She and Amber would have argued which side was best, then raced up opposite stairways and, once at the top, insisted they'd beat the other. They'd explore their summer residence as ghosthunters, competing to find the item most likely to be "haunted."

A black-and-white crying baby photo—*absolutely*

haunted.

A screaky step in the stairwell.

The old candy in the vending machine. *Definitely haunted.*

A cat she'd pet on the porch. *What cat? There hasn't been a cat here in thirty years*, the other would say.

The bed she'd chosen. The chandelier above *your* bed. *Oh yeah? Your* face in the mirror.

Blon-n-n-ng! A grandfather clock clangs one solitary chime. Rose leaps out of her skin. It chimes the essence of her soul:

One. A broken pair.

The shoe with the more-worn heel.

One shoe belongs nowhere.

She can't figure out how to go on without Amber.

Gripping her bag into her chest, she weaves right and creeps up the west set of stairs, alone. The stairway moans and yawns with each step, as if awakening to human footsteps for the first time in a long while.

If she finds proof of the supernatural, will anyone believe her? They didn't, *last time.* She shivers off the sorrowful thought like a bedraggled cat shaking off water and refocuses her attention.

Where is the entrance to that tower? She ducks into each bedroom, opening creaky doors to reveal oversized frilly beds (possibly haunted), lush crimson curtains, and marigold rugs.

One door halfway down the West Hall does not open. It's old and weather-beaten and gnarled like driftwood, with hardened black tar filling the worn crevices so no light passes in or out.

Her top pick for haunted object, for sure.

She jiggles the brass knob, rattling the door in its frame, curiosity flaming through her.

When she was nine, she asked Dad what he kept in the locked drawer of his desk. He said it was human nature to need to know what was "on the other side." Rose challenged him, asking if cavemen would waste energy rolling away a rock blocking a cave just to see what was inside?

"Totes," he answered, making them both laugh and cringe at his dorkiness. She reminded him—even back then—that word was *so* five years ago, and no adult should ever say it.

She toggles the doorknob one last time before giving up and hurries onto the next room.

"Hellooo! I'm moving in for the summer. Is anyone haunting any of the bedrooms? Please let me know which one is yours, so I can select another one," she calls out. *Let's not incur the wrath of an angry spirit.*

She pauses for an answer. A flickering light, rattling furniture, a temperature change. She automatically reaches into her back pocket for her phone to look up other signs of poltergeists, but shrinks back.

There's been no reception since they corkscrewed up the mountain highway, long after the car ferry crossing, beyond a country border—so far away from her normal world. A phone full of contacts, but not a single human she can talk to. Dad points out that the writers of the classics never had internet, anyway.

"I know you exist," she whispers into the long, dark hallway. "You must…"

The floorboards creak as she shifts her weight from

one foot to another.

"Rose, did you pick a room yet?" her mom calls from downstairs. "Your dad and I will be in the master bedroom. East Wing."

"She's probably straightening all the crooked paintings," Dad replies. He knows her so well.

A tilt here. A tap there.

Relief, from crookedness. Relief, from being different.

She stoops to eavesdrop on what else her parents are saying about her.

Dad continues. "Opaline, look. Much of this has been here since the Peacocks built the Manor. You know, *she* would've liked these historical details." His voice catches, but he clears his throat. "And the library…"

Rose's insides twist. Poor Dad. It's difficult to ignore that when her dad mentions "*she…*" her mother responds with silence. *She*. Amber.

In through the ears, down into her heart to be buried. Mom, raised by pastel-suits Grandma and pocket-squares Grandpa, learned to silence anything unpleasant—and to bury her sorrow in mindless tasks, like her baking.

Heartache turns into a lemon meringue pie.

"Rose, are you still upstairs?" her mom calls.

Rose pivots, moving down the hallway. "I'm here!" she replies.

A hot current of perfumed air passes through her, as if she'd stepped in front of a fireplace. A stranger's perfume. The back of her neck prickles. Who else is here? She sniffs. Lilies, definitely lilies, like in her grandparents' backyard. Magic and tragic, Grandma used to say about their fragrance.

Sniffffff-fff. Rose draws another breath, struggling to pick up the direction of the scent. She sniffs too hard and snorts. *Oops.*

Someone giggles. Hollow footsteps follow.

Clunk. Clomp-clomp.

Rose is not the only one upstairs.

Gripping the banister, she resists the urge to run back downstairs.

"Who-oo's there?" Her voice wavers, betraying her astonishment, and her eyes dart up and down the shadowy hall. *Where are all the light switches in this place?*

She presses on, needing to know if the laughter and footsteps are real. If they're real, and spirits exist in the Manor, it means they could pass through the veil here. Certain places are hot spots for spirit activity.

Maybe here, the summoning she tried before will work? Maybe, just maybe, she can see—or even talk to—her better half, one more time? There are too many unanswered questions about that day.

To know her sister is okay, to hear her say it, is to know she herself might be okay one day.

She doesn't dare hold those thoughts for long.

Because, wait. Footsteps and a little girl's laughter? How unoriginal. Her shoulders drop from their hunched position, but she doesn't allow herself to relax; instead, she scours the shadows for movement.

No other signs of poltergeists. Her heart sinks. Were the sounds fake, set up for guests expecting a haunted house? That would be clever.

Disappointed, she sidesteps into a bedroom, tapping her fingers along the velvety wallpaper, finally finding a light switch. She toggles it a few times before a dim chandelier reluctantly sparks on, casting dreary blue-gray shadows around the bedroom. The tips of her fingers sting where she burnt them in her last attempt at summoning a spirit. Stupid phony witchcraft book. Over the desk, a sepia-tinted photo of an unsmiling family (definitely haunted) needs a little tilting before she can lie down.

She swipes a paperback from her bag and belly flops onto the bed. She and Amber started the first book in the series together. Grandma brought books over, and they took turns reading chapters aloud to each other. That seems like forever and a day ago.

There is no one left to do that with anymore.

Her throat tightens, and she clenches the book into her chest for a long moment.

With a heavy sigh, Rose flips the pages, escaping the only way she knows how. Into a book. She doesn't fit in here anymore—all by herself—but within the pages, she soars in the shadow of a dragon's wings, magicks an orb of light as a sun goddess, rescues a parallel universe just by being herself.

Here and now, she is none of that.

Here and now,

she is only a rainstorm that lasts all week,

mushrooms growing under a log,

the stump of a candle lit with an almost burnt-out flame.

****

She arrives at the last word and re-reads the paragraph. It's hard to let go at the end sometimes. She shuts the cover hard enough to emit a muted *ploof!*— one of her favorite sounds of all time, comforting and final.

A whorl of mountain wind slams her bedroom window fully open with a THWACK! The air this deep into the night chills her, so she leaps up to lock the glass pane into its frame. She gazes down into the square courtyard within the Manor, but…

staggers
backward
in
astonishment.

A beautiful older boy with inky black hair stands tall and rigid in the night, next to the fountain, staring into the water. He's dressed in a well-fitting dark suit—the gloomy kind you wear to a funeral.

She presses her forehead against the glass. Her movement catches his attention, and he curves his striking face upward, slow and graceful, as if in a dream. His eyes flash silver as they catch the glint of a hanging lantern in the courtyard, and his red lips move slowly, forming words.

She leans out the window, but hears no words, even as he continues speaking to her.

He aims a slender hand at the fountain, pointing. He stoops and reaches into the water, but she can't see what he's doing. She adjusts her stance—still shamelessly gawking—intrigued by an attractive local her own age even though he could be something else entirely. Was he the figure haunting the window before? Or had she dozed off after such a long trip and momentarily fallen into a dream?

Without thinking, she shoves back from the window to sprint out of her room, but trips over her bag and crashes onto her knee with a thud. She ignores the pain and limps downstairs, desperate for a closer look. She slides open a door opposite the front entry and steps out into the inner courtyard.

By the time she reaches the fountain, the courtyard is empty.

Human or spirit? Gone, either way.

She spins around, scanning the small space, and her calves hit the low stone edge of the fountain. She twists to avoid falling in and turns her attention to the flowing fountain.

He must have pointed at it for a reason.

Its centerpiece is a stone octopus grasping a lantern with one tentacle and spouting water from the other seven. Weird, but has character. *Oh hey, kind of like me.*

The lantern, though. She's seen it somewhere. It scratches at her memory. Has she been here before, in a painting, a book, a dream?

As if it knows she's staring at it, the lantern begins to glow a jade green. Strange bubbles bob in the water. She leans inward, placing her palms on the cool stone edge. Fish eyeballs! Not bubbles at all. Fish eyeballs, not attached to fish. Silver and disgusting. One after another, small and large, streaming out of the octopus like a broken gumball machine.

She jolts back as if struck.

The fountain hums and water spews faster, turning black as ink. With a deep rumble, the fountain explodes, shooting the octopus into the starry night sky—water, stone, fish eyes, spinning up and up.

From inside the Manor, rushing water gurgles as if pouring from every faucet, as if every pipe within the walls has burst.

Glass snaps, rupturing like crackles of lightning ripping through the air. Rose teeters and falls, cowering. A torrent of water dotted with rolling eyeballs gushes out of the shattered windows. A tidal wave of nightmares!

She screams, but her mouth is dry and she chokes. Left and right, the black water tears down the stairways, pulling off doors and splintering wood beams toward her.

In the time it takes her to throw her arms up and duck, preparing for impact, everything rewinds as if sucked backward into a drain. All is still again. Except for her heart. Her heart drums the insides of her ribs the way someone pounds against a door for help.

****

Her thoughts lurch as she peels herself off the pebbly ground of the courtyard and retreats into the Manor.

What did she just witness? Was the boy warning her with a message—from the past or the future? Spirits are inter-dimensional beings, affecting time and space around them. She'd researched spectral phenomena extensively before arriving at the Manor. Just in case.

She creeps past a sitting room, hung floor-to-ceiling with oil portraits overlooking sheeted furniture that, in the darkness, give rise to looming beastly spirits. She briefly wonders who all the people in the portraits are before moving on to the next room, sliding open a door to a formal tea room—but doesn't bother closing it before swerving upstairs, taking the long way back.

When she passes the master bedroom in the east wing, Dad's snores rumble through the door—her parents said goodnight long ago. *They* didn't see or hear anything unusual, though she suspects grownups only believe in what they already know to be true.

Mom would *never* admit to seeing a ghost.

Upon returning to her bedroom, she's surprised to find a small book lying open on the floor, fallen off a shelf built into the wall. Did she knock it down when she tripped? Or did someone place it there while she was outside? This night could not be more extraordinary.

She crouches to scoop up the book. *The Graveyard.* She thumbs through the stiff yellow pages of the short novel and finds herself wondering if there is a cemetery on the property.

On the last page, there's handwriting, so she bends back the cover.

Scrawled in pencil:

THE BOOK OF LOST SPIRITS is Here, So Is The Key

By Amaryllis A. O. Peacock

Last over the ocean on a sailing ship,

Dying stone falling from the night's grip,

The bottom half of the page is torn off. She flips the pages again and shakes the book, but the rest of the poem is missing.

Whoa. *The Book of Lost Spirits is Here*, it says. The legendary book that contains the secrets of communicating with the dead? Would she be able to contact Amber—? Her breath catches. She would give *anything* to do that.

Or, is this just a poem? Who is Amaryllis?

She'll need to do some research—there's no way the book is real. It's a myth, like the Fountain of Youth and Blackbeard's Treasure…Right?

Rose doesn't allow her hopes to linger on the biggest reason why she wants the book.

Still rattled by the night's eerie events, she sets *The Graveyard* on the nightstand and unfurls the quilt on her four-poster bed. The darkest part of night wanes into the first glimpse of dawn. She sinks deep into the mattress and rolls over, staring up at the canopy of the bed. Her mind spins.

The figure of light, the laughter, the boy, and the horrific dark water vision: *Phantasmagoria* is the proper term. The handwritten poem—where is the rest of it?

She suspects it's all related. Something is here, she is certain of it. It rings through her bones. Who was the boy? If there are ghosts haunting this place, whose are they, and…what if they are malicious? Her pulse doubles its pace.

What would she do then?

The edges of her vision narrow, and darkness devours her.

Chapter 3

February Peacock

Noon arrives out of nowhere, its stark light illuminating the rich emerald wallpaper of the bedroom.

Rose jolts awake with a gasp, gulping for air. "I had the weirdest dream, Amb—"

Ah, shoot. She's still not used to waking up alone after sharing a room with her sister all her life. Amber would've reminded her that nightmares and dreams were woven by Dream Spirits supplying glimpses of "the other side." If there *were* an afterworld—a heaven or a purgatory—then you never quite knew in the strange, convoluted elixir of dreaming, which side you were sampling. Especially these days.

Her chest tightens. She presses her fingers to her eyes, knowing what always comes next: she begins to ugly cry. She was never a crier as a child, yet here she is now.

Every. Frickin'. Morning.

She chokes on the sorrow and heartache that feeds the monster in her—the monster that swallows her hope and says to her, "No amount of time will ever be enough to escape the sadness." She takes one more ragged inhale and wipes her nose. Onward. This summer will be different.

Old Rose would wallow. Summer Rose is all about

change.

Not cut-micro-bangs change, but *real* change.

She doesn't want to belong to grief anymore.

She smells warm butter swirling into cinnamon, flaky pastry, and sugared red fruits. Her mother's baking has begun.

She glances at the book, *The Graveyard,* on the nightstand. Last night's events still trouble her. She commits the lines about the ship and the stone to memory and decides the manor graveyard would be a good place to start.

With images of the elegant boy and the dark flood still stamped into her mind, she swings her legs over the edge of her bed. Her foot lands on something

squishy

and

cold.

"Eek!" she yelps, collapsing back onto the bed. Cringing, she bends back her knee to inspect the bottom of her foot.

A fish eyeball—stuck to her foot—stares back at her.

She squeals again and hobbles to the bathroom to kick the eye off into the toilet. She begins scrubbing the oily brown spot where the eye had been but decides it isn't enough and continues into a shower, washing the night away. Could a vision like last night's manifest into a real physical object, like an eyeball? Or did she track in roadkill from last night?

She shudders in disgust.

The outfit she chooses is colorless. She represents slobs everywhere, in her free T-shirt from a spelling bee and soft leggings. Amber was the stylish one, and Rose still can't bear to look at her sister's clothes, so she only chooses attire they never shared. Spelling bee tee it is.

When she stomps downstairs in her short gray boots that make a lot of noise, her mom calls out, "Is that you, Rose? I made cardamom-pear pixie cakes."

She switches directions, drifting past a dining room with the longest table she has ever seen, and twists around the corner, into the massive kitchen.

Her mother is clinking and clanking near the oven. The early afternoon sun angles in through the kitchen skylight; dust floats in and out of the sunbeams.

She lingered in bed for so long that half the day is gone.

Pixie cakes, though. *Yum.*

She plucks two frosted cubes from the basket on the breakfast table—carefully, to avoid still-warm icing on her fingers. *Thanks, Mom.* Inhaling the warm spices, she skids across the foyer's turquoise marble before slipping sideways through the front door.

There was a creepy statue garden she saw from the car last night. Could that be part of a cemetery? Once outside on the porch, she chomps off a piece of pear from the cake and pedals down the wide stone stairway, swerving left where the stairs split.

She tosses her brown-sugar-colored strands out of her face and spills down the hill.

A honeybee zigzags toward her, drawn to her sweets, so she dodges while quickly shoveling a cake into her mouth. She treks past a giant boulder deposited long ago by a glacier.

"Hey, rock, you're like me, dragged here by someone bigger." She spits out a laugh and wanders toward the first group of marble statues.

From memory, she repeats the two lines of the poem out loud. What the heck was *last over the ocean on a sailing ship?* A *dying stone falling* at night. A meteor, maybe? The lines could be instructions. Or a spell. She recalls another "spell" she found in a new-agey book promising contact with the dead and mumbles it half-heartedly, in case it might magically work here.

With the last bit of cake in her mouth—

A flash of dark hair catches her eye.

She stops mid-chew, melted frosting pooling in her mouth.

A small, feminine face peers out at her from behind a narwhal statue across the lawn.

Behind, or *through*, the marble statue? Rose berates herself for forgetting her sunglasses as she squints into the sun streaming from behind the statue.

A spectral being, in daylight?

"Are you—?" Rose says with her mouth full. She swallows and scrutinizes the pale wisp of a face. "—haunting this place?" Her voice trails off, afraid the apparition will vanish as quickly as the figure she saw last night.

A teenage girl steps out from behind the narwhal.

She is alluring. Radiant mahogany hair cut into a bob with bangs, sea-foam-green eyes, glowing skin. A creature of beauty from a lost era of folklore,

a firefly under starlight,

new frost on spider's silk.

Rose peers down at herself. *I should've put on a better shirt.*

"You believe…in *ghosts*?" the girl asks, her voice high-pitched and silvery. She wears a white summer

24

dress, and a pocketwatch hangs on a chain around her neck.

Rose clears her throat. "They exist. Physics," she replies, hoping she doesn't sound stupid. Of course, this girl isn't a ghost.

"How so?" the girl asks. She sidles up to Rose as if approaching a wild animal.

Rose doesn't blame her. She quickly finger combs her hair again.

"The First Law of Thermodynamics says energy can't be created or destroyed. It's constant across the universe." A ready answer—she's been hanging onto all her ghostly facts for a while. "The electrical energy we have has to go *somewhere* when we die."

"Where?" She stares at Rose, cocking her head to reveal a single emerald earring she wears on one ear only in the most charming way.

"It's possible that leftover energy changes form— into a ghost. I've seen one before, you know." Rose regrets it as she says it. She just met this girl and is geeking out already. Is it too late to say *just kidding*?

She plasters a flimsy smile on her face.

The girl replies warmly, "You sure know a lot about ghosts! I'm sorry to disappoint, but I'm February. My family calls me Feeby, 'cuz I'm smallish for my age—seventeen, but bet you wouldn't have guessed."

February, like her wintry name, is delicate and pale.

"I'm Rose Green."

"*Why* do you want to see a ghost?" February presses, her green eyes widening. She angles in close enough for Rose to see that the gold pocketwatch around her neck hangs upside down.

Rose shrugs coolly, pretending not to care, even though it matters to her more than she wants anyone to know. *We saw a spirit together. Amber and I. Then, she died. What caused the accident? Whose fault was it?* She pushes away the uninvited memory and snaps back to the here and now.

"I dunno. It's something to do during vacation," Rose mumbles, mortified by the long silence while her mind spun off the rails for a second. "Do I get a prize when I collect enough awkward moments?"

"Ha! Welcome to being a teenager, right? If you don't already have an insecurity, one will be randomly assigned to you," February says. She has the kind of smile that puts strangers at ease.

She adjusts her pocketwatch. "I live nearby," she says, flinging her wrist in a vague direction. "My family—the Peacocks—own the Manor. Tourists love to rent this place, so we don't live in it. I'm dropping off extra keys and checking to see if your parents need help figuring anything out. It's an old house with idiosyncrasies."

Rose lifts a brow. She likes that Feeby used the word *idiosyncrasies*.

February glances sideways from under her long, dark lashes. "Have you seen much of the Manor? There's the ballroom, the Garden of Mistakes, the music room, the library, a graveyard—"

"Graveyard?" Should she mention the book, the poem? Part of her doesn't want to share her discovery. Not yet. If it can help find her sister...she wants it for herself.

"Ooh yeah, it's out back, but I know a shortcut—it's where my grammy's buried. Maybe you'll see your ghost there." February's small frame contains so much energy, she practically bounces in place, reminding Rose of a helium balloon ready to float away once untethered.

"Sure," Rose agrees, and off they march, along the manicured lawn, past a stout broccoli-shaped tree.

She swears she can make out a door in its trunk.

They duck under a grove of smaller trees, crunching over unraked leaves.

"These are cherry blossoms, cotton candy pink in the spring. C'mon, long legs, this way!" February calls back to her.

Rose is a head taller than February but speeds up to keep pace with her. They press through a field of waist-high grass, golden like summer wheat. She swats away the teeny flies whizzing out of the scrub they disturb.

"Have you ever been to a cemetery?" February asks, bending to pluck wildflowers as she walks.

Rose shakes her head. "No."

Well, that's a straight-out lie. She remembers when her sister was laid to rest. It was autumn, and the trees wept scarlet, yellow, and bitter orange. Rose was there, and the last to leave. But she doesn't want to talk about it.

Anguish cleaves her gut. For lying. And for remembering.

February doesn't notice. "My great aunt September is buried with every gold object she ever owned! Including my great-grand uncle's gold teeth," she says, as they approach the Peacock family cemetery. "My loony relatives didn't believe in 'can't take it with you.' There are gems, swords, wine casks, even a statue of Grandpa Jules—short for July—buried in here."

She speaks fast, not out of nervousness, Rose supposes, but out of trying to fit all her ideas in one breath.

Thorny hedges of winter holly around an iron fence guard the graveyard's buried treasure. Rose pokes one of the long needles, leaving an imprint on her fingertip. *Ouch.*

Luckily, the heavy door built into the shrubbery is wedged open, so there's no need to climb the prickly hedges. Thunderstorms the week before mired the entrance in thick, chocolatey mud.

"Door's been stuck in the same spot for years. It can't be moved," February warns, neatly stepping around the sludge.

Carved with glyphs, the door offers enough room for Rose to squirm by with a sideways turn and a held breath.

She finally thinks of something to ask her guide. "What does the door say?"

"It's a protective spell," February says, stopping abruptly. "A long time ago, locals here used these glyphs." She raps the door with her knuckles.

"Protection from what?"

"Oh, folks in the past were superstitious. Afraid their souls would be snatched away by dark spirits. Spirits that break through the barriers between our realms on summer nights, when the light is weak—at dusk, twilight. The hour when humans can fall into the spirit realm too, winnowed away forever." She shimmies her fingers in front of Rose's face when she says "winnowed," as if one of them were fading away.

Rose shrinks back, frowning slightly. "I love old legends. Feeby, are any of the rumors about Peacock

Manor true? I read online that for every few families who go up the mountain and stay at the Manor, someone *disappears* and doesn't come back down the mountain." She'd scrounged for information, but only found a few vague mentions of individuals and objects *"last seen at Peacock Manor."*

The thought thrills her as much as it terrorizes her.

"It certainly keeps the tourists coming!" February skips ahead into the cemetery.

It's impossible for Rose to overlook that February didn't answer her question. She falls back into silence, trailing behind once again.

They skulk past tombstones mottled with lichen and moss. Stone shrines push out of wild grass, resembling hunched, dormant creatures. Each one perched over a dead body. Rose's skin pricks into gooseflesh, even as the summer sun beams onto her skin.

February spins around and waves at her to follow faster. Her movements convey familiarity with the graveyard. "Look at this tomb here—twin babies, died 1793," she announces like a macabre tour guide.

Twins. At least they died together.

"Are you an only child?" February asks, interrupting Rose's doomy thoughts.

Her heart nearly stops. "Yup." Only half a lie this time.

"Me too. It's just me and my mom," Feeby says with a hint of regret.

"My parents want another baby, though. Picked out names and all. They're trying to replace—" She catches herself. She almost said too much.

"That's exciting, the thought of having a brother or

sister," February says, bright again.

Rose wants to tell Feeby that she already has a sister and that she doesn't want a new sibling at all, but she's afraid the cheery grin on Feeby's face will turn into a pitying look. And no one wants to be friends with someone they pity.

February prattles on, but the nice thing Rose already noticed is that Feeby doesn't need an answer to everything she says. So it isn't tiring to listen. Rose follows along without a reply.

They loop around the newest marker in the yard, shiny and clean and modern. It seems out of place. Rose does the math: he was only nineteen when he died last year. Jarring, any death not from old age. Why do some souls get fewer years than others? Much fewer.

She can't peel her eyes away. A deep hollowness threads through the pit of her stomach. As she shivers it off, a shadow back at the entry catches her attention.

A boy shifts out from behind the stuck door.

The somber boy in the crisp dark suit from last night.

He scans the grounds, searching, but stops in surprise when his gaze lands on her.

Rose stiffens. "February. Don't freak out, but there's an actual ghost here. I saw him in the courtyard last night. Turn. Around. Slowly," she whispers.

"Where?"

"Him. There." Rose jabs a finger toward the glyph-carved door.

"Oh!" February laughs. "That's Kamdyn—we go to school together. Have you heard of the Charbon Ski Resorts, Charbon Chateau and Lodge?"

"Nope."

"His family owns half the mountain. They're helping me and my mom fix up the old manor, so it doesn't fall apart in the next winter storm. Kamdyn's the oldest son, heir to all the properties and the Charbon empire."

"As in, 'one day, this will all be yours'…cue evil laughter?" Rose exaggerates a laugh. "Why was he here in the middle of the night, though?"

"You're sure it was him?"

"Fancy suit. Dark hair. Sharp features. Serious-looking." She ticks them off on her fingers.

"Lemme ask. Kam!" Feeby waves her entire arm as he crosses the long cemetery.

"I've been looking for you, February."

Now that Rose sees him up close, his unblinking gray eyes shine like the new grave marker two rows behind—his penetrating gaze devouring all he sees. *What's he got to be so serious and intense about?* His hair, dark as raven's feathers, matches his suit. Well-built, tall, and strong. None of the boys at her school look anything like this.

Everything is different high up on this mountain of mystery.

"Kamdyn, this is Rose. She and her family are staying for the summer. What the heck were you doing at the Manor last night? You scared her."

"Rose." He speaks her name, low and smooth, like breathing out smoke from his mouth. He smells like lavender soap and something sweet, but she can't quite place it. "I'm sorry if I frightened you. I was repairing the fountain earlier in the day, and I lost my keys. Thought I dropped them in the fountain. I didn't know you were arriving last night. My apologies."

The intensity of his silvery glare, and now, the timber of his voice, complements the solemn lines etched between his brows.

Rose wonders what he'd look like if he ever smiled.

She regards him with silence for now, but nods. She's made a fool of herself twice already in front of February, insisting everyone here was a ghost.

He anchors his attention on her. Assessing her.

She's not sure what he sees in her—what he's staring at—and embarrassment creeps into her cheeks.

She breaks first, scowling, afraid she looks as ridiculous as he's making her feel, and pretends to study a nearby gravestone instead.

"What do you need *me* for?" February asks him.

Rose can't stop herself from looking up at the surprise in February's voice.

"I need to talk to you about the, um…" Kamdyn clears his throat. "Manor." He cuts a glance at Rose and suddenly appears less sure of himself.

"More repairs? It's gonna be expensive, huh? Come by my mom's later—we can chat then."

"Sure, that works. I'll see you there," he replies. He flicks off lint from the lapel of his blazer and straightens his collar with a well-manicured hand.

Without another word to Rose, he turns on his heels and strides away in effortless, long steps.

Rose doesn't bother to acknowledge his departure either.

"Bye, Kam!" February calls after him. She turns to Rose. "He's incredibly handsome, don't you think?"

"Hm," Rose scoffs, neither agreeing nor disagreeing.

"He's an elite alpine skier who's won a bunch of titles, but his parents want him to focus on the family business."

Competitive skier. That explains the physique. "I dunno, he was creepy last night."

"He can be really serious and intense! I'm sorry, he didn't know you'd be here. Please don't write a bad review for the Manor, ha-ha."

"Nah, it's all right."

"There we are." February scuttles over to a large, weathered headstone several rows over, engraved with an amaryllis bloom, and crouches down.

The worn, crumbling edges of the temple-shaped marker suggest that Grammy died many, many seasons of sunshine and snow ago.

She clears away dried flowers from the base of the grave and lovingly replaces them with blossoms in magenta and canary she collected on the way over.

"Grammy said every single day is one more advent calendar door to Death. Gotta appreciate every door you get to open. I wish you were here, Gramms."

"A bit morbid, your grammy," Rose mutters to herself, but her breath catches at the inscription:

Amaryllis August October Peacock, 18-something to 18-something.

Rose's heartbeat quickens. The poem was by Amaryllis A.O. Peacock! But the faded numbers don't make sense. Grammy had to be Feeby's great-great-grandmother?

She bows forward, pressing away the grass.

"How old was Grammy? How did you talk—?"

—but stops at once. Above the numbers, a red gemstone flashes, glimmering at her.

It glitters more than expected from only reflecting sunlight.

She braces her palms on her knees. It bothers her that the jewel hangs off-center, falling out of the gravestone. Rose reaches out to the ruby-and-shadow-colored gem, but pauses out of respect, hovering her fingertips.

"That's a bloodstone. You know what it's used for?" February asks.

Rose shakes her head. "Nope."

"It guides lost souls, Grammy said. She collected crystals."

Straighten me out, it pleads, and Rose can't help herself. She presses it with a firm finger, but the stone only loosens more. "I'm so sorry—" *Oh no, don't mind me, breaking your beloved Grammy's grave.*

"Ooh! What is it attached to?" February scrunches next to her and wriggles at the jewel like a loose tooth. The bloodstone slides out, attached to a red glass tube.

February holds it to the sun. It glows crimson like a vial of blood.

Rose leans over her shoulder. "There's a rolled-up piece of paper in it."

"Impossible! Who put this here? I visit Grammy's grave all the time." She unscrews the bloodstone top, tips the vial, and a yellowed roll of paper slides out. "How'd you see this?" February asks.

"It was crooked and I had to fix it. What's it say?"

February scrambles to unravel the rigid scroll that insists on curling back into itself.

Rose reads the two lines:

"*Desert illusion,*
Your arthropod, the scorpion."

The second half of the poem!

"What's that supposed to mean?" February asks.

"No way," Rose murmurs. "You're not going to believe this, but I think…it's a riddle. I found the first half last night in the back of a book." She repeats the lines she's been spinning in her head all morning:

"THE BOOK OF LOST SPIRITS is Here, So Is The Key

By Amaryllis A. O. Peacock

Last over the ocean on a sailing ship,

Dying stone falling from the night's grip,"

February whistles a long exhale. "Why didn't you say something before?"

"I wasn't sure if it meant anything."

"But, *The Book of Lost Spirits? THE Book of Lost Spirits?* You've heard of it, right?"

"Uh, of course. It's a lost text. A frickin' legend. My dad referred to it in one of his adventure novels—"

"It hasn't been read in centuries—" February cuts in.

"They say the ones who wrote it figured out how to summon spirits and talk to the dead—"

"Last known location was Peacock Manor, after it was found on a tiny island in the Pacific."

"But it's all a myth. Isn't it?" A tingle creeps up Rose's spine.

"I was told something happened, and it was hidden away. I thought the stories were made up, to make our family history exciting so we would listen to the rest of it," February says.

"Maybe your grammy found it and is passing it to you? Do you think it has powers, like they say?" *Powers, allowing me to summon Amb—*

"I have no idea. But the last line—*your arthropod*—has to be for me!"

"Why?

"Arthropods were my favorite. I was a funny little kid, right? Wanted to be a biologist—study life and the living," February says.

Rose doesn't respond. Her mind is elsewhere, reeling from their astounding discovery.

She isn't sure if she believes the book can summon and commune with spirits. But the possibilities! A supernatural book, proof of the paranormal?

No, be realistic, Rose. All her research into conjuring and communicating with spirits has amounted to nothing so far.

Still. This is how things could be different.

February hands the scroll back, disrupting Rose's spiraling thoughts.

"My mom and I take care of the Manor, but my uncles want to sell it and split the money. They've all been arguing over it for years. Grammy didn't believe in wills."

Rose takes this opportunity to ask, "How did you talk to Grammy if she died in the 1800s?"

"She left a diary, and my dad told me stories he'd heard."

Oh. Not supernatural at all.

February goes on. "If we found the book, it wouldn't be an issue anymore. A collector or museum would pay a lot of money for it, don't you think?" She peers at Rose from under her dark bangs.

"For sure," Rose says, knowing secrets never stay hidden forever, surfacing like the time she and her father discovered a raccoon skeleton pushing its way out from the garden soil after a heavy wash of rain.

Secrets claw their way back from the dead, out of their buried caskets lined with lies.

The Manor is only beginning to reveal its treacherous mysteries—and Rose holds proof in her trembling hand.

****

"Rose. Promise me we'll find the book before you leave at the end of summer," February says, hiking toward the Manor across the back lawn.

"I might know the answer to one of the lines," Rose says, eager to prove herself useful. Maybe she can make a real friend this summer.

"Already? I definitely need you, then. Let's go take a look at the half of the clue you found."

She threads her arm into Rose's and drags her along into a skip across the grass. Rose can't resist grinning like a doofus. February's blue shoes dance up and down, while her pocketwatch swishes with them.

Affection comes easily to February, and Rose is drawn in. She normally wouldn't have this much to say to someone new, but Feeby has ignored all the unusual things she's said and done. Rose spins toward her with a half-smile, but February's silent gaze has drifted elsewhere.

They stop in front of the fishing lake. February drops her arms, unlinking herself from Rose, and inches toward the water's edge.

Her voice lowers. "This…"—she kicks a few pebbles into the water, creating ripples— "…is where those twins were found, they say. It's a lot deeper than it looks."

The curves of the small lake twist through craggy

trees and high grasses, tall enough to hide a grown man.

"What happened?"

"No one knew how they got out of the Manor—they couldn't even walk yet."

Rose squints at the murky water, the color of seaweed. Even in sunlight, every corner of the Manor bears a shadow of the unknown. The sticky, sweet pixie cakes churn in her belly.

Twin babies died 230 years ago.

Dead Grammy and her secret, lost book.

Mysterious, grim Kamdyn and his icy gray eyes.

Her insides twist, so she sips in a slow, tight breath. The strangeness of a new place must be getting to her.

She slogs up the stairs to the Manor. Mom is in the entryway—on her way out to church, ready to pray for Rose's soul like all moms with a teenage girl. The older Rose gets, the more Mrs. Green attends services. Rose takes a little morbid pleasure in this.

Rose aims a thumb at February. "Hey, Mom. Look who I found. Her family runs this place."

"Hullo, Mrs. Green! I'm February. I've brought over another set of keys for you."

"Thank you! I'm glad Rose has company her age this summer," Mom says. "Help yourself to pastries on the breakfast table; they're Rose's favorite. Once, she ate so many pixie cakes—she threw up."

"Oh, hey, thanks, Mom. Way to make me sound so awesome in front of a new friend." She narrows her eyes at her mother before turning to February, who is cracking up at the story.

"This way." Rose herds February toward the stairs before Mom can tell any more barf stories.

"Okay. It was nice to meet you, Mrs. Green!"

"Later, Mom."

"Your mom's nice. I'll take a pixie cake on my way out."

"They are kind of the best. There'll be lots. All Mom talked about in the car was baking, going to church, and wanting another baby. Her three goals this summer."

"Where's your dad?" February asks as they ascend the stairs to the left.

"Dad's gotta finish his book by September, so he'll be isolating himself in the study. Sunrise to moonrise," Rose says with a long-suffering sigh.

"I like your melodramatic description. What's he write?"

"The kind of book you buy at the airport because the cover promises excitement."

"Hah, cool! Would you believe I've never been to an airport?"

"Really? I guess we mostly do road trips. One year, we rented a famous author's antique cabin. Exciting, for no one *but Dad!* Another summer, we stayed in a secluded lake house for what felt like a *thousand* days, where a Lady of the Lake haunted—supposedly."

"Sounds lonesome for you. What did you do?"

"I counted frickin' squirrels. At the lake, at least I had a rowboat to take out on the water, with my books."

"No cute tourist boys?"

"There was nobody else around."

"Well, you have me this summer."

"Nice. Already beat expectations," Rose says.

When they enter Rose's bedroom near the top of the stairs, February exclaims, "Oh, you picked the room with my favorite chandelier! It's like an upside-down wedding cake of rainbow crystals."

Rose forces a smile, pretending to agree. She doesn't have the heart to admit that her withered soul picked the room not for its light, but for the deep emerald wallpaper. A green so intense and vibrant, she might go as far as calling it viridian, only because it sounded otherworldly, and she and Amber liked otherworldly. At night, the dark walls turn into a moonless forest, where she imagines she's hidden so deep that she can no longer

see dead faces or

hear lost voices or

feel any feelings at all.

That's when she can finally fall asleep.

She can't tell February any of that. People don't want the truth all the time. Lies keep them happy. She hands February the copy of *The Graveyard*, flipped to the penciled-in writing.

"This is unbelievable. Someone wants *us* to find the book?!" February says as she matches the torn edges on both halves of the riddle.

Before Rose can think of a reply, the doorbell to Peacock Manor rings.

The bell's echo interrupts the phantom of emptiness forever lurking in the cold, cavernous hallways. Rose swears the papered walls ripple a little with the hollow ringing from below. A shudder sweeps through her, despite herself.

"Is your family expecting someone?" February asks, one eyebrow lifting into her chestnut bangs.

"No. We don't know a single soul here."

Chapter 4

Peacock Manor
Day 146,601

I let those twins out. They wanted out, so I opened the door, and they crawled down the stairs, their chubby thighs propelling them downhill toward the pond. The young ones always want to explore my hallways, like the tall girl. I shall call her Pixie Cakes because she left cake crumbs all over my front stairs—she is very curious, and kind of clever and morose. The other one, the small Peacock girl, used to come over with her dad when she was little, but ever since he disappeared, she hasn't been here much.

I know what happened to him. But I couldn't do anything about it.

There are many things I can do: move walls and furniture, open doors, summon visions and sounds and voices, compose messages, and alter the temperature.

But there are even more things I cannot do. I am not good at helping. I thought I was helping those twin babies. I am just a house.

Chapter 5

Robbie and Kamdyn

"DOOR-BELL! Dad!?" Rose hollers. Her voice carries downstairs into the labyrinth of hallways but does not reach him.

She suspects he's blissfully tip-tap-typing away on his laptop, classical music on repeat (she likes it when he plays Beethoven's Moonlight Sonata and Chopin's Nocturnes), and coffee nearby. Coffee, reinforced with a dash of whisky and a handful of chocolate chips. A fantastic cure for writer's block, he dad-splained to Rose.

February rushes to the bedroom window and flattens herself against the glass. "It's a boy. Here's your cute guy for the summer. Hold on—I know him!"

"Who is it?" Rose presses her face to the glass. A sturdy, rugged boy waits in front of the balustrade, his muscular arms hugging overfilled bags of groceries.

"It's Robbie. He goes to my school, but a year ahead. His family, the Skylers, own the local grocery and run a farm nearby. They have this amazing goat cheddar cheese, ooh—and the best persimmons in the fall. Your parents must have ordered groceries," February says. "I hope they got—"

"Can you go open the door?" Rose interrupts.

"Go talk to him. He's sweet and super cute."

"Ugh. I'm not good at talking to new people. Really dismal."

"You're talking to me just fine."

Rose scowls. "I was hoping you were a ghost at first. Plus, you've done all the talking. I only listen and nod."

"True. My mom says I buzz more than a bag of bees."

Impatient knocking echoes off the columns in the foyer. "Anyone home? It's Robbie!" he calls out.

"I'll come downstairs with you," February offers.

"Fine. But don't think less of me, okay?" Rose grumbles, dreading February seeing a shameful side of her. She can't talk to boys. As in, she's horrendously awkward. She got away with it in the graveyard with Kamdyn because he didn't care to interact with her, anyway.

She creeps down the stairs, hoping Robbie might leave before she arrives at the entryway. Sweat forms on her palms with each downward step. *Be normal*, she reminds herself as she pries open the heavy door.

Her eyes shift upward to a wide, friendly smile on a decent-looking face. More than decent-looking. He is sunshine and ocean-blue skies, golden retrievers, and lake sports. She can't imagine anyone finding him unappealing. Why is everyone around here gorgeous? Sample size of three so far, but still.

"Hi, delivery for the Greens?" He wears red shorts and a white uniform shirt with a name patch. His sun-kissed wavy hair is cut on the shorter side, and his cheeks are rosy from hauling deliveries on a sunny day. He smells salty. Hints of hay and sage. *Stop sniffing the delivery boy, Rose. My god.*

She starts to say "Hello, Robbie," but her throat catches, words tangle, and…

"Haaa," comes out instead. She cringes. Oh no, not normal at all.

Robbie's smile fades and his brows lift, confused. Perhaps concerned she isn't okay.

She stares chagrined, speechless, and blank. She may as well be a decorative plant by the door.

The grandfather clock *tock-tock, tock-tocks* endlessly on in the hallway. *Oh hell—*

Luckily, February bounds in with a "Heya, Robbie!"

Peeling the grocery bags from him, she sets them on the entryway table. "You keep getting taller and more muscle-y. Did you start kindergarten when you were ten years old, or what? What're they feeding you on the farm?"

"Feebs!" he says, cornflower blue eyes agleam. "Cute as ever. What're you up to today?"

"I'm helping Rose settle in. She's here for the summer." She rolls up as high as she can onto her toes and wraps him in a hug, but her face only reaches the curve of his collarbone.

Behind her, Rose resists the instinct to coil up and hide after that terrible first impression she just made. She shows her teeth in an attempt to smile, adding a weak wave to demonstrate normalcy.

"Rose, huh? Welcome, welcome!" his voice booms. He ducks his head through the doorframe, scanning the grand entry of the Manor. "This place is amazing! Here, lemme take the groceries to the fridge before the frozen stuff melts."

"I'll help ya." February chatters away as they each

take a bag, leaving Rose standing alone.

Rose glances at Robbie's red car. To her surprise, Kamdyn waits in the passenger seat, window rolled halfway down, flipping carelessly through a magazine.

She squints past the glare of the car window.

He turns, flicking his coal-colored strands out of his face. He skims right above the half-open window, but he stiffens when he catches her studying him and straightens up, stony and expressionless.

His eyes flash as he holds her gaze from afar, two circles of fiery white, like a wild animal's eyes at night. Except…in broad daylight.

Whoa. Weird. Cool? How'd they do that?

The sharp angles of his face contrast with his soft mouth. He remains still, unblinking and unwavering.

She does the same, staring.

Well, now we're both being weird. She raises a hand to wave.

He drops his head and begins reading again.

Rose frowns, taken aback. If Robbie is a sparkling summer sky, then Kamdyn is the woods at midnight— the threat of unknown danger looming when one lingers too long, precarious even at a distance.

Yet…she can't look away.

She considers this for a moment, frowning. It's unlike her to be drawn to risks. For anything—least of all boys.

February and Robbie return, making plans to hang out more this summer.

"Please lemme know if you need more supplies. I've got a few more deliveries, but I know I'll be seeing you again soon." Robbie's grin is wide enough for the both of them, but all Rose can muster is a lame double thumbs up.

Before she can do anything else, the front door bangs shut with a draft of wind.

February lets loose a low whistle. "Whew. Rose. *That* was the most awkward encounter I've ever seen! Did you have to slam the door on him?" She laughs, giving Rose's shoulder a friendly squeeze.

Rose presses her fingertips into her temples. "I didn't! The wind did it. I warned you. What's wrong with me? RIP me, five minutes ago."

"Hah! *As useful as a burp for blowing dandelion*, Grammy would've said. You weren't like that around Kamdyn, though."

"I haven't said anything to Kamdyn either. Speaking of—he was in Robbie's car. He was...unfriendly." She can't admit how intrigued she is by something she saw *in his eyes.* How unoriginal. She wants to roll her eyes at herself in mild disgust.

"I didn't see anyone else," February says, confused. She fidgets with her pocketwatch. "Kamdyn, really? Robbie must've run into him on his way here and offered a ride."

"He seems stuck up." Ashamed at the possibility he was unfriendly only after seeing her, she drops the subject. "Maybe it was me. I can't talk to boys."

"Rose, you can! I'll help you. I can already tell we're going to be best friends this summer!" she promises, lunging to capture Rose into a crushing hug. February smells like red apples and honeysuckle.

"You don't want to be best friends with me. I'm a weirdo. Sung depressingly like that old Radiohead song."

"Vintage. Don't worry. A true friend ignores the

cracks in your eggs, and helps you make custard tarts, Grammy said."

"Yum, custard tarts. Are you my cracked egg?"

"Ha! I *am* kind of a cracked egg in life. Aren't we all? But I know the only thing you heard was *custard tarts*," February says.

"Hmmm…My mom can make us some good ones, if we ask."

"*You're* a custard tart," February says.

They cackle at each other. It's been a long while since Rose laughed like this.

A very long while.

Rose supposes the best an introvert can do is to wait for an enthusiastic extrovert like February to take her under her wing. Make friend, keep friend. Perhaps it can be as simple as that?

She promises herself to try harder.

Chapter 6

Peacock Manor
Day 146,601

Yes, I slammed the door on the grocery boy.
There's something odd about him. He never has a
single rotten or wicked thought. Is he human, then?
From what I've seen, it is abnormal. Believe me. I've
been here long enough. So for now, I do not trust him.
Although, he does look at February with admiration in
his eyes—the kind I've seen many times in the past.
The Peacock women have always been gorgeous.
Gorgeous, but a little batty.

There was a September Peacock a few decades
back; she was obsessed with gold. She painted my
music room and my ballroom in gold, with 24-carat
gold leaf in the trim.

She went too far when she coated the sea lion
fountain in the middle of the ballroom with gaudy gold
plating.

That night, I changed it all back to mint and black.
September fought back and had it all redone the next
day. It was an all-out war. The Peacocks are persistent.
In the end, we settled on gold and mint. When she
passed, she demanded in her will to be buried with the
gold sea lion, but I held onto it. The other Peacocks
could not remove it for the life of them.

The two girls have funny conversations. They worry about everything they do and say. But they are not worrying about the right things.

Danger lurks, and they need to be more careful.

Chapter 7

Hidden in the Laboratory

"Do you want to see a hidden laboratory? We can work out the riddle down there," February suggests after Robbie leaves. She glances askew for Rose's reaction.

"That wasn't in the brochure!"

"I knew you'd say that! You get the VIP tour because you appreciate science."

"Hell, yeah. Science nerds deserve more. Why did the Manor need a lab?"

"The early Peacocks were explorers and found all sorts of weird stuff like new minerals and plants. In the old days, they searched for a potion to extend life, but later, they were more realistic—they invented an ink." She laughs. "There was even a patent for it!"

February slides open a door between the entryway and the mint-and-gold music room, exposing a deep hallway closet full of heavy winter jackets, boots, an old movie projector.

"The lab is in the closet?" Rose asks, skeptical.

Feeby leads her into the back and says, "Pick a jacket, spin around a hundred times...nah, just kidding!" She pats along the back wall and pulls a lever, springing open a door down into the Manor's stone foundation. Eight deep twisting steps later, they arrive in a windowless stone chamber.

Large painted glyphs, similar to those on the graveyard's door, glow in aquamarine blue across the floor.

February clicks on a lamp near the door, and the glyphs vanish in the bulb's yellow light.

Like a school chemistry lab, long worktables display burners, Erlenmeyer flasks with iridescent liquids, scattered notes, and an insect collection. A colossal telescope angles upward in the back corner. The entire room smells of herbs and nail polish remover.

"Looks like an escape room. Horror-creepy factor nine out of ten," Rose says, eyeing a jail cell behind iron bars inset into one wall corner. Who or what was caged in there?

"Do you want more spooky or less spooky?" February darts over to a large brass crank and winds with both arms as if stirring a cauldron. A domed ceiling gives way, splitting open to a skylight above.

"Whoa. What kind of sorcery is that?" Rose marvels as daylight streams through.

"The dome doubles as a planetarium," February says. She sweeps her arm across a table, clearing away a stack of stained books, and slaps down a few clean sheets of notepaper. "Ew. What's this purple goop?" She sniffs her fingers, making a face. "Let's use a different table."

"You should wash your hand, Feebs." Rose squeaks onto a tall stool and flicks on a lamp.

February perches next to her scribbling a pen on her paper to test it, her legs kicking back and forth as they dangle. Rose's own feet practically drag on the floor.

Rose recites the riddle from memory as February transcribes it.

"THE BOOK OF LOST SPIRITS is Here, So Is The Key

By Amaryllis A. O. Peacock
Last over the ocean on a sailing ship,
Dying stone falling from the night's grip,
Desert illusion,
Your arthropod, the scorpion.

"—Did Amaryllis like riddles?"

"No! Are these instructions? We need to travel on a ship—find a stone—in a desert? That *is* where scorpions might live," February suggests.

"Each line is a direction to a location?"

"Holy moly. That's too many places to go," February says, chewing the inside of her cheek.

"This second line. '*Dying stone falling*.' It's a meteor, right? It burns up in the atmosphere as it falls to Earth. That's dying, isn't it?" Rose made air quotes with her fingers as she emphasizes *dying*.

"Meteor." Scritch-scratch. February jots down their answers.

"And, the shortest line," Rose says, "an illusion in the desert. That's got to be a mirage."

"Not *oasis*?" February asks as she writes.

"No, the illusion isn't always an oasis. I'm certain 'mirage' is the answer."

"Oops, that went over my head like a migrating bird." February rips away the top sheet of paper, bunching it up and flinging it aside.

"What do you think is *last over the ocean on a ship*?"

"Whoever's at the back of a ship?" February suggests.

"Everyone on a ship's deck moves around. What about a part of the boat?" Rose asks, not having been on a sailboat before—only a large rowboat at the lake from last summer. "The rudder? It's like a tail at the back end of a boat."

That rowboat at the lake had a rudder. Rose shudders involuntarily.

"Rudder. We'll go with that for now." February scribbles. "Next line."

Rose tilts her head over February's notes, but senses something wrong beside her. She holds her breath as she listens to the small clock hanging off her friend's neck. "Feeby, your pocketwatch needs winding. It's ticking dismally slow."

"Yep, this is my dad's. It doesn't work very well. It says it's midnight now—see the moon on the dial?" She holds it upright for Rose.

"Very cool. Looks antique."

"It's old as heck. Probably why it's tired and slow."

She lets it drop back on its chain so it hangs upside down again, and dismisses the subject, tapping her pen on the riddle. "What about this final line?"

"You said it refers to your love of scorpions," Rose reminds her.

"Yep, this is where I shine. Scorpions have been around since before the dinosaurs." She continues quickly, "They've got eight legs and are *not* insects."

"Like how spiders aren't insects?"

"Right. Spiders and scorpions are arachnids. That's it! A scientific way of looking at it: Arthropod-arachnid-scorpion. Phylum-class-order. Simple biology," February says.

"Nice thinking, Feebs." *Feebs*. That's what Robbie called her, and she seemed to like it.

So finally, the four answers:

Rudder. Meteor. Mirage. Arachnid.

"Now what?" February frowns.

"Are they describing an object, a location, a person? The first three words all have six letters. 6-6-6...wait, that's kinda creepy, right? But then, *arachnid* has eight letters..."

"Rudder, meteor, mirage, arachnid," February says.

As she completes the words, a monstrous howl rips through the room, aching and sad like an out-of-tune violin. "Ah-WooOoooOoooO!"

Rose shoots up at the noise, jerking her head around.

Beside her, February jumps. "Wha—!"

"Ah-WooOoooOoooO!" Again. From inside the laboratory!

Rose whirls on her heels, elbowing February and spinning her off her stool. February tumbles off, smacking onto the hard floor. She remains on the ground, absolutely still.

A daytime haunting? "Did we unleash something with the four words of the riddle?" Rose asks. After her first night, anything is possible.

"You think it's part of the scavenger hunt? Where's it coming from?" February whispers, her voice tight and low.

"Near that monster furnace."

Rose silently gestures to a pair of hefty candlesticks on a shelf beside them. They each wield one as a weapon and shuffle forward together, unsure if it is the right decision, though the howling has subsided.

She clutches her candlestick out in front of her, ready to shake it ineffectively should anything attack.

From inside the brick furnace, a pile of half-burnt notebooks shifts and crackles as Rose approaches. She recoils, falling on her backside. "Ahh!! It's moving! Feeby! There. See?" She prods the air with her candlestick.

February rushes over, offering a hand to pull Rose upright.

"You check. It's your manor." Rose moves behind her, trading places. Her longing to find something from the spirit realm pushes against her desire to stay alive in her current world. After all, the last time…

"You!" February sidesteps and crouches behind Rose, her cold fingers gripping Rose's arm.

They laugh nervously but don't take their eyes off the furnace.

Together, they crouch forward, lowering themselves eye-level to the grate, ready to leap back. Rose nudges the pile of moving paper with her candlestick.

"Something's in the ash chute underneath," Rose determines, swiping away papers and ash. She lifts the grate with her candlestick, hoping it's gone away.

"Oof," February says, as a cloud of cinders blows into their faces.

A pointy-eared dust ball shakes off his fur.

"Wait a minute. He's stuck." Rose crawls deeper and scoops out a fuzzy puppy, brown and gray. He tried to get in from the outside through the ash chute and made it halfway through before becoming trapped.

She lifts him to take a good look at his dopey face and over-large paws. He unfurls his tongue and laps her face as if they'd been reunited after a long time apart. He must be smelling the pixie cakes she ate earlier. His own breath is a mixture of meat, grass, and gasoline.

"Is this your dog, or a neighbor's?" Rose asks. He hangs in her hands, wagging his half-tail.

"No. Huh. Interesting," February mutters.

"What?" Rose asks, expecting a story. What does Feeby know?

"Oh. Nothing. I think he's a stray. I've seen him wandering around before, but he wouldn't come to me."

"He looks part wolf. No wonder he's a howler. Do you have a name, Sir Meat Bones?"

His charcoal-tipped coat is wild with sticks and grass sticking all over him. He is missing one of his canine fangs and, based on the length, part of his tail.

"Ha-ha, Meat Bones—he *is* the same kinda brown, with burnt edges! Why was he trying to get in here?" February asks.

"Was he hiding from something?" Rose asks.

"Poor pup. Are you going to keep him?"

Rose presses her face into the large ball of fur folding over her arms. He wiggles in delight at the attention. Her parents said no to another pet after their old dog Pancakes passed. But she and her sister launched a stubborn campaign for a new one, and Mom and Dad finally gave in and promised them a *small* pet a while ago. Then, her sister's accident derailed plans.

Still, she would keep Meat Bones a secret, until she house-trained him. That was the best way to go about it with her parents. He isn't the "small pet" they imagined, and based on the size of his chunky paws, he had room to grow.

"Of course, if he needs a home. And a bath." He's sticky like a scummy pond. But she knows they belong together. If only it were this simple with people.

"With a dog around, you always have someone to blame for weird smells," February says, leaning in to sniff him.

He wriggles in protest, so Rose sets him down to dust the ashes off his fur. She glances sideways at the furnace again—a handwritten word catches her eye. In the pile of burnt notebooks, she glimpses the word *spirits.*

"Feebs. Did you ever think of searching through these?" She lifts the handwritten pages and makes out other curious words in the scorched notes.

Wayward spirits. Use The BoLS, Dawn and Dusk, use 3 on Scraythe? Perhaps then—

"Whoa. No—It's not as if I'd hang out down here by myself…"

"What do you think this means? What *wayward spirits*? Wayward, as in evil? What's a *bols* or a *Scraythe*?"

"Is this a clue?" February asks.

"BoLS…B.O.L.S. Book of Lost Spirits?" Rose suggests.

"Use the book at dawn and dusk. I don't get it."

"So they possessed it at some point? The book is real!" Rose's pulse begins to race.

"It has to be!"

"Or did previous Peacocks use it, and something bad happened, so they hid it, never to be used again? Why else would they burn the notes?" Rose flips through the rest of the pile, but most of the pages disintegrate upon her touch.

"I have no idea; I haven't heard any family stories like that." February sinks to her knees to see if there are any other legible papers in the furnace.

Still. Someone was investigating spirits of some sort, and the notes clearly say, "use the BoLS."

Use it how? And *Scraythe*. She's never come across that word in her research. Is it possible then to use the book to summon spirits of the dead?

Rose's wildest imagination whispers to her, *yes, it's possible.*

"Heya, Rose. Come back to Earth." February waves her hand in front of Rose's daydreaming face and glances up at the domed skylight above. "I told my mom I'd be home before dusk, but I'll come back tomorrow. We've gotta solve this thing."

"Dusk curfew, huh? Sure. I'll be here. Meat Bones and I. *All day, every day,*" Rose says, as she scratches his back.

Although now, this summer isn't going to be nearly as dull or lonely as she predicted.

Chapter 8

Peacock Manor
Day 146,602

I've done my best to keep out pests and vermin. Not a single mouse or squirrel in the rafters, nor an owl or sparrow in my eaves, and certainly never any termites chewing away my cypress columns. But yesterday, I let in a fuzzy puppy dog. Dogs are disgusting.

However, he was being chased—by evil. He'd run and run from something dirty and rotten, and I could not let those parasites get him, so I let him in for safety. The girls seem to like him.

Hopefully, he won't leave messes or chew up my insides.

No one else has visited the laboratory in so long. It reminds me of my younger days when there were many Peacocks here. I vibrated with activity, feeling like a bell constantly rung. There were countless humans I could observe, parties at which I could show off some of my powers, visitors I could entertain and harass and scare. Once, I grew exhausted of seeing the same guest in my upstairs hallway mirror—fussing with six or seven or eight dresses and complimenting herself—that I changed the reflection she saw. She screamed and

Yun Johnson

fainted, rolled over the banister, and broke her neck in the fall.

Humans are so frail.

Chapter 9

The Answer

Amber appears in a dream that night, from beyond the ether.

Vivid and bright, as if Rose were speaking to her mirror reflection in daylight, Amber whispers...

Find me, Rose. Rudder, meteor, mirage, arachnid.

"Amber! How? I want to. What do those words mean? I need you. I miss—"

You're in the right place at the right time.

"Is it the book? Can I find you with *The Book of Lost Spirits*?"

I am Lost. Find the Book. Hurry. It's not safe here. I'll be gone by the end of summer.

"What? No! Amber, don't go yet. What's not safe? I need to talk to you. It wasn't my fault, right? I couldn't save you..."

Rose shudders from under the covers.

Rudder. She used one to steer the boat. There was a rudder on the rowboat *that* day at the lake—the day she'd lost Amber. The ghost. The accident. How did she escape and make it to shore, but not Amber? Rose grasps at the brutal memory.

She keeps her eyes closed to see Amber's face, even as the tears leak out. Stupid tears.

Does the Manor have anything to do with her

dream? She'd stopped dreaming of her sister months ago. *Find the book.*

Rose wants to take control of her life this summer and part of her plan includes another serious attempt at summoning her sister's spirit. A quest for proof and answers. To find out what happened. Closure. *The Book of Lost Spirits* is her best and last chance to contact her sister.

She's tried everything. Once, she thought she'd succeeded—that she'd called up a spirit—but it was only a neighborhood power outage. Another time, an incantation she purchased online infected her computer with a virus. She held a grudge after that and gave up for a while.

She forces herself to re-focus, repeating the riddle half-heartedly out loud.

The doorbell dings twice, as if her words have conjured a distraction.

She glances at her reflection in the mirror, appearing more awake than she feels. When the bell dings again, she wonders why no one is answering the door.

No—she knows why. Dad and Mom leave her alone most days, now that she is old enough to go without a sitter. They have writing and publishing, or baking and church.

In middle school, Dad sought out her opinion on how his book was unfolding, so she'd read his manuscripts. Together, they controlled the fates of villains, heroes, and everyone in between. She loved the thrill of knowing that *anything was possible* in those other worlds, and that Dad cared to know her thoughts.

These days, his series is formulaic, and he no

longer asks for her input. Just as well. She'd grown weary of his hero, always making it out alive for the next book. Over and over again. Dad's protagonist would survive and vanquish the vengeful spirit in his current novel. She'd bet her first edition of *In a Hundred Dreams* she'd inherited from Grandma on it.

Rapid knocking follows the doorbell. Someone wants in. Now.

"Be right there!" Rose wipes the side of her face one more time before hurrying down the stairs.

She swings open the door.

Dark-as-night hair, sharp all-consuming eyes.

Kamdyn. Refined and reserved and grave. He dresses like he's going to an interview. This guy knows his brand.

She's filled with a strange mixture of burning curiosity and cold dread.

Since words fail her and she remains silent, he speaks first.

"Hullo. I hope I'm not scaring you. I'm supposed to meet February here today. Her mother wants the old glass replaced, and I need to take window measurements." His voice is low and wooden, and he barely looks at her—instead, his dark lashes flicker upwards as he eyeballs the windows of the Manor, searching for something.

Behind him, mauve clouds gather on the far side of the mountains. Rose breathes in the metallic air. Rain today.

"She's not here yet," Rose replies, as toneless as he.

He scratches his pointed chin absently and surveys the upstairs windows. "I could start the work now; I

63

need to know how many there are," he says, attempting to gain control of the awkward silence.

He reaches a long arm out and for a wild second she thinks he's going to touch her shoulder for some reason, but he indicates the windowpane behind her.

"Sure," she says, peering up at the darkening sky. "If it begins to rain, you can let yourself in."

"My dad would say, 'We are not made of sugar,'" he remarks with a straight face.

"Funny. I wonder where you get your stoicism."

Despite himself, his rosy mouth tightens into a straight line for a second. A smile? A smirk?

She isn't sure why she can say anything to him at all, except that he's distracted, counting windows, and isn't even looking at her.

Relieved to see a flicker of white crossing the red garden bridge, Rose cranes her neck around Kamdyn's tall frame.

February speeds up the path when she sees the two of them and races up the stone stairs, greeting them with her endless smile.

"Rose! Kam!"

"I need some numbers, then I'll be out of the way," Kamdyn tells her. He hands her a neatly folded note— thick stationery from someone's fancy desk.

"Super. We'll be in the library if you need us. Rose and I are working on a project," February says, but he's already descended the stairway to examine the windows on the other side of the Manor.

February stuffs Kamdyn's letter into the hidden pocket of her dress. She wears the same single emerald-on-gold earring and white dress as yesterday.

She returns her attention to Rose.

"You're frowning," February says, pinching Rose's cheek in an attempt to mold it into a smile.

"I'm not a morning person. Kamdyn throws me off." Her eyes feel puffy; the left one stings more than the right one from rubbing too hard earlier. Rose drags her hands through her short hair to spike it out.

"Throws you off...in a good way?" February asks, an impish gleam in her eyes.

"Good, how?"

"Like if you're on a rollercoaster. Does he throw you off like you want to vomit, or are you a tiny bit thrilled?"

Oh. *A little of both*, if she's honest. Rose avoids answering out loud and dodges the subject completely.

"Feebs, *you* might be a ghost because you have the same outfit on," Rose points out instead, as they turn toward the Manor library.

"True. *You've* got the same shirt on as yesterday," February retorts. "You can tell it's the same one by the pixie cake crumbs." She reaches over and pretends to dust off Rose's collarbone.

"Doh. Yes. Yes, I do." Rose winces, peering down at her favorite black top, worn and washed so many times it's turned a purply-charcoal gray. She's cried into it many times, but charcoal gray is a good color to hide lonely pastimes such as crying.

"Look at this." February's hand slips back into the pocket of her dress. "I collect dead animal skulls I find outside. *This* one is good luck. It'll help us with our task today," she says, opening her palm to reveal a crow's skull. It is yellowish, except for the dark pointy beak, tinged like a bruised toenail.

"How morbid of you," Rose says. *Yet, kind of*

intriguing.

"The biggest skull in my collection is part of a bear's jaw I found in the forest."

"A bear? Did it die of old age or something?"

"I'm not sure what killed it. There's lots of stuff in the forests here."

"Like wolves?"

"Predators, yes. Have you seen the rest of the Manor yet? I should've given you a better tour yesterday, but my mom doesn't want me out when the sun goes down. *Home before dusk.*" February mimics a voice but glances down at the skull in her hand.

"Is she overprotective? What happens after dark? It's such a sleepy place. My mom rides a bike to church. That kind of sleepy."

"Well…my dad disappeared a while ago. We don't know what happened." February's effervescence has suddenly deflated.

A disappearance. Loss of a family member. Rose's stomach twists. "Geez, I'm so sorry."

"After dinner, around dusk, he came to fix the lights at the Manor and didn't come back." February's throat bobs. She traces her fingers over the curved beak of the crow's skull.

There is more to the story, but she offers nothing else.

"Oh crap, that's terrible," Rose sputters, shocked into a lack of more eloquent words.

Feeby's words ring through her. *Dusk, twilight.* The hour when spirits and humans can pass into each other's worlds, she said yesterday.

Rose's bones shiver. No matter how high the summer temperatures reach outside, the Manor is freezing inside. She rubs her arms, trying to erase the goosebumps. Could the book help locate February's father? Is that why she seems to want it as much as Rose does?

February bows her head—her silence dismisses the subject.

Meat Bones decides that now is a good time for violence. He launches himself from behind Rose, stabbing the back of her knees with his claws, painfully raking her skin. *Aah!* She spins around. He isn't a big guy yet, but he's working on it.

"Heya, M.B." February bends forward to pet him, but he ducks back with a low wag, still unsure of her.

"Why are you scared of Feeby?! You're not going to claw up her legs, just mine?" Rose scoops him up when they reach the end of the hall.

She and February each heave open one double door into the monstrous library and at the same time, tilt their faces skyward. Normally, sunlight would be streaming from the skylight, but today, dark rain clouds hover.

Rose flicks on the entire panel of switches to a dozen hanging lanterns and copper lamps, illuminating the room with a ripened apricot glow.

"This is amazing. After my vacation is over, can I just live here and be the manor librarian?" she marvels. Tall sliding ladders stretch up ceiling-high shelves. Books upon endless books.

February whirls around, holding one hand at her sternum to steady the pocketwatch twirling with her. "Right? It's bigger than my house!"

Rose indicates the dusty, uppermost shelves. "Do you think there are old, cursed books here?"

Muffled thunder rattles the glass windows. Meat Bones snarls back.

"Good dramatic timing. Things get dark with you fast, huh." February giggles. She empties her pockets onto the desk beside her.

Their notes from yesterday.

The crow's skull.

The letter from Kamdyn.

Rose eyes the letter. She can't make out any words through the thick, twice-folded stationery.

February clambers up the nearest ladder to the top. "Grammy's old books are up here; I bet there's one that'll help us. Some of these books have been here since the Manor was built!"

Her head angles sideways as she tugs on spine after spine.

The storm settles over them, smelling of salty grass and rotting soil—the scent of sky meeting earth.

Rose can't help but check the windows to see if Kamdyn is still outside, caught in the rain. She imagines him and his impeccable suit standing out there drenched but suffering in quiet dignity.

She sees no sign of a dark suit and tries not to think about him any further.

"You think *The Book of Lost Spirits* used to be on one of these shelves?" Rose wonders aloud, but February doesn't hear her over the splatter of rain.

Rose brushes the burgundy leather of a text written in a language she doesn't recognize. Who read this and what journey did it take to end up here? She sniffs the vanillic, mushroom scent of old paper. Paper decaying.

How can she get back to where she wants to be?

She slides out a book with Peacock Manor on its

cover, except with a blue roof instead of green. She rifles through a few pages, stopping at a sketch of a stone lantern, similar to the little temples in the graveyard.

"The Five parts of a Lantern, from bottom to top, represent: Earth, Water, Fire, Wind, and Void (or Spirit)." Spirit, huh? She reads on. *"When a Physical form dies, it returns to its Elemental forms."*

Elemental forms. This sounds useful for her own research. She sets the book aside on a desk to take upstairs with her later.

February cocks her head. *"Spirituality in Architecture.* What're you searching for?" she asks.

"Oh. Answers."

"To?"

"Life, Death…Where you go when you die?" *Where is Amber now?*

"You think about that? You're kinda profound. I was having a contest with myself looking for the oldest book." February draws out a large tome from the highest shelf. "Like this—it's handwritten!"

"Before the printing press?" Rose asks.

"Yep. A six-hundred-year-old book makes me feel like a bumblebee. Robbie told me that bumblebees only live for six weeks. *Six tiny weeks*! They collect pollen for the hive, and then they're just…gone. They don't even get to see all four seasons of the year. Isn't that heartbreaking?"

Don't get to see all four seasons of the year. That *is* incredibly sad.

Rose is jarred out of her melancholy thoughts with the next snap of silvery lightning and thunder—louder, nearer than before.

The lanterns flash off and on as the sky weeps.

February calls down to her from the ladder. "Summer thunderstorms. They're wild here! Do you wanna take a look at our notes...?" Her extended finger lands on an empty table. "Wait, M.B., what're you chewing there?"

Rose rushes over and kneels before him. "Aww, Meat Bones, don't do that. Come here!" He refuses her. He's also knocked down the letter Kamdyn handed February, and Rose quickly unfolds it as she plucks it off the floor.

It is blank, except for a Charbon hotel logo and five numbers written with care:

10-13-2-5-13. She's crouched with her back turned to February, so she folds it back up and replaces it on the table.

She captures Meat Bones and pries the rest of their crumpled notes from his jaws even as he tries to dip his head to avoid her. It's too late. He's swallowed half the sheet.

She uses her thumb to iron out the remaining half—the half with the riddle written in full. "I guess it doesn't change the fact that we still only have four words to go on."

February gracefully slides down the ladder in a flurry of white cotton and quick limbs.

They each plop into ruby-red armchairs by the empty fireplace. February reaches for the nearest lamp and snaps twice on the cord for extra lighting.

Rudder. Meteor. Mirage. Arachnid.

"*THE BOOK OF LOST SPIRITS is here, So Is The Key*," Rose reads.

"Key to what? They are both lost. As am I,"

February balks. She slumps deeper in her chair. "We need a key and a rudder and…"

"I said that before. You said it was too many steps and you didn't want to do that."

She laughs. "Oh, yeah. That sounds like me."

Rose studies their chewed-up notes with piercing scrutiny. Rain lashes the windows.

Certain letters pop up at her, emphasized by the wrinkles and creases and—

"Wait. I see something. That's clever," she mutters. Her pulse quickens, working its thrum into her ears, keeping time with the splattering rain.

"What, where?" February asks.

"I've figured out the riddle," Rose says with certainty.

Chapter 10

A Windy Whisper

"Shut your face! I don't see what you're saying," February says. The storm outside churns, and the howling wind rattles the windows.

"It says right here, 'S-O is the key!'"

"Huh?" February scrunches her face.

Rose explains. "Anytime there is a letter S and O, the letter in between spells out the clue! The answer to this clue is: a-t-t-i-c!"

THE BOOK OF LOST SPIRITS is Here, So Is The Key

By AmarylliS A. O. Peacock

LaSt Over the ocean on a sailing ship,

Dying StOne falling from the night's grip,

Desert illuSiOn,

Your arthropod, the ScOrpion.

"You're a genius!" February shrieks, clapping Rose's back.

"How do you get to the attic?" Rose asks as they rush out of the library.

"Through the middle tower. It's the third story."

Rose pivots toward the nearest stairway.

"No. You don't take the main stairs. The tower entrance is a hidden panel," February says.

"Where?"

"In the banquet room on the first floor." February does an about-face down the hallway into the West Wing.

"The dining room? That's why I couldn't find the door to the tower."

The two of them squeak past the long table in the midnight blue room.

"Over here." February motions toward a long woodblock scroll depicting a scaled sea beast with a mane, four tiny legs, and a tail.

"What's that? Looks like a dinosaur."

"It's a powerful sea spirit that drives away diseases. And it can foretell the future." February leans her shoulder into a wood panel next to the painting.

It spins like a revolving door, opening to the bottom of a spiral staircase.

"Cool. So, if it can tell the future, then the future is pre-determined?" Rose asks.

"Interesting. Never thought of it that way. I think everything that happens is random and chaotic. Can't control what's next." February starts up the stairwell.

They race up the creaky stairs into the highest tower at the center of the Manor, hoping the attic door will open up to a golden beam of light shining upon a magical book.

At the top, February throws on a light switch as Rose trips over the threshold, emerging to face a stained-glass window. It's the circular window she saw from the driveway.

Shades of blue glass form a mosaic of a ship, and hand-painted letters label the window, "HTRON." The lettering appears backward, meant to be read from the outside, looking in.

"How are we going to find anything in all this junk?" February wails, flailing her arms at the stacks of boxes.

"Clearly, this is where things go when you never want to see them again," Rose says.

The attic smells of dirty rugs, the rotting wood of broken furniture, and moth-eaten dresses. February fans the air. "Stinks like stewed beans in here," she says, wrinkling her nose.

Rose sputters with laughter. "That's weird, but you're not wrong."

February slides past a mannequin with no arms and begins flipping open hat boxes. She shoves an ostrich feather hat onto her head and twirls like a possessed feather duster. "I wish I had fancy clothes. Why don't people wear crazy hats anymore?"

"Your hat is haunted, for sure. It works on you, though," Rose tells her.

"What does that say about me?!" February laughs.

Rose opens the nearest box lid. "Seashells and ocean-themed decor. Kitschy."

She crouches to pick up a large conch shell and holds it to her ear, expecting to hear waves, though she knows the sound is only air moving inside its curved walls.

"Whoooo…Roooose, Rosse, Rose," a girl's voice whispers.

What the—? She spins the bone-colored shell over. Empty.

She holds it to her ear again.

"It's me," rasps a windy whisper from a faraway place, possibly from her own deep desire to hear the voice of the one person she knows she may never see

again.

"Ammmber…Rooose…Amber…Rose…What happened to me can happen to you."

Dizzying from holding her breath, she strains to hear more. A warning, or a greeting from beyond? Does this mean contact with a spirit is possible?

Before, she might have paused in doubt, but here in the attic, the thought has already grown into something more than a seed of potential.

The Book of Lost Spirits. It has to be close. She is near the book, and its magic allows—

"ROSE," comes a real voice.

"Ahh!" She drops the shell, jumping at the sound of February's voice.

"Hell-oh, you've spaced out!"

Rose swallows and takes a deep breath. What is wrong with her? Did she drink too much of her dad's coffee this morning?

"You scared me," she scolds February.

"Oh, sorry. It's so quiet up here. I was reading these old letters. Look! Lovers used to write to each other and wait weeks to hear back. Sounds so lonely, right? Do you ever…feel lonely?" she asks.

Rose recomposes herself. "Yep. All the time." *Truth.* "You?"

"Sometimes. I miss my dad. He and I were always close."

"I'm sorry about your dad. My parents and I aren't close. Anymore."

"What do you do when you're lonely?"

"I think you know the answer. Read. You?"

"Don't laugh, but there's a tree I like to sit in. Hah. I'm not intellectual like you."

Feeby's answer makes Rose like her even more. "You be you."

"For sure. If you had one wish, what would it be?"

A deafening silence ensues. *Find the book, find her sister, find out if*—she can't say it out loud, not to herself, not to February. "I need to think about my answer. Own a hundred dogs, start a dog rescue. You?"

"Sometimes I dream…well, I've never been far. I wish for my dad back and that my parents and I lived by the beach, somewhere tropical and flat."

Away from this house are the unspoken words.

"That's a good wish. You don't go on vacation?"

"No, not really. We don't have much money. Look at this thing, a seashell lamp?!"

February smiles, perking up again, and resumes rummaging.

Rose wonders if her perpetual cheeriness hides darker feelings.

****

February treasures the knick-knacks they uncover. She pretends they are archeologists digging up artifacts.

Rose doesn't see the value in any of it, but February claims for her bedroom:

—an old-fashioned hotel counter bell cast as a sea turtle,

—a large pink sand hourglass (possibly haunted, they agreed),

—coral inlaid brass candlesticks

—and a ballgown in sequins of lavender, Rose's favorite color.

By the late afternoon, the rain subsides, and February packs up an armful of goods to take home. They've found no sign of a second clue. But they solved the first clue, which meant they were one step closer.

And Rose found something surprising in the attic— something she hasn't had in a very long time. Companionship. Something shifts in her, deep down, and she lets herself hang onto a sliver of hope and possibility. Hope and possibility of finding her sister, yes, but also of knowing that things will be okay, with a teeny chance at getting back to how they were before. Before…

Before that horrendous day at the lake.

Chapter 11

Happy Birthday

The very next day, June 18, is Rose's seventeenth birthday.

She remembers when she turned thirteen, and she and Amber decided to save the world. Instead of presents, they donated the money to an animal charity. That year was elephants, the next was orangutans, then marine mammals. Dad gave them his credit card and trusted them to do their research to pick an organization.

She hasn't celebrated her birthday since her sister died. Why did she get to go on, but not Amber?

It feels like gloating to her, to celebrate.

On the dining table, lavender-yuzu pixie cakes are arranged on a platter, each little cube with one colorful frosting letter:

H-A-P-P-Y B-I-R-T-H-D-A-Y.

Mom must have taken the rest (twenty-four pixie cakes in a batch) with her. Dad probably doesn't remember what day, or even month, it is. He'll remember after he receives an alert for a charge on his credit card she uses to make her animal charity donation.

"Habby Burfday," she says, with H and A in her mouth. She sets aside Y and A from the right-hand edge of the platter.

"You can start at the other end, Amber," she whispers inaudibly, trying to concentrate on the sugary sweetness rather than the saltiness of the tears spilling into her mouth.

Chapter 12

Peacock Manor
Day 146,603

Pixie Cakes is always eating cakes alone while crying.

It seems sad in the way that I am sad.

Her sorrow feels the same as mine.

Chapter 13

The Dead Dolls

The *idea* of a treasure hunt is much more romantic than is the reality, Rose grumbles under her breath, after long days of sorting attic antiques—though she's happy that February comes over for so many hours of the day.

"I need a nap," February says, flat on her back, staring up at the peaked ceiling of the attic. "But my uncles are pressuring my mom to sell the Manor. We need this book." She rolls up off the floor and picks cobwebs off her dress.

Rose chimes in. "What're we supposed to find— another vial? Look at these windows, though!" After dragging and sorting trunks and boxes all afternoon, she's exposed three more circular windows. They are a matching stained-glass set:

North (a blue ship),
South (gold coins in yellow glass),
East (a red flower),
West (trees and green waves).

Light filters through the pigmented glass, scattering shards of color on the crates and chests stacked all around them.

Meat Bones sniffs an immense wooden toy chest in the southeast corner, his half-tail confidently pointing straight up in the air. He barks bravely at a porcelain doll whose eyes have fallen out.

"Thanks for the warning, M.B. That is one terrifying doll," Rose says.

February plucks it up by its armpits and walks it over. "I just clawed myself out of a doll coffin. I come to life when you go to sleep, and I'll take your eyes for my own."

Meat Bones pulls his ears back and unleashes a loud snarl, *Grrrrrrrrr*. The brown and gray hairs on his neck inflate, and he barks once more before fleeing the attic. His doggy nails click-clack all the way down the tower.

They ignore his warning.

"Haa! You scared him, poor guy." Rose opens the toy chest to find the doll's family. Vintage dolls in lacy dresses and cherry lips ogle her with glass eyes and blinky eyelashes. Some are the size of a small child. She stoops closer—they smell like mothballs. The dolls reveal their true age in their missing eyes, broken limbs, and the cracks in their skulls. They died a long time ago from lack of playtime.

"I'll take puppy eyeballs too, Meat Bones!" Feeby calls after him.

"Don't worry, buddy, I found a worthy opponent!" Rose draws out a large doll in a white dress with a shiny ceramic face and short mahogany hair that feels like real hair. "This one looks like you, Feebs! It just needs a green-and-gold earring and pocketwatch."

"Shut your face. That one's awful. I don't look like that!" Her hands are on her hips in false outrage. She laughs.

Rose lifts the doll by its neck, ready to attack, but

her attention shifts to the bottom of the trunk.

She's exposed a mouse hole where the doll was sitting.

Casting the doll aside, she kneels by the chest, using her knuckles to rap the bottom of the trunk. "Sounds hollow!" She strikes the base again. "Could be a false bottom?"

"You think?" February asks. She folds over and works quickly to remove the rest of the dolls.

With the trunk empty, Rose hooks a finger into the hole and pries up the wooden board.

"Oh, I cracked it."

Feeby pulls up the broken panel the rest of the way and throws it aside.

"There IS something here—a doorknob!" Rose ducks into the trunk.

She and Feeby crash heads when they both cram in for a look.

"Ow, oops!" February reaches in and twists the doorknob, lifting a trapdoor. "Whoa, a secret room, between the attic and the second floor?" She tips forward over the edge of the trunk, hanging upside down. "There's a bed, a desk, and a little wooden chair…Hey, this would be the thirteenth bedroom! I bet one of the dolls lived here," she jokes.

Rose's face crumples in disgust at the thought of anyone living in this dark, windowless room.

"What else is in there?" She can't see much past the back of February's head and shoulders.

"Look for yourself," Feeby says.

They trade places, and Rose hangs upside down through the door. February's pocketwatch dangles next to Rose's ear. Today, the little clock is ticking faster, but unevenly.

Tick-tick-tick, TICK. Tick-tick-tick, TICK.

The bedroom beneath them is long but low, complete with small furniture.

The only way into the thirteenth bedroom is to lower down into the trunk feet first or jump. She'll have to pull herself up to climb out. Can she even do a pull-up?

Rose turns to her friend.

At the same moment, they each jab a finger at the other, saying, "*You go in first.*" It breaks the tension for an instant, though they don't recognize the nervous, too-high laughter that comes out of them.

"All right, all right, I'm going in," February says. She steps over the side of the trunk and lowers herself with a reverse pull-up, feet first. Rose watches her fall into the darkness. She hears February tug on the cord of a lamp, but the bulb is out.

Rose folds over the edge, peering in. "Are you okay? Is there another light switch?"

Feeby skates her hands along the walls. "Got it." The sconces on each side of the bed flicker on.

"Will I fit?" Rose dangles her feet, slithers halfway into the thirteenth bedroom, and quickly lets go before she can change her mind, hoping she can get out. She drops into a deep knee bend.

The raisin-brown wallpaper peels in places, patterned with floral vines the color of mold on bread.

They stand side by side in the secret room, built between walls, between floors.

Rose surveys the room. "That's strange. This furniture set looks just like the one I had when I was little, except smaller. And...I had that violet quilt," she says, gesturing. Cautious and guarded, she circles the room.

"That's super creepy. Was it a common design?"

"Arranged the same way, though," Rose murmurs. "Desk to the left, lamp on the right…"

"Is this what the riddle wanted us to find?"

"I'm not sure—did someone live in here?" Rose's mind races, forgetting about their search for a clue. *This is unreal.*

A secret room. That looks like a replica of her childhood bedroom—except without a second bed. Amber's bed is missing.

A secret room. Used to hide something. People tend to hide what is wrong or dangerous or shameful.

Cold dread seeps into her blood. What is this place? She shudders.

February shakes her head no. "That's disturbing," she says as she hunts around the desk drawers, pulling them in and out. Empty.

Rose isn't sure if February even believes her, so she kneels beside the familiar-looking bed, flapping the quilt before prodding under the small mattress. She sweeps an arm under the tiny bed, patting the wood floor, stopping when her hand lands on a sheet of paper, folded in half.

"Hold on…Feebs, I found something!"

"What?" Feeby asks, equally surprised.

Could it be the next clue? A piece of paper tossed under a bed seems a little easy, a little crude, even in a secret bedroom.

"Looks like a one-line note." Rose unfolds it and holds it to the light.

A jolt of disgust hits her. Too frightened to move,

she remains rooted silently in place as her blood thrums.

"Rose? What is it?" February asks.

Rose passes the note without speaking, afraid if she parts her lips, she won't be able to stop herself from screaming.

Scribbled in the thin red ink of
mistakes,
danger,
and warning:
IT'S TIME TO GO HOME, ROSE.

****

Rose thrusts the paper in Feeby's face. "What the hell—what is this?!" She hurls the note across the floor in revulsion. It whirls twice in the air, dropping like an autumn leaf before settling next to February's foot. Rose searches her friend's face for answers—any sign that this is a joke—but finds nothing but confusion and fear in February's wide eyes.

Not a single coherent thought comes to mind, and she is certain she's about to pass out. She last glimpses February raising both hands to her mouth to muffle a whimper as the lights in the thirteenth bedroom flash and die.

Muted light casts down upon them from the opening of the trunk, their only source of faint light, and it isn't enough to see the now-dark corners of the thirteenth bedroom. The edges of Rose's vision register movement, but as she seeks them out, the shadows are still again.

The sound of gushing water hisses inside the walls of the room, as though a pipe has burst. Now they are in a boat or a wooden crate, sinking rapidly to the bottom of the ocean.

Rose holds her breath as if she were already underwater, despite her hammering heart demanding more air.

"What is happening—?"

"Rose?" February's voice falters, but Rose is lost inside her own head.

We aren't drowning; it isn't possible. Old pipes, ancient plumbing, she tells herself. *Old plumbing, old plumbing—or it's raining outside again.*

February shrieks as the trunk door above them slams shut. The last of the light vanishes, and darkness swallows them whole.

Rose's eyelids may as well be sewn shut.

Water gushes from behind the walls, its gurgling sounds alarmingly forming words.

Come with me, we belong together, the voice calls. *I know you can hear me. We can help each other. I know what you seek. I am here.*

"Amber?" Rose whispers. She covers one ear with her hand as the other arm swipes at the dark in front of her. "Do you hear that?" she asks February.

Feeby doesn't respond, but Rose feels her tugging on her arm, wanting to link elbows the way she likes to do. Rose steps sideways to find her friend's hand. She needs to know February is still there, through the dark, watery voice.

Instead, from across the room, February pleads, "Rose, I'm over here, where are you? I can't see anything. The chair! I need the chair to reach the door."

"Aaahhhiiiiiii! You're not touching my arm? Who's here?" Rose flails, brushing her arm as if casting off bugs, and flings herself toward February's voice.

Just a spider, a large spider at worst. Think logically. Imagination only gives life to nightmares.

"What? Rose, I'm over here! I found it!" February stammers.

Rose hears her dragging the chair, wood against wood. A doorknob rattles, and light floods down, illuminating their escape.

She stumbles forward and grabs February's calves to propel her upward through the trunk opening, then claws herself up the sides, reaching for a hold on the edges. Splinters and pain tear at her hands, but she doesn't care if she is bleeding.

Rose surges up and over the edge of the trunk, twisting her way out, and knocks her head against a wood beam. She collapses limply onto her side. Tiny white flashes of constellations appear in her vision.

"Is somebody here? Feeby, is this place haunted? I heard—the first night, and now—fingers...touched...water sounds..." She swallows hard, bracing herself for the truth.

"There are legends and rumors, and that's what guests come here for, but—but," February stutters.

"Who put the note there, then?" Rose interrupts her. "Spirits can manipulate objects and send messages..."

Folklore given form and flesh mortifies Rose to the bones. She wants to believe—wants to seek out and discover—but what if she becomes part of the legend? *Rose Green, taken by Peacock Manor, never to be seen again....*

No! No part of her wants that.

"You think?" February stares round-eyed at her, awaiting an explanation.

Rose's mind wriggles and writhes. "Who—how—why..." she sputters. Is this proof of the paranormal? Her name is on the note. *Could it be Amber contacting her?*

She rolls off of her side and rummages through her thoughts. "Is someone *trying* to scare us?" she asks. "Is there someone who would want to stop us from finding *The Book of Lost Spirits*?"

"My family gave up searching a while ago. But now that we have a clue in hand, maybe there's renewed interest. I told my mom what we found on the headstone, but I don't know if she would tell my uncles...Have you seen anyone sneak around here?" February asks.

"No. But I heard laughter the first night I was here. Could one of your relatives have hidden in the Manor?" Rose's nerves rattle, but she grows defiant. If someone wants to scare them out of looking for the book, it means they too believe it exists. If the book is up for grabs, then Rose wants it for herself, and February. Still, her courage falters, knowing someone snuck in while she and her parents were in the house. *No one is here now, are they?*

"I'll ask my mom if anyone else was supposed to be here, if anyone could've heard us talking about the book," Feeby says.

They rush to gather up their belongings. Rose is about to exit the tower when the low afternoon sunlight seeps through the circular window on the left wall, lighting the attic with an unsettling ruby glow. The same red—*as that ink*. She retches silently, the walls closing in.

But that light.

It comes from the red stained-glass flower in the window.

The lettering at the base of the round pane reads, "TSAE."

East.

"That window. It's wrong," she says with certainty.

Rose points to two windows, left and right. "The sun sets in the west. Everyone knows that. But look. West's window is green, and all the light is coming in through the red window right now. The west and east labels are wrong. The red flower, is it an amaryllis bloom, your grandmother's namesake? Same as on her gravestone?"

Together, they inch toward the red window and peer outside. The jagged skyline of mountains and trees seems both near and far from high up in their attic tower.

The sun lurks near the horizon in front of them. West.

The north window facing the front of the Manor and the south window opening to the back lawn are correctly placed. East and west are swapped.

"What does it mean?" Rose asks.

"East and west switched, huh," February says cautiously. "I might know this one. The Garden of Mistakes. The sundial in the bird bath is mislabeled, too. Same thing on a sea captain statue."

"Garden? Let's take a look?" Rose asks as her hand tightens around the door handle.

The two of them hurtle down the dim spiral stairs, hoping never to return to the attic. They exit through the dining room panel.

February glances out the window before answering

and blanches.

"Um, how about tomorrow? The sun is getting pretty low. It's time for me to go home." Her cheeks remain pale. She's still visibly shaken by the thirteenth bedroom but promises to come over tomorrow, to explore the Garden of Mistakes.

Rose walks her to the front door, doubting February would be back after this.

February rushes past her, out of the Manor, her bangs flying out of her eyes as she hurries down the front stairs to the driveway.

"See you tomorrow, Feebs." Rose waves at her, but February doesn't look back.

Rose lingers outside long after February disappears down the lane into the line of dark alpine trees, their jagged outlines in sharp relief against the dimming sky. The twilight hour today is ultramarine, with ribbons of the palest pink.

Always home before twilight. Because her dad stayed out past twilight and vanished. But there is more to the story, more February refuses to tell.

Rose doesn't press her because it's none of her business, but she is certain the Manor isn't the only one with secrets. What is February hiding?

The stinging of her fingers, raw from clawing the wood of the chest, reminds her of the horror coiling within.

What have they set in motion?

She shivers off the prickle creeping across the nape of her neck and shuts the door.

****

That night, she lies numbly in bed, her limbs made of stone—as cold and heavy as the boulders of the mountain. Nothing explains how or why the note would be in the attic for her to find. She swallows back the urge to vomit.

If it's a prank or scare tactic, she doesn't want those responsible to win. If it's a more sinister phenomenon, she is powerless to stop an unknown terror in an ancient house. She slams her eyes shut, imagining her walls have fallen away into a deep, dark forest where thoughts no longer exist.

Her mind reaches for her sister, the way a small child grasps a beloved stuffed animal for false security.

Someone or *something* here doesn't want her searching for the book.

What will they do to her next?

It might be more than a threatening note.

She reminds herself that she is in charge of her fate, but fear ruthlessly overwhelms her resolve. With one ragged inhale, Rose makes a traitorous decision right then and there.

Chapter 14

Peacock Manor
Day 146,610

I am not sure if the Peacock girl heard me in the attic. I have decided to try to help. I changed the room around—to make it familiar.

Humans like to support each other in their endeavors. Pixie Cakes has been assisting with the riddles, and February seems grateful. I have hopes that February Peacock will like me if I help her.

However, looking back, they both appeared frightened out of their wits.

Chapter 15

Dad's Betrayal!

February's cheery face falls when Rose announces that she doesn't want to continue the hunt for clues.

"I'm creeped out. I quit," Rose says. The treasure hunt doesn't belong to her. The note says so in its own way. *You don't belong here. You're not in charge of your own fate here*, it warns her.

"I am too, but it must be a prank. To scare anyone looking for clues."

"Likely. But still—it had *my* name on it. I feel gross about it." She crosses her arms, refusing to change her mind despite Feeby's pleading eyes.

"I understand. I do too. I talked to my mom, and she said the housekeepers are here Mondays, and the landscapers come on Fridays. The repair guy is new, but he works for the Charbons, and Kamdyn helps with maintenance too, as you know. That's it."

"Huh. I haven't seen any of them, except Kamdyn that first night."

"If you woke up before noon, you'd see more people," February remarks, leveling a knowing look at Rose.

"Hah! Right, for sure."

"But I want to keep searching—if the book is here, my mom and I need it. I'll go snoop around the Garden

94

of Mistakes. If you change your mind, come hang out with me."

Rose retreats inside, but peers out the window at February.

Once her friend disappears around the corner, Rose slinks down the hall into her dad's office, whose bay windows provide a view down the back of the hill where the statues dwell. Even in the daytime, the Manor lets in very little sunlight. The wiring is old—bulbs flicker, exhausted from lighting such a shadowy place.

Dad isn't around. His desk is littered with open books, a plate with crumbs, and a neat row of drying mushrooms. The computer screen is still on a half-written page.

He must've left to get more coffee, and Rose can't help herself. Whose life is he creating today?

She scrolls up the screen a bit, and begins reading:

"One cold and rainy March when she was nine, she found a bumblebee floating lifeless in a puddle.

'It's dead, honey,' her parents said.

'No! If you give up now, you're as good as killing it.'

She fished it out with a leaf and placed it in a heart-shaped jewelry box, insisting it was merely cold and in shock. Her parents pitied her; they'd have to console her when it dried and fell apart, and she'd weep over its tragic life.

She ignored them and warmed the bee with a hairdryer.

As it dried, its antennae began to flinch. It wasn't dead at all. She fed it sugar water with a dropper. Her parents warned her how clinging to the edge of life also meant hanging over the precipice of death. She transferred it to a shoebox and placed it near the heater overnight.

'Bees can't fly when it's below 50 degrees,' she said. 'It just needs heat and some food.'

Mom and Dad expected it to be dead by morning.

The next day, when she opened the lid, the little bee buzzed its wings in place, eager to depart.

Her parents looked at the other in astonishment. 'Did you replace it with a live bee just to make her happy?' they mouthed at each other.

The sun was out now, and she released it in the garden, watching it crawl onto a camellia bush before pushing off and disappearing into the sky.

'You go and have the best life ever!' she yelled, waving it on. She'd saved the bee, let it go, and trusted it to survive and live its life. She believed in life. And moving on. And surrendering to wherever it takes you."

Rose gapes at the screen in a mix of confusion and horror.

Hold on. What the hell?

This. Is. A. Familiar. Story. Dad is writing about…Amber?! He's out of ideas and has stolen Amber's life stories to flesh out a character in his book?

She lets loose an exasperated snarl and pounds her fist on the solid wood desk so hard it hurts. Their family can't talk about her sister, but he can use her life to fill a page of his fiction. Because he can't think of a better character!

Fury builds until it burns her insides. She wants to punch his laptop. She doesn't understand him anymore. She and Dad used to be buddies.

She clicks and swipes a few times and erases the

entire passage. "There. Edited for free. You're welcome, *Dad*." She feels wicked, but embraces it, slamming the screen down so she doesn't have to see it anymore before twisting away to glare out the window.

February glances up and waves enthusiastically.

Rose ducks, flattening herself against the desk. "Gah. Too late, she saw me," she mumbles, guilty of not helping her friend, but still nosy enough to spy.

"Roooose." February's faint little voice travels up and through the window. "Come out here!"

Rose folds over the desk and swings open the window only enough to lean her head out.

February beckons her. "Please help me. I can't reach the taller statues. I think I see something. I thought we were best friends! If someone is trying to scare us, you're letting them win, you know!" She throws her arms up and pushes off of the ground as hard as she can in a pathetic attempt to touch the horn of the narwhal statue she's searching.

"Oof." Feeby exhales as she lands once again, teetering and almost falling backward.

She thinks we're best friends.

"Grrr," Rose grumbles, still grumpy and deeply hurt by what she read on her dad's computer. She mutters about dysfunctional families.

"Don't growl at me. You're being a feral cat!" February yells up to her. "I'm not as clever as you. I'll never be able to do this on my own and the book will be lost for eternity—eternal failuuure, Rose!"

"Fine." Between her outrage at her dad using her beloved sister's memories and February's stark reminder that she needs friends *and* the book more than anything now, Rose decides to brave it out for another clue.

A voice from behind spooks her. "Rose, did you close my computer?" her dad asks.

Rose bangs her head on a brass lamp as she straightens up, knocking it over.

"Ah-ow!" She lurches backward.

As she spins around, furious again, she wonders how he snuck up so silently. Her dad, suspended mid-step through the doorway gripping his large mug of caffeine, can't take his eyes off his laptop.

In his eyes, she expects surprise, but it is fear that flashes across his face.

He knows what I read. She rubs her forehead, feeling for a bump.

"What are you doing here? Why is the window open?" he asks calmly. Too calmly.

She glares at him. "I saw what you wrote."

The mug in his hand is unsteady. He knows. But, like always, he dodges around uncomfortable topics. "What's wrong, sweetheart? Are you—?"

He avoids mentioning what she's seen: the character sketch based on Rose's sister.

What a nauseating betrayal. Rage spikes through her, but she stands her ground, hands on hips, and refuses to shed a tear or let him finish.

It all comes spilling out. All the feelings she's collected and bottled up about her family, her absent parents. Anger. Sadness. Loneliness. Back to anger again. She bares her teeth.

"I. Saw. What. You. Wrote!" she repeats emphatically, hurling a hand toward the laptop. "How can you make Amber a character in your stupid book?!"

She punctuates her statement by pounding her fist

on the desk, and swipes a notebook off, hitting the wall. A painting of a sea eagle tilts off at an odd angle. She'll have to fix that later—

"Don't be angry, I just…" His hand slips and he drops his coffee.

They both jump as the mug crashes to the floor, shattering. The shards fly at their feet, and Dad's now-empty hand shakes, but he remains rooted in place.

"Just what…?" She glances down at the puddle of coffee between them. The chocolate chips he threw in haven't fully melted. She needs to get her words out now or she'll never have the guts to say them later. "You know what? Dad, that's super crappy, using Amber and her bumblebee in your story! You don't understand! Geez, Dad, what the hell?"

He heaves a breath.

Here we go. He's going to let me have it for yelling at him.

"You know, Rose, I miss…" his voice cracks, and he pauses.

Oh? She straightens. Will they finally talk about real feelings? *I miss Amber*—say it. Say it, Dad.

"…I miss when we used to read my stories together. Don't be mad," he says quietly.

Nice sidestep, sir. "Don't tell me how to feel!" *I miss spending time with you, too.* No, that's not the point. "I miss her! Don't you? Why can't we talk about that?"

He says none of that. He is quiet and uncomfortable and can't meet her gaze. Her anger boils up again. He can't include Amber in the conversation.

The Greens do not discuss true feelings.

Deep, hurtful feelings, like invisible worms

tunneling through their hearts—not for mentioning, but for keeping sealed safely inside their shuttered heart jars.

He's only telling her that he misses her to calm her down. She doesn't want to do this. Her family is dysfunctional as hell. Before she allows herself to push the boundaries too far—to say something truly terrible—she gives him one last glare of death. Then, fury wins, and she hisses like the feral cat February claims she is and blows past him out the door.

She doesn't offer to help him clean up...

Doesn't care that she slams the door into the wall so hard the tilted painting comes crashing to the floor.

Doesn't look back at him at all, standing there, befuddled, and speechless.

She can't look back.

If she did—if she dared to glance over her shoulder—she would've seen the silent tears streaming down his face.

But she doesn't. She can't because she wouldn't be able to stand it.

Instead, she stops in front of the tea room, bracing herself beside the sliding doorway. She presses a hand over her lips to still the trembling.

Only anger prevents her from sinking to her knees.

Right now, it is easier to be mad than sad—though she wishes she had a third choice.

Meat Bones bounds toward her from the kitchen and spends his next few breaths sniffing her shoes. There are coffee stains on the canvas of her high-tops.

"Well, buddy. Let's go where we're wanted," she says coarsely.

Chapter 16

Peacock Manor
Day 146,611

Family drama. The closest I have to family are all the Peacocks who have stayed here on my hill. I see them live their lives—I see them grow up and grow old. I see them turn to dust.

I have been here since the first Peacock, and I am certain I will be here for the last.

I've made a decision. I will try to communicate again with the small Peacock girl. She needs help. The other day, she was crying on my front steps, telling herself she could "do this on her own." She was frightened. I am not sure what she was referring to, but she puts on a brave face though she feels alone in this world. I can feel her trepidation when she is here. Pixie Cakes is sad in the mornings when she wakes, too. I do not like to see so many tears in my house.

I whispered to February. She was polite about it and wasn't spooked. She whispered back this time! She said she *can* hear me and feels my presence. I offered to help. She said thank you but explained it was all up to her and only she could do it, and that she had to do it all by herself.

Chapter 17

The Garden of Mistakes

When Rose heaves open the front door of the
Manor, Meat Bones broadcasts his delight by howling
wildly as he waggles his shortened tail. They journey
across the clumpy green lawn to meet February at the
statues.

He chased butterflies,
Gobbled down two yellow ones,
But then, threw them up.

Rose wonders if February would appreciate her
haiku poem about Meat Bones, but then decides it'd be
too dorky of her to share.

Now that it's almost July, the chrysanthemums
along the front hedges are blooming.

She inclines her chin at February. "What've you
found so far?" she asks casually, ignoring the fact that
she'd abandoned their hunt earlier, but entirely relieved
that February still wants her company.

"Thanks, Rose. I don't want to do this by myself.
We need to stick together. If someone else is after this
book, I need your brain to help me solve the clues
faster. You got the last two so quickly. Grammy's
tombstone, the attic…"

Their three silhouettes—one lanky, one petite, and
one fuzzy—stand facing the main statue in the Garden

of Mistakes, a sea captain.

"You think one of these statues has our next clue?"

"Want to know something creepy?" February asks.

"Sure."

"My dad said each statue is built around a corpse. So this captain has a real skeleton."

"What? Gross!"

"Uh-huh."

"Why would anyone do that?"

"Eternal punishment," February says grimly.

"Whoa."

"And the statues…change at night. That narwhal wasn't lying in a rowboat last time I was here."

"No way. You're trying to scare me."

February grins, turning away.

"Look at his inscription: *Westward into the Unknown*." February kicks the base of the plinth with her foot. "Westward. Westward!" she shouts.

"You know what it means?"

"No, sorry, I'm just very excited."

"Right. But the captain is looking *east* through his backward telescope," Rose says, swinging her head around to trace the captain's line of sight. "He's aimed at the Manor's kitchen ceiling or one of the bedrooms upstairs."

Besides the sea captain, a dozen other fondant-white marble statues crop up unpredictably on the lawn, like chess pieces mid-game.

Rose can't look at them the same way, knowing now there are skeletal remains entombed inside each one.

A narwhal lying on its back in a wooden boat, its unicorn tusk skewering the sky. *Human bones inside—*

gross.

Two enormous crabs interlocking claws, one trying to flip over the other. *Bones inside.*

A mermaid clutching a glass orb. *Bones in—*

"What do you think? They're all nautical-themed," February says. "Which makes sense since the Peacocks were sea-farers back in the—"

"But everything's slightly wrong here. These giant crabs only have nine legs, not ten. Is that a clue?" Rose asks.

"Garden of Mistakes. The narwhal is upside down; its blowhole is on its belly," February says. "Rose, did you know that narwhal means 'corpse whale?' Sailors mistook its mottled gray skin for a drowned human corpse that had been in the water awhile."

"Ew, gruesome. You're full of 'fun' facts today, Feeby."

"All instances of west or east are swapped. Even this compass etched into the mermaid's orb is incorrect," February says, tapping the glass sphere gingerly.

"What's it telling us? Why wouldn't anyone check to see if they were correctly aligned?"

"What about motto? Do we go west from here? The brass telescope itself is backward," Rose says. She studies the captain. "If we turned it the right way…"

February climbs onto the captain's platform and reaches for the brass telescope. "Can the scope be moved?" February asks. "You might be able to check it, you're tall."

Rose steps onto the plinth and stretches overhead. The cold brass telescope creaks and twists in the sea captain's hand.

"It's rotating, but it's stuck in his hand. Does it retract?" Rose pushes the eyepiece end of the backward telescope toward the captain. "It does! There's something here, inside the scope."

A small heart-shaped box drops out of the wide end, near the captain's eye.

Rose catches it with her free hand. She immediately thinks of the heart jewelry box that housed Amber's bumblebee. She winces, but also remembers what Amber would do. Move on.

February squeals. "Pretty! Is the book inside? Kinda small, but no one knows how big the book is." She leans a shoulder into Rose to inspect their find.

Wooden panels run along each side of the box, engraved with symbols and patterns.

"How do you open it?" Rose asks.

"It's a puzzle box. You hide valuables in them. My grammy used one for her gemstones. You slide the panels and hold them in the right order to unlock it."

Rose skims her fingers over the delicate panels. Some slide parallel to the edges of the box; others, diagonally or vertically.

"Crack it open," Rose determines. The thin wood won't be hard to dash apart on the marble of the statues.

February gasps. "Ooh, no! We can't do that!"

"Why not?"

"Sometimes there's water or acid inside that ruins the contents if broken!"

"Ah. Forever lost to history, until the end of time and beyond." Rose fiddles with the box and accidentally fumbles it. "Oh shoot—oops!" She hurtles forward to catch it before it hits the ground, landing on elbows and knees.

"Rose! You're impossibly doomy."

She laughs. "That's me, all right."

Meat Bones sees her on the grass and drops off an old baseball he's unearthed, begging Rose to throw it for him. "Here you go, buddy," she says, tossing his slimy ball far across the lawn.

Still an uncoordinated puppy, he misses the catch.

The ball plummets down the driveway.

At the same time, a red car pulls up—

"Meat Bones, no, wait! Stop!" Rose yells. She darts forward, but the eager pup is already too far away.

She won't reach him in time.

Chapter 18

A Shadow

The ball rolls toward the car with Meat Bones at full speed right behind it.

The red car, upon seeing the bouncing ball cross its path, screeches to a full stop, as both dog and ball tumble in front.

Whew.

Meat Bones is safe.

Whoever is driving is aware that a rolling ball means a child or animal will follow. Careful and attentive. Rose wonders if how someone drives reveals anything about their personality.

February waves. "That's Robbie's car. Think you'll manage a greeting today?" she teases.

Rose's face stiffens into her natural frown.

Robbie hops out and waves back. Jacaranda trees fleck light purple flowers onto the driveway, cascading his sturdy outline in a backdrop of periwinkle. He's wearing sunglasses, looking like he stepped out of a magazine ad selling summer.

"Hey again!" he says.

"That's Milk Ball's bone, err, I mean, Meat Bones' ball," Rose blurts. *Bleh.* She can feel warmth in her cheeks.

Robbie scoops out the ball from under his car and

effortlessly throws it back in a smooth arc. February snatches it out of the air. Meat Bones' short legs are surprisingly fast. He pounces and continues through February's legs, disappointed he couldn't get to it first.

"Great catch. What's up, buttercup?" Robbie calls out to February across the empty drive. Rose's mom had baked bread this morning for her church group and couldn't transport it all in the bicycle basket, so she took the car.

"Robbie! Do you know anything about puzzle boxes? Rose and I are trying to open one," February calls out.

"Puzzle box? Let's take a look," Robbie says, eager to help.

Don't be awkward, don't be awkward.

February holds it out to him on her palm. He shifts his sunglasses to the top of his head, pulling his hair away from his face. His large hands turn the heart-shaped box with care, as if afraid to crush it.

"No instructions?" Robbie asks, peering underneath it.

Rose can tell he has no idea what it is.

"Oh right, there were very specific instructions, but we didn't think to read them and want to do it the hard way." February smirks at him.

"You're so kooky. I'm not good at puzzles. My brain's thick as pig poop. You've seen my grades. I'm stupid." He laughs at himself as he hands the box back to her. A honeybee buzzes around him, but he doesn't bother swatting it away.

"No, you're not, Robbs, don't say that. You know lots of things. Everyone has different skills and knowledge. You can take care of any animal. Rose loves animals."

"Oh! That reminds me; I've been meaning to tell you. I recently took in a miniature horse. He's a baby, but his mama rejected him. If you want to come over to the farm, you can meet him. You and...Rose, is it?"

Tiny baby horse. That sounds too good to pass up. "Sure," Rose musters.

"We can come over this weekend," February suggests.

Rose exaggerates a smile.

"Awesome. Can't wait for you to meet him," Robbie says, always enthusiastic. His happy look lingers on February, but she doesn't notice. "Groceries in the same spot, then? I snuck in some honeycomb for you two. Feeby said you like sweets, right? I'll be right back."

Honeycomb? Rose nods appreciatively. "Thanks."

Meat Bones returns with his ratty ball, and Rose pitches it across the lawn again for him. It lands inside a bush, so he circles and cries, whining for help. As she jogs across the lawn alongside the Manor, she glimpses February hurrying to Robbie's car. Her voice is lowered from its usual exuberant volume, but she is speaking to someone Rose can't see.

Rose dives into the bushes to fish out the ball and throws it back toward Feeby. She barely makes out the last bit of the conversation upon approaching.

"Have you—" February asks.

"I still haven't located it yet. I think it's been moved," a low male voice grumbles.

Kamdyn.

"No! It's been all year."

"I know. I'm still searching, but at least I've

narrowed it down." His voice is velvet. Smooth and even. "The code I gave you last time doesn't work anymore."

He's restrained, concealing his frustration well, but his brows knit together toward the bridge of his long, straight nose.

"But you're ready to go through with it? When you do find...it," she says, fidgeting with her pocketwatch.

"I am," he says. There is a grave weight behind his words. A finality.

Rose edges toward the back of the car, behind February, to get a better glimpse of Kamdyn. Glowering brows and scornful lips.

His solemn steel-gray eyes shift right, catching sight of Rose. Instead of returning to his conversation, he drags his piercing gaze over her. She knows her face has stiffened into whatever expression it makes when surprised, and she hopes it's not a scowl.

His mouth moves, but no words come out, as if he's changed his mind about speaking.

She doesn't know what makes her do it—perhaps the urge to provoke a reaction to break his somberness—but out of nowhere, she drags her fingers through her hair and draws the shorter strands near her temples out to the sides. She pulls a monster face at him, baring her teeth and scrunching her nose as hard as she can, before dropping back into an expressionless face, mirroring his.

For a second, she thinks he hasn't seen her, that he's looking at something else, but his eyes widen in surprise.

His lips curve into a grin, and he's forced to suppress his laughter with a cough as if he'd sneezed.

He tosses his dark hair out of his eyes and goes blank again, but continues to watch her, seemingly intrigued at what she may do next.

Rose smiles ever so slightly as one…two…heartbeats elapse.

Three heartbeats. She doesn't turn away, and neither does he. February's eyes skip back and forth between them, wondering what happened in the exchange.

Kamdyn manages one—amused?—nod before ducking back into the car, busying himself with what looks like organizing the dash of Robbie's car.

But to Rose's satisfaction, right before he slouches away from view, he turns over his shoulder for one last glance at her.

She's made an impression.

She remains in place, as Robbie dashes down the front stairs, bounding toward them—wide grin, broad chest, and all.

"I'm done here, but I'll see you this weekend, right?" He holds his palm up.

"Yep! Rose and I will be there," February promises, returning his high-five with an enthusiastic smack.

"Sounds good. You know where I live, Feebs. Good luck with the puzzle box. Let me know what you find." He pauses, wanting to say more, but—

"Bye, Robbie!" February shouts, and turns away, puzzle in hand.

"See you later," Rose says.

February pats Rose on the shoulder. "That was less sad than last time. At least you said something this time. That's progress."

Rose has accepted that her friend is an eternal optimist. Someone who believes in a happy future no matter what. It is comforting to know that someone believes.

"Thanks for noticing. I. Said. Words. Ha! What were you and Kamdyn talking about?"

"I was just saying hello," she says, a bit too casual, a little too dismissive.

"Hmm." Rose's eyes narrow, assessing her cheery friend.

"What?"

"Hmmmmmmm," Rose exaggerates, glaring suspiciously.

February laughs. "Kamdyn's like you; he can be uncomfortable around strangers, but he's great. You know, like when you have to tell people your dog's not friendly, but they're a terrific dog—to you. Did you notice you have an easier time interacting with Kam?"

"Ha. I get it, I get it—I'm an unsocialized dog." Rose concurs. It hasn't crossed her mind until now that her shyness might lead people to think she is unfriendly also.

"Oh, Rose, don't be so hard on yourself. Like I told Robbie—we all have strengths and weaknesses. I think you're fabulous."

"Thanks, Feebs," Rose replies. "Let's go inside for snacks while we work on the puzzle box. I smelled something besides bread baking this morning. Strawberry cupcakes, maybe?"

"When you have a problem that needs solving, a good cupcake can help," Feeby says, dropping the puzzle box into her dress pocket. She links her arm with Rose's and begins to drag her along into a skip.

Despite telling her, "You're such a weirdo, Feebs," Rose accepts.

She and February are four skips into their journey when,

a large shadow…

r

ri

rip

ripple

ripples

ripple

rip

ri

r

across the back lawn.

Next to her, February tightens her grip and yanks back on Rose's arm before she goes utterly still.

"Whoa. I saw it too," Rose says, glancing up at the sky to see if a hawk or a plane has thrown a shadow. The sapphire sky is bare, cloudless.

February isn't looking up. Her head swivels from side to side, scanning the lawn, her dark brown hair swishing with the movement.

"That's impossible," she mutters.

Rose cocks her head at Feeby. A rapid clicking drowns out the thrum of her own pulse. "What's impossible? What's all that noise?" Rose asks. "It's coming from you—your pocketwatch is out of control today. It sounds like a racing heartbeat."

February picks it off her chest and shakes it twice. The color leaches from her cheeks.

"We should…get inside…but manor…too far," she fumbles for a response, weighing their options as if they're in danger.

Her friend's rising panic takes Rose by surprise and floods her with worry.

"What're you thinking?" Rose asks, abruptly unlooping her arm to face February.

"Nothing. It wasn't anything," February insists, but her uneven tone does little to reassure Rose.

"Is someone else after the book?"

"I don't really…it can't be." Her voice drifts off as she scans the grounds again.

"Why are you so concerned?"

"I'm not." February's brows soften, and she finally smiles. "Hey, want to see a secret passageway?"

She's evading the question. February always knows how to distract her from asking more questions. It is frustrating that she's withholding information, but at the same time—who can resist a secret passageway? Rose's skin prickles at the words. "Where?!"

Feeby tugs her toward the broccoli-shaped oak tree beyond the statue garden. "It begins there."

"The tree? I thought I imagined an outline of a door!"

Just then, the mystery shadow—now more clearly a human-sized figure—flashes across the garden and darts around the back of the Manor.

Rose swings around in place. "There it is again! Who is that?"

February's hand tightens on Rose's wrist. "This way, let's go."

"What is—"

"Hurry." The tremble in Feeby's voice gets Rose's legs moving.

They sprint to the tree, with Rose twisting back

over her shoulder for a look, but February tows her forward. She's surprisingly strong for someone so small.

Once alongside the oak, February crouches down. Her hands slip into a crevice at the base of the tree trunk. She heaves upward, sliding a board covered in bark to reveal an entrance.

"Get in."

Rose ducks in and finds herself at the top of a narrow slide, but she doesn't have time to marvel at the magic of this door in a living tree. February shoves her in from behind. As Rose plummets straight down the chute, Feeby follows, shutting the door behind them.

The darkness engulfs them, filling them with a nameless dread. The passage stinks of rotten wood, but Rose inhales the musty darkness as if breathing it in will make it brighter.

"There should be candles and matches at the bottom of the slide!" February calls after her.

Rose swipes her hand across cold, rough gravel and damp soil. "Can't find them."

"I'm coming."

"Is someone trying to scare us again?" Rose asks. "A man in a dark suit? Maybe a cape?"

"You okay?" February lands behind her and rummages around the ground until she finds what she's looking for. She strikes a match, illuminating their faces in a way that accents the hollows of their eyes.

"So far. Just tell me what we saw."

"I dunno. What do you think it was?"

"When I get a closer look, I'll let you know—oh wait, you shoved me into a tree before I could see."

"We're okay now." February lights a candle and

blows out the match. The scent of burning wax and wispy smoke weave around them before fading into the dark tunnel.

The dim light illuminates a low, subterranean passageway. In any other circumstance, Rose would be delighted.

"What aren't you telling me, Feebs? You knew enough to be worried."

"I don't know what we saw—a swarm of bees? The gardener? A wild animal? I'm sorry. Don't be mad at me," she pleads.

Her tone is sad and frightened and makes Rose almost want to hug her. She doesn't feel like she's being a good friend to Feeby, so she wills her attention to the passage ahead instead of the fact that her friend is lying to her.

"Where do we go now?" Rose asks.

February circles past Rose, holding up her candle, her composure now regained.

She lowers her voice as if sharing a secret.

"A long time ago, the cook of Peacock Manor married a warrior, who was called into battle for the lord he served. While he was away, she tried to poison the entire Peacock family.

"A year later, her warrior husband returned home. The cook greeted him at the door and prepared dinner for him. The next morning, he woke up next to a skull with her long hair. When he asked his neighbors what happened, they told him she'd died the year before— after attempting to murder the family here, the groundskeeper confronted her and killed her in this very passageway! The warrior brought the skull back here and left it with the rest of her body, ashamed she tried to murder everyone at the Manor."

"Whoa. She came back to haunt him? Why would she poison the family?"

February shrugs. "Resentment? Insanity? In those days, cookware and paint contained lead or arsenic and other toxic chemicals. It could drive people mad."

"Ooh. Is it *her* ghost haunting the Manor?" Rose asks.

"Ha-ha. You're obsessed."

"I am."

"You're not wrong though. They say if a soul doesn't have proper final rites or isn't allowed the goodbye they wanted, they'll come back to haunt as a lost spirit, eventually corrupting into something wicked."

"A vengeful spirit?"

"Yep."

"Yikes. Like…what was chasing us?"

"This way." February disappears to the left when the tunnel splits. "That way is a dead end." Her voice is muffled, muted by the earth.

Rose rushes to catch up. "Where does the passageway lead?"

"You'll have to go through it to see!" she says, cheery again.

"Oh man, the mysteries are bottomless at Peacock Manor."

"That's right—I'm making sure you're getting your money's worth."

Rose can't see the end of the passage or any exit at all. She shuffles along the damp, serpentine path. Her hands fly up to her head—*pffth*—she blows sticky webbing and perhaps a spider or two out of her face.

117

She drags a hand along the unfinished walls encrusted with seashells and fossils. Dead things. Dead, for a very long time. Her finger traces a dusty spiraling nautilus. She draws back, shuddering. This land was under the sea an eon or two ago, and this creature of the darkest ocean depths never imagined it would spend eternity trapped within a mountain, high up in the skies.

How can anyone know where they'll end up? *Where do we go when we die?*

Hazy circles of light flare off the dirt walls as February's candle leads them deeper into the winding tunnel.

After a while, roots push through above them, scratching like witches' claws at Rose's head; she guesses they are under the statue garden. The cool air of the tunnel blows through her.

She swears the walls pulse and writhe as she creeps through the inky blackness, as if journeying through the insides of a living, breathing creature.

The tendrils of dead sea critters squirm alongside her, while roots crackle and grow unnaturally fast, and a wickedness creeps out of the crevices of loam and rock, crying out for her.

She tells herself it's shadows and loose roots tricking her mind, but she can't shake the feeling that Peacock Manor *changes* things.

Is it changing her?

Her hearing dulls. February is talking to her, but Rose can't hear anything she's saying. She shuts her eyes for a brief moment. Did the sprint at high altitude make her dizzy? Is she that out of shape? She wills herself to overpower the wooziness and speeds forward toward February, edging closer to her friend.

Rose cups her ears, hoping Feeby understands that she can't hear. Will February believe her if she describes what's happening? Rose smells the decaying soil, feels the loose gravel beneath her feet. Her palms scrape along the rough edges of the seashells embedded in the tunnel wall as she steadies herself, so she knows not all her senses are failing.

But her vision? Her vision falters.

Because before her, fossils wriggle, waking up after an eternity, worming their way to her and—how can this be?—seaweed slips between the cracks, their slimy, slug-like fronds lashing until the wall crumbles, giving way to a tunnel beside her. Rose leans inward. Deep within, a foggy green light glows, and…a tentacle writhes.

A tentacle *holding a lantern*. Again!? It's déjà vu, back to the first night at the octopus fountain when she saw Kamdyn. Where has she seen this before?

She glances at February one last time.

Her friend's eyes widen, and she shakes her head no.

But Rose needs answers, and Peacock Manor is trying to tell her something. She's never been more certain of anything in her life.

She backs away from February, toward the unexplained hole in the wall and the lantern and presses through the seaweed. Her stomach drops as the ground gives way beneath her, and she screams as she plunges downward into water, plummeting into the unknown.

Chapter 19

The Secrets of the Passageway

Rose drifts and floats with the deep-sea creatures in the wall. They sway together in a dreamy trance, the creatures in bioluminescent gem tones of teal, indigo, and fuchsia. Where does this tunnel lead? She chases the moving light of the lantern. Bubbles float up. Or is she sinking downward? *Do I need to breathe?* As the thought enters her mind, she gasps for air, but instead, swallows water.

Panic flares and she flails, struggling to breathe.

She spins around, but the way back to the tunnel is no longer there. Only deep green water as far as her eye can see in every direction.

How do I get out of here?

That is her final thought before her head bumps into a hard wooden panel above her in the water, like the edge of a dock or boat. *Ow!*

The pain blinds her, and everything dims and fades to a thundercloud of gray, then black.

February stands over her. "What happened? Are you all right?! You ran into the wall and passed out. Did you freak out or something?"

"Huh." Rose blinks her eyes open to see Feeby's concerned face hovering over hers. Her forehead hurts. She pats around her face, checking for blood.

"You okay?" February asks, her voice finally coming through. "What the heck? Your wheels are falling off."

"Yeah, I'm pretty clumsy," Rose mumbles. "I'm good," she lies, her world still spinning. What's wrong with her?

How embarrassing. Is she claustrophobic and never knew until now? February didn't see the walls moving, the watery side tunnel, the lantern, and the glowing creatures.

Just her, then?

February clasps Rose's wrist and pulls her to her feet.

"Sure you're all right? I thought you wanted a bit of excitement. Do you need to stop?"

"I'm fine," Rose insists.

But is she? Another instance of phantasmagoria, like the exploding octopus fountain. Why do all her visions involve dark water?

Who, or what, is haunting this place?

They huddle together and creep forward. Rose doesn't have any more time to think about what happened, because when she sees what lies ahead, her stomach sours.

Brown muddy splatters on both walls of the tunnel.

Brown that must once have been a deep, thick red.

Torn cloth, a broken bottle, a lead pipe. Next, a dirty knife—not the largest, but the sharpest. The kind used to separate meat from bone, lacerating flesh before detaching ligaments and tendons.

She knows what it had done. Murder. Here.

Already woozy, Rose fights the urge to vomit when she sees…the bones.

First, the remnants of feet, toes loose like marbles. Then the leg bones, femurs splaying, leading to a beige skeleton. A *human* skeleton, slumped against the tunnel wall. An empty-eyed skull with matted reddish-brown hair; upper jaw inset with three gold teeth.

To her horror, small triangular pits perforate all the bones, as if pecked by birds. She gags.

"What the hell is that!? You knew this was here?" Rose asks, glancing at February to make sure she is seeing the same revolting scene, that she isn't hallucinating again.

"I told you. The cook was murdered here, like a hundred years ago."

"But you...they...*left* it here?" Rose has never seen death up close, magnified like this.

A large wooden spoon hangs from the cook's tattered apron pocket as if the skeleton had been in the middle of preparing a stew and stepped away for a bit.

"Apparently." February grins.

Her cheeriness makes it worse. She's like a creepy clown, smiling, while stabbing someone to death. *She* isn't fazed by this passageway of death.

Rose suspects Feeby knows much more than she is willing to reveal. What dark secret hides behind her perpetual smile? Where is the lie?

"Barf." Even though she's disgusted, Rose can't look away. The arm bones, crossed in their last moments, had hugged the dying body, now loosely held together by a stained cloth. The skeleton's jaw hangs open, still shocked by her own horrific circumstances.

"Right? Total barf. We're almost at the end of the passage."

"Sure." Rose scuttles sideways like a crab, past the

skeleton, never taking her eyes off of it until she reaches the end of the tunnel.

Another short set of stairs leads to a small door in the passageway ceiling. Soft streaks of light sift through the cracks. February yanks the rope handle and opens the hatch, leading them out and up into the kitchen.

The image of the skeleton burns in Rose's mind. She can't help it—she turns over her shoulder for one last morbid look at the skeleton, as the passageway is now illuminated by the open doorway.

The dust on the path behind her contains one set of footprints.

Just one.

Strangely, she and February have taken exactly the same steps down the dusty tunnel. It isn't impossible, and her head hurts, so she hurries to get out instead of giving it too much thought.

She crawls out of the trapdoor on her hands and knees. Her gaze travels up the kitchen's red brick walls that extend up into the second story, opening into an immense skylight like the one in the library at the opposite end of the Manor. Ocean blue sky. Silvery tendrils of clouds.

Meat Bones sniffs at them as they emerge from the kitchen floor. He licks Rose's face and yowls until she stands up. She suspects he is more wolf than dog.

Seeing the radiant sunlight and that familiar wagging tail, not only does relief wash over her, but also…appreciation.

Appreciation of life, *her* life.

She can't remember the last time she felt this way.

February pulls up on the circular iron handle, slamming the trapdoor into the floor. Dust and bits of dirt puff up through the cracks.

They walk past an immense stone hearth, designed in the days when the Manor ballroom held lavish parties and feasts. Rose wonders if she'll ever know enough people to host a ball.

"How many loaves of bread do you think this oven's made?" she asks.

February laughs. "You're always thinking about snacks."

"Imma big eater." Rose veers toward a tray of colorful baked goods. "My mom must be at a church bake sale today. Look, I was right—strawberry cupcakes. And black currant marzipan pixie cakes! Three o'clock cake appointment!" She crams one into her mouth.

Despite her stomach churning in the passageway, her relief upon exiting has made her hungry.

"How do you know what flavor it is?" February asks.

"Rah pieces on rah top..." Rose says with her mouth full. She swallows. "...give you a clue to the filling inside. I wonder if Mom used the black currants from the side yard?"

She scoops up a ribboned bag of milk cookies and tucks them into her front shirt pocket. "For later." She pats her pocket.

"What did you think? You wanted the scary tour of the Manor," February asks, threading her arm through Rose's, guiding her past a corridor of larders, the banquet room, the tea room, and the sitting room. They stop at the front door.

"I did, but with more warning. *More* warning, please. I wasn't prepared to see...a dead person."

"Next time," Feeby promises.

"What? There's more like this?" Rose practically spits out the words.

"No, that was the best thing I had to show you," Feeby admits.

"Best? Or *worst*. Thank God." She lets out a too-high laugh.

February giggles.

"Sometimes I wonder about you," Rose says.

Her thoughts churn—the new clue, the rippling shadow, the moving passageway, February withholding information from her. She hides a secret—Rose is certain. She regards her friend with narrowed eyes before deciding it isn't worth it to press. The more forcefully a secret is removed, the deeper it wriggles to conceal itself.

"I'm an oddball, it's true," Feeby agrees, casual and calm. Her glance lingers on Rose, her lips tensed as if she had more to say but holds back.

Rose can't read her thoughts. But she vows to find out what her only friend is hiding.

Chapter 20

Peacock Manor
Day 146,615

February talks to me a lot now when Pixie Cakes isn't looking. She told me that I should have tried harder when they were being chased, and under no circumstances am I to frighten Pixie Cakes again with any more visions, like in the tunnel. I like changing things.

I didn't mean to cause trouble for Pixie Cakes. February said to call her Rose. I thought *Rose* wanted a scare. I thought it might help her remember. Since I know what happened. She keeps talking about wanting to see a ghost. If I could shrug, I would.

Chapter 21

The Miniature Horse and the Next Clue

"How many words will you say when we're at Robbie's? Sample words: Hello. What's up? What do you feed the horses? How come your wavy hair is *always* in place?" Conversation starters are February's specialty. "At least you're much less nervous today— good job!"

Rose replies with a snort as she fidgets with the puzzle box, trying to figure out the right panels to move.

"Blackberries! Like candy growing by the side of the road!" Feeby gingerly bites one off of the bush with her front teeth like a wild deer, avoiding the thorny spines.

She offers one up, but Rose laughs and shakes her head.

Today, as always, February is stunning—filled with light and energy and enthusiasm. She radiates life, and it mesmerizes Rose. Unlike most people, the mundane doesn't jade Feeby. She celebrates everything, from blackberries to Rose's measly accomplishments like talking to a boy.

"Will you grab some of the big ones up there for me?" February asks.

"Sure."

"I always think you look like a tall pixie, I don't know why. Your chin plus your hair? You're gor-gee-ous. Hold on—is that why your mom calls them pixie cakes? Because she makes them for you and you like them so much? That totally makes sense now."

"I guess so. Yeah. Ever since she came up with them, like five years ago."

They snake down a smaller dirt path toward the Skyler's neighboring farm.

From afar, a tall silhouette approaches them, heading away from Robbie's house. With the sun behind him, Rose can't be sure who it is, so she lifts a hand to block the light and squints.

Slighter in frame than Robbie, but still solidly built so that his white button-up shirt hangs perfectly off his muscled chest and shoulders, his sleeves rolled halfway up.

Kamdyn.

"Kam!" February bounces in place. "Whatcha up to? Visiting Robbs?"

"Yup. He just finished feeding the animals. He's in the house now."

"Rose and I want to see the animals."

"Hi, Kamdyn." Rose allows herself to linger. *Staring a little is okay, right?* His black hair contrasts with his gunmetal-gray eyes; the sharp angles of his finely structured face are more elegant, more sophisticated than Robbie's carefree golden retriever look. Edgier. His narrower, pointed chin and curved rosy lips impart a feline, feminine appearance.

"No monster face today?" he asks Rose. "That's disappointing. Just a normal and entirely pretty face, then?" Too confident, too sure of himself. His tone is restrained, though, as if carefully concealing something wilder underneath.

He picks off a non-existent particle from the cuff of his sleeve and re-rolls it.

She shrugs coolly. "That's how the cookie crumbles." Beside her, February suppresses a giggle and mumbles under her breath so only Rose can hear, "You and cookies."

He shoves his slender hands into his pockets. "Are you...liking it here so far? We have mountains."

She can't tell if he actually wants to have a conversation with her, or if he can't stand her and is only being polite in front of February.

"It's all good. Feeby makes it fun," she says casually.

He presses his lips into a straight line; from here, he could either smile or frown, but does neither, and has nothing else to say to her.

"Oh, uh, Feeby—" He glances sideways at Rose. "I'm pretty sure I've discovered the location of what you wanted...for, you know. But I need a—a key." He trails off, clearly not wishing to divulge any more detail than he has to, but February understands him.

"Okay, don't give up. You're *so* close." February touches his arm reassuringly.

Rose strains to comprehend the hidden meaning in their words. She catches herself looking overeager and lowers her brows, feigning indifference.

"Agreed. I'll keep you updated. Later, then." He turns to Rose. "Hope to see you around, Rose. I like monsters."

As he passes by Rose to continue down the lane, his shoulder accidentally brushes hers as he strides by.

Yun Johnson

Or else, she *may* have shifted the tiniest amount—or did he?—to get in the way, and before he moves on, the back of their hands graze each other's for a long, slow moment.

His fingers extend to brush hers.

Oh.

Time stops. She is surprised at the warmth, and the sensation running up her arm. It's embarrassingly delightful. She follows him with her gaze as he strolls onward.

His hand has curled into a fist, but he casts a sidelong glance at her with the smallest turn of his head—she levels her eyes at him—and his lips twitch and spark into an irresistible smile.

She knows it wasn't an accident.

He strides smoothly on with long, light steps. She grins to herself.

Feeby shakes Rose's shoulders. "You. Said. Many. Words."

Rose laughs. "I did! Why is he so serious all the time? What were you guys talking about?"

"He's got a lot of responsibilities and family drama. He's doing me a favor, for the Manor. Since my dad isn't..." She can't seem to finish her sentence. "Kam's a good guy. He's in Robbie's class at school, practically best friends since first grade. His parents do business with the Skyler farm and order produce for the restaurants at their hotels."

"Fancy."

"He's adorable, though," February says. "Always dresses nice. Good manners. Neat and organized—you know, opposite of Robbie, who's always rumpled and scruffy." She laughs.

"You think everyone's adorable. You even think *I'm* fun."

"You *are* fun."

They continue walking down the dirt path, changing direction when they reach an oak-lined lane.

"Here we are. It's right up there." February swings her arm toward a chocolate brown house with a large sloping roof, encircled by a wooden fence containing a single goat.

"Hey, goat!" Feeby says. The goat lifts his bearded chin and continues chomping. "Robbie, your goat is eating the fence!" she yells, even though he isn't in sight. Her voice carries across the sun-yellowed grass slopes of the farmhouse property.

The creaky screen door swings open, and Robbie's large frame darts down the porch steps, shooing the goat toward a bale of hay.

"Gorgon! I just repaired that fence yesterday, you troublemaker," he says, good-natured and unperturbed as ever. "This guy's in a head-butting mood, so we're keeping him from the other goats today."

"Gorgon?!" Feeby laughs. "The monster from Greek mythology?"

"Nope. The cheese," Robbie replies. "Gorgonzola."

Rose sputters a laugh, catching herself before she snorts.

"What a great name, Rob-berry!" February says, hugging him tightly.

"Hello, sunshine," he replies, returning her embrace.

Rose makes it through hellos, and Robbie gives them a tour of the farm, the dairy cows, and the goats.

They stop to pick fruit—peaches and pears—

before the tour ends at the barn.

He leads them to the small pasture where his miniature horse is munching on hedge flowers he isn't supposed to be eating. "What else have you been up to?" he asks.

"We're still stuck on the puzzle box," Feeby says.

"Oh yeah? This little guy," Robbie's words are deliberate and thoughtful as he rests his forearms on the fence and dips his head at the foal, "has a whorl that reminds me of one of the symbols on that box. I was thinking, they resemble the ancient carvings in the caves on the east side of the mountain. The ones archeologists aren't sure what they mean or who used them."

Rose whips her head around. *Ancient symbols?* "What carvings?"

"The Impenetrable Glyphs of the East Ridge," Feeby says. "Ooh, interesting."

He inflates at her approval. "Could the symbols be clues to help open the box?" he suggests. "*If* you can figure out the meaning."

"We need to check that out," February says to Rose.

Rose nods once in agreement, wishing she had something clever to add.

Robbie always has a grin that rolls warmth and charm all into one upturned mouth. How can anyone be so unbothered, so carefree all the time? Kamdyn's personality somehow seems more realistic to Rose.

Why is she thinking of *him* again? How mortifying.

Robbie's mini-horse trots to him for a carrot, throwing an eager buck halfway over. The foal's head is way too big for its body. Rose reminds herself to add

132

baby miniature horses to her list of cutest animals ever.

"My little brother named him Jellybean—I don't know what flavor bean this color brown would be, but it was the smallest candy he could think of. Jelly likes these baby carrots. I think they make him feel like a big horse."

"Ahahhaha!" February screeches, startling Jelly into snorting and pawing the ground. "*That* is hilarious, Robbie." She chases the chickens around them, hunching forward with her arms outstretched. The birds scatter like billiard balls around her.

"Feeby, Meat Bones is better behaved than you," Rose chides.

Robbie erupts into laughter.

Rose flattens her hand against Jelly's side and brushes his coarse cinnamon coat. His skin twitches and ripples under her touch, especially when she goes over the whorls; his long eyelashes kiss his cheeks.

"Chickens like to be hugged. Let me show you, if I can catch one of these guys," February says, speeding after a russet hen. Her emerald earring falls off and she pauses to replace it, laughing at herself. "This is probably how I lost the other one."

"You're a lunatic, Feebs," Robbie says, kneeling next to Rose.

He extracts a hoof pick from his pocket to clean Jelly's small hooves, then runs a bristle brush over him, from withers to flank. Flecks of dust billow off of Jelly with each stroke. While Robbie's handling of the puzzle box was clumsy, his movements here are practiced and efficient as he scrapes off one hoof after another free of dirt.

"Always. You know that," Feeby says.

"That's why I love you, sunshine," he replies softly, so only Rose next to him hears. He wrenches his gaze downward and his cheeks color, but he swiftly recovers and resumes brushing Jelly.

Rose glances at Robbie. He's caught her off-guard. His tone suggests more, and she detects a sweet longing in his voice. Also, he hasn't taken his eyes off February since they arrived. How did she not see it before? Robbie *likes* February! *Like* likes.

Does February feel the same way?

"Thanks...for letting us play with Jellybean," Rose ventures.

"Yeah, thank Jelly for the fun afternoon, Robinson Skyler!" February shrieks, wiping a hand on her dress. She's caught a chicken, but it pooped on her.

"Anytime! Come over anytime," he says. "Heh, I never liked my name much, but I gotta love the way she says it," he mutters to Rose and Jelly, shaking his head and fighting down a smile. "My mom was the only one who called me that, before she got sick and passed."

From his matter-of-fact tone, Rose gathers that it happened a while ago.

"I'm sorry to hear that," she says.

"We'll be back," February promises, oblivious to his adoration. "These chickens can't hug themselves." She rakes her fingers over the feathers of the hen nestled in the crook of her arm; it roosts contentedly despite the initial chase.

On their way home, Rose kicks a little gray rock ahead of her every few steps as she weighs the question of whether she should tell February about Robbie's feelings.

Will Feeby hang out with him and forget about her

and the treasure hunt? Rose would become a third wheel. Or worse, an uninvited wheel. She feels like a terrible person, but she doesn't want to lose her only friend.

She gives one final frustrated kick to the pebble, shooting it off the path down into a ditch.

"See, you had fun like I promised," February says, her hands in her skirt pockets, swishing the dirt and chicken droppings off the fabric as they walk.

"Robbie's nice." *Kamdyn—she isn't sure about either way.* Yet, she finds herself thinking about him more than she wants to. "How are Robbie and Kam friends? They're opposite personalities."

"Robbie told me in first grade, they had a Parents' Day where your mom or dad come to class and do a science project with you. Kam's parents were too busy and forgot, and Robbie's mom had just died, so his dad was trying to keep the store going while taking care of Robbie's baby brother. Kam and Robbs were the only kids without a parent there, and Kam, who dressed the same when he was six as he does now—you know, little suit and all, to imitate his dad—asked Robbie if he wanted to join his company: The Forgotten Boys Club.

"Robbie thought that was too sad, but Kam insisted it was the opposite. If Robbie joined as vice president, then their motto could be "Never Forgotten," because they'd have each other to not forget, he reasoned. Their business would be *not* forgetting important things. Robbie finally agreed, and they've been best friends ever since. They're both popular in school now, but they go out of their way to include everyone. If someone seems lonely, they sit with them at lunch or invite them to stuff."

"Kamdyn does that? That's different."

"Yep, they're good guys," she says. "Robbie's heart is in the right place. Lotsa girls at school ask him out, but he says he's too busy. I wonder why he never has a girlfriend, never seems interested in anyone," she chatters to no one in particular.

Because he's in love with you. But Rose doesn't say anything about it on the way home.

Maybe after the next clue. Or not. She needs February to focus on finding the book.

She knows she is being selfish, and Rose doesn't want to be *that girl*.

She reminds herself she needs to be the kind of friend she would want to have.

Chapter 22

Heart-Shaped Box

"There are literally tens of thousands of combinations," Rose says, exasperated.

The main gate to the Manor appears at the end of the lane ahead of them. "Whoever left the box for you couldn't have left it to chance. Robbie mentioned the symbols might be hints…"

"What do six spiral glyphs mean?" February wonders.

"Some panels are longer than others but don't have more symbols. A few are blank."

They halt halfway across the red garden bridge.

Rose balances the box on the railing. "If the symbols are a hint, let's try number order. This long panel only has one spider-looking thing." She slides it and holds it.

"That panel has two tree characters," February says, gliding her finger over that panel, pressing it aside.

"Then these three squarish glyphs," Rose says, pinching her fingers to set it in place.

Four, five, six. When they get to the six spiral glyphs, the panel glides off and the wooden box collapses, pieces cascading down at their feet.

A scroll drops out with the wooden pieces.

Rose fumbles to catch it, but February is faster and snatches it out of the air.

In that instant, acid fizzles and consumes the remaining panels into an unrecognizable muddle.

"Whoa! You were right about not forcing open the box," Rose says, kicking gravel onto the debris to stop the reaction.

They curl over the scroll, forehead to forehead. Rose can smell Feeby's apple-scented shampoo.

They unroll their next clue:

I can be one color, or I may change in light.

You might look upon me, or see through me, morning to night,

I'm around for one season, or else I'm always there.

I can be many, or sometimes, just a lonely pair.

"Woooo!" February exclaims. "What do you think?" She leans on the red railing of the bridge, staring down at the trickle of water underneath them.

"Another riddle, huh." Rose secretly resents not knowing how many more there are. She hopes this isn't a wild goose chase. Will she have to leave before they find the book? She only has six more weeks of summer vacation left.

"What is one color, but can change in light?" February asks, waving the clue.

With a brilliant flash and a sizzle, the ink catches fire in the sunlight and the paper in February's hands bursts into blue flames, burning away in seconds.

"It's on fire!" February wails. "Oww!" She flicks her fingers as the ashes spiral downward, dotting the water's surface before dissolving away to nothingness.

"No! How did it—"

"We can't solve it now!" February throws both hands into the air.

"Yes, we can."

"How?"

"I know it." Rose taps her forehead.

February whips her head around, mouth open.

Rose has seen this look before—on the faces of classmates—whenever she quotes books, vocabulary definitions, and math formulas.

"You memorized it? That quickly?" she asks.

"Sometimes, I just...remember things." Words have always etched themselves easily into Rose's mind, flowing from ink to paper to memory.

She recites the clue, from "*I can be one color...*" all the way to "*just a lonely pair.*"

"You're incredible!" Feeby says.

"Don't be impressed. That's the one thing I have going for me," Rose assures her.

"No way. I like so many things about you!" February replies.

"I don't."

"Ha-ha, well, you're improving what you don't like. That's impressive. Look, you didn't freak out when you were talking to Robbie."

"Ha. Oh, speaking of Robbie...he *likes* you." Rose traces a heart in the air with her hands. February deserves to know.

February scoffs. "What? Aw, you're teasing me."

"No. I can tell. I'm not good at talking to people, but I'm good at observing."

"Pfft. He thinks I'm nuts. More nuts than in a squirrel's nest. Seriously," she says.

"You're wrong, Feebs. He likes you. Should

139

I...ask him?"

"You wouldn't dare!" She laughs.

"I'm braver now, like you said," Rose teases. "Well, do you like him?"

"What's there not to like, right? He's such a sweetheart and nice to everyone."

"So...yes?"

"I'll have to think about this. But, I'm telling you, he likes me the way a kid likes a circus clown."

"Then he has a clown fetish. But that's not how he was looking at you. He had hearts in his eyes, like the emoji." Rose turns away and trudges up the grassy hill to the Manor.

"You're ridiculous!"

"You know I'm right," Rose calls back over her shoulder.

February falls into silence, polishing her pocketwatch, not knowing what else to say. Possibly, thinks Rose, for the first time in her entire life.

Chapter 23

A Ghost in the Bathroom

"Rose, are you running the water?" her mom yells upstairs to her later that evening. "I need it for the wash."

Rose kicks a soapy foot out of the tub to shut off the hot water, spinning the gold handle with her toes. In the bedroom next to hers, one away from the locked mystery door (which she'd given a good rattle before her bath), she'd discovered the most luxurious, black marble claw-footed tub. A bottomless pit in which to abandon her worries.

Surrounded by candles in the dark, she sinks deeper into the abyss, tipping her head back to gaze up through the skylight above the tub. The moon has yet to rise. Infinite stars shine with such ferocity this high up in these mountains, like holes gouged in the thickest of black paper and held against the sun.

She crams a milk cookie into her mouth. Is there anything more relaxing than eating cookies in a balmy tub of bubbles? An exquisite pairing. She's lost in her thoughts, encased in a soft cocoon of steamy comfort. A cocoon. Silky webbing. Cobwebs. Cobwebs on the cook's skeleton in the passageway. Dead bodies.

Yuck. She doesn't want to see the pecked skeleton in her mind anymore.

Instead, she focuses on the riddle, reciting it aloud:

"I can be one color, or I may change in light.

You might look upon me, or see through me, morning to night,

I'm around for one season, or else I'm always there.

I can be many, or sometimes, just a lonely pair."

A lonely pair. She was never lonely when she was part of a pair.

Through the steam and vapors purling around her, a glint of movement reflects in the large hanging mirror over the sink. She curses and slips and splashes until she's fully upright. A silhouette of a child's head—like an old-fashioned cutout—emerges in the otherwise foggy mirror. By the shape of the bowl haircut, it seems to be a boy, in a high collar, his profile facing away.

She collects herself and stretches her neck over the edge of the tub. The head swivels and the outline of his nose points toward her. His handprint appears on the mirror, as if he were about to press through the veil, as if the steam from the bath connected their two realms, but his features don't fully appear.

Instead, he folds three fingers down, one at a time. Two fingers, like bunny ears.

"Two?" she says aloud. "Two what? Who are you?"

She is in the presence of a spirit. It has to be.

I need to get as much information out of him as possible. Previous phantasmagoria were fleeting, so she acts quickly.

She looks away for an instant to reach for a towel. In that tiny moment, the mirror mists, and the silhouette vanishes, as if absorbed into the most nebulous fog.

"Wait! Are you helping me?" she calls out. "With the riddle? Come back! Two is the answer?"

Her pulse hammers. What is he trying to tell her?

Think. Two is not in the riddle. One color, one season, lonely pair. One item with changing properties.

How can anything have two opposing attributes, as if they are two separate items?

Yes, of course! *Two* different objects! *Looking at* one, *seeing through* the other.

The first half of each line refers to one thing, and the second half, another!

But the answer sounds the same for both.

She has the answer.

Chapter 24

Alone and Screaming

February doesn't come by the next day. Or the next. It occurs to Rose that she has no idea where her friend lives. Feeby flings her hand in a vague direction when Rose asks, and always pops up at the Manor whenever Rose starts wondering where she is.

Rose holds the answer to the riddle but doesn't know what it means.

She needs February.

Rose attempts another summoning. She positions the requisite candles, burns the herbs and crystals, and speaks the incantations she's collected in her latest research. She feels a little silly. There's no real reason they'll work now if they didn't work before. Smelling of singed leaves and incense, she scoffs at her own desperation and failure. Back to the library.

She takes a detour down the hallway, determined to get into the locked bedroom door. With a hairpin in hand, she carefully inserts it into the keyhole and jiggles it. No luck. She picks at the tar in the cracks, hoping to gouge out enough to peer through. She's sure part of February's secret is behind that door.

At least she's uncovered a hidden nook beside the fireplace.

The bookcase swings outward on a hinge to reveal

a brick enclave with its own lantern and one oversized chesterfield against the bricks.

She and Meat Bones slip into it and stay all day with a stack of old books on the side table next to them. She's searched the highest, deepest shelves and discovered lore on avoiding mischievous spirits, honoring nature spirits, and entering the afterlife properly, but nothing useful for her own purposes.

Nothing on calling forth a specific spirit.

The shadows now stretch long and thin, slinking lower and lower down the walls.

She lets her eyes close for a second and nods off.

When her head tips forward off her palm, she snorts and jerks awake—and finds a small boy standing in the nook beside her.

"Ah! Who—?" Rose scrambles to sit upright. Where is Meat Bones? He is no longer at her feet, and the library doors are closed.

"You're in my seat," says the little boy with black hair in a bowl cut. His silhouette is familiar. The same one in the mirror last night.

"Huh?" She's groggy and confused.

"Get out," he sneers.

"That's aggressive. Did you help me yesterday? Who are—?"

"You can't change your fate." He begins to scream. Rose can't tell if he's throwing a tantrum at not being able to change one's fate or if he's displeased with what she said.

"Shhh. Stop it!" She clamps her hands over her ears. "What do you want?"

His mouth closes and he pauses his vicious scream.

"Do *you* know how to get through the locked door

upstairs?" he asks.

"No. I've tried. Is there a key or—?"

He screams again.

Shaken, Rose squeezes her eyes shut—cringing—and when she opens them again, the boy has vanished.

What just happened? She glances around wildly, her breathing ragged.

Her stack of books has been put away. All except *In a Hundred Dreams*, which lies open on the side table. Her favorite book.

"Meat Bones?" she calls weakly, rattled.

She stands just as the library door slams open into the wall beside it, and a rush of air blows in.

Dad drifts in, glancing over his shoulder, surprised the door swung so violently, but otherwise lost in thought. He scans the stacks before looking vaguely up at the skylight.

She's not sure he notices her in the nook.

"Mom home yet? Dinner?" she grunts at him, still completely baffled as to where her books have gone. Did she sleepwalk and put them back on the shelves, or did Meat Bones carry them elsewhere? The boy—?

"Huuh. Yes." He bobs his head, his dad brain prompting him to answer her automatically, but his writer's brain is lost in another world, wherever his book resides. He doesn't share her interest in food.

Instead, Dad scribbles something on his notepad and leaves. Inspiration must have struck.

His novels do well, so Rose doesn't question his methods. It's a miracle he answers her at all when he's working. He's much more interactive after the launch of a book. For a bit.

No dinner, then.

Rose remembers a time when her mom used to cook dinner. They would all eat together. Mom sticks to baking now, but once in a while, she'll concoct a soup to go with the fresh bread. Rose and her dad snack all day on whatever comes out of the oven, but they haven't sat down together for dinner in a long while. Definitely not since Amber died.

In fact, she can't remember when they last did. The walnut dining table at home has become the saddest rummage sale ever— a hoard of half-sorted mail, a dog collar belonging to a dog no longer with them, a large glass bowl that doesn't fit in any cabinet, and broken odds and ends no one has strong enough feelings for to either repair or throw away.

One evening, she took a walk and saw families at their tables eating dinner together through windows lit with an amber glow.

She realized then what was carving a hole in her heart—and also, that her family would *never* be the same again.

Rose finds Meat Bones sniffing around in the kitchen.

"You did an incredible job guarding me from screaming ghosts while I napped," she says sarcastically.

He thumps his tail in agreement.

She pilfers a few more cookies before shuffling back to the library.

He springs into her lap once she settles back into the overstuffed chair in the nook.

"Where do you think February is, Meat Bones?"

He cocks his head and stares at her with his butterscotch eyes.

Yun Johnson

It occurs to her that she actually *has* a friend to miss. She knows it might sound pathetic to most people, but to her, it's one tiny indication, one inkling of proof that *time does move forward* and that *change is possible*—even on a day when she has nothing to show for living through another sunset, except the reaping of bitterness that comes with knowing that she has nothing to show.

Chapter 25

Peacock Manor
Day 146,618

That wasn't me in the bathroom. Or the library. I already promised February not to manifest more visions. I wonder why that little boy appeared. He looks very much like the other Peacocks I have known over the centuries. I can't remember when in my timeline he was alive. Time flows so differently for someone who has been around as long as I have.

Or perhaps I am finally getting old and am becoming rather forgetful.

Chapter 26

The Next Stage

"Rose, we're giving you a makeover," said the girls at the last sleepover she attended. "You could be *so* pretty."

"Makeup can't hide tall, scrawny, and shy," she reminded them. She waved her new book at them from the corner of the attic where she'd set up her sleeping bag.

They giggled at the cover. "What is that—a dude with wings?"

"*Spirit Mythology From Around the World.* This is a tengu, a spirit that lives in remote mountains and forests. They can protect travelers, or be tricksters, but are also harbingers of—"

"This is why you use stuffy professor words." They relented and spent the night endlessly texting hot boys named Ash and Julian and Cade.

Rose had grown up with these girls, in the same neighborhood, in the same classes, living the same lives. *Mostly.*

It's funny how the more similarities you share, the deeper your differences cut.

Now, Rose scrunches her face, even as she tries not to think about it. It causes her little twinges of pain, quite like paper slicing into skin.

Not fatal, not the end of the world, but still wicked and painful.

She has no reputation at Peacock Manor, in the middle of nowhere. She could outgrow her awkwardness this summer. Maybe a local boy will fall in love with her. *Be normal, Rose.*

She returns her attention to the psychology book she's brought up from the Manor library for bedtime reading. It's part of her research on taking control and moving on:

"The Many Stages of Grief—

Shock. Denial. Anger.

Fear. Searching for Answers. Bargaining.

Loneliness.

Depression.

New Relationships. New Patterns. Helping Others.

Hope. Acceptance."

Her fingers drum the U-shaped chart next to the loneliness-depression stage at the bottom of the U.

Just checking. It appears to be upward from here on out, although the text mentions that zig-zagging around the chart is normal. Hopefully, her friendship with Feeby counts as a "new relationship."

She is on the up and up, then. She snaps the glossy textbook shut and smiles.

Either way, she'll return home in the fall, changed.

Chapter 27

A Memory of the Lake

Rose wrenches out of a disjointed nightmare about the screaming little boy from the day before—the images swirl away upon awakening, but the rotten feeling remains.

She exhales slowly. Just a glimpse from the other side.

It's still morning, judging by the angle of the light streaming through her windows.

Frantic knocking rouses her out of the covers. *Why no doorbell?*

She flies down the stairs to answer the door.

"I'm sorry I couldn't come over the last few days," February says, breathless, with a different edge in her voice. "They found my dad."

"Your...dad?" Rose asks, snapping to attention. February's missing dad. The reason she isn't allowed out after dark.

"A hiker found him in the woods," she says. Her face is tense, but otherwise expressionless.

Rose resists the urge to retreat backward into the house. Dead or alive? She can't bring herself to ask it. The words claw at her throat.

"Is he—" This is all too familiar. When they found Amb—

"He's alive. My dad's alive. He's in the hospital right now," February says. The edges of her eyes water and redden. "He isn't talking, though. I was taking care of him, so I couldn't come over."

"I'm glad you have your dad back. I hope he'll be okay soon. No one knows what happened to him?"

"Not yet. He's back, but...he's not the same..." February trails off, unsteady. Her hesitation gives away that there's more to the story—but Rose doesn't know what question to ask.

Feeby pretends to check for dirt on her blue canvas shoes and fiddles with her pocketwatch.

Rose senses she doesn't want to discuss details surrounding her dad, so she steps forward to wrap her in a quiet hug.

"Aww, thanks, Rose. I needed that. How are you?" she asks.

"I've been reading. Hey—is the library haunted? A little boy told me to get out of the chair in the secret nook yesterday. Or else it was a weird dream. You know me, I can sleep anywhere," she says dismissively. She still isn't sure if the boy was real or not, but she's certain February is not as into ghosts as she is.

"You found the nook! My dad said it was his favorite spot to hide from chores when he was little. Grammy said he loved sorting books back on the shelves once he'd learned the alphabet. What did the boy look like?"

"Black hair, green eyes. Mean."

"That sounds like my dad, except for the mean part."

"Ghost or dream?" Rose asks no one in particular. "Also, I saw something in the mirror that led to an epiphany about the riddle."

"*Epiphany*—ha—you and your words. What did you come up with?"

Rose recites the riddle again:

"I can be one color, or I may change in light.

You might look upon me, or see through me, morning to night,

I'm around for one season, or else I'm always there.

I can be many, or sometimes, just a lonely pair."

"They're two things: Iris, the flower, and iris, the part in an eye," Rose says.

"Hmm, iris…iris! I would not have come up with that in a million years," Feeby marvels, shaking her head.

Rose recounts how she came up with the answer.

"Which bathtub were you using?" Feeby asks.

"Black marble, in the room next to mine."

"My dad's old room when he was little!"

"What do you know about it?"

"Dad never mentioned it being haunted or seeing anything in his room."

"That mirror is haunted for sure. Unless I drifted off to sleep in the tub too?"

February only shrugs and doesn't ask for further details, so Rose drops it altogether. In the truth of daylight, the audacity of her claim sounded delusional. Why would a ghost child help her? How would he know the answer? Plus, part of her wants to take credit for solving the riddle by herself. She is Rose Green, and she figures out answers to things. It's her best and most useful trait.

"Where are there irises, besides our eyes? The

garden? The pond?" Rose asks.

"There are irises on the walking path out back—oh, the Iris Room!" February claps Rose on the back. "Let's go!"

"Inside the Manor?"

"No, no, it's the indoor pool behind the library. It looks like a giant birdhouse made of glass," February explains.

"I haven't seen it." Strange, the pool wasn't advertised in the brochure for the Manor.

"The pool isn't filled right now, but the footpath to it is lined with purple blooms in the spring. This way."

They take a shortcut through the library to exit via the rear double doors, stepping off of the pavilion onto the grassy lawn behind the east side of the Manor.

"I know you're not a morning person, but you're making an angry face." February's eyes widen in false concern. "Is it too bright for you? Is the sun coming in at a funny angle? That's called *morning*, you know. What the sky looks like before noon," she snickers.

"Apparently, all your sarcasm comes out in the a.m. You've got to pace yourself, like I do, so you don't run out by the afternoon and become too warm and fuzzy," Rose retorts, rubbing the last bit of gritty sleep from her eyes.

"You think I'm too warm and fuzzy?" February asks as they walk the pebbly path. The sun-faded irises are in decline, petals wilting as the days have passed the summer solstice.

"Like a frickin' teddy bear at Christmas time. But I don't mind. We can't both be Halloween," Rose says.

"Maybe if you wore another color besides doom-and-gloom gray?" February jokes.

"Haa! Do I need a makeover?"

"Nah, you're fabulous the way you are." February crushes Rose with a hug.

"You're a squeeze-from-the-middle toothpaste person, aren't you," Rose wheezes, her breath pressed out of her.

"That's right; blind enthusiasm is my thing. A Peacock trait. You be Halloween, I'll be Christmas."

"I like it."

"This is it. The Iris Room."

The Iris Room's roof and walls are made of glass trimmed in chalky white, to let in as much sunlight as possible to heat a long, rectangular pool. *An aquarium for humans*, Rose laughs to herself. Lavender tiles line the bottom of the pool, with darker purple squares bordering the upper edge.

Aptly named, the room glows purple.

"Your favorite color, right?" February says.

"Yep. This place is such a throwback—look at the viewing balcony."

As might be expected in such an ancient relic of a pool, a few missing tiles at the bottom leave white plaster squares where no one bothered to replace them.

"Let's clean it up and fill it—we could have a swim party," February says, stepping down the short set of stairs into the empty pool to mimic swimming.

Rose laughs. "I bet we find a clue quickly. There's not that much in here."

February sweeps a few leaves out of the bottom of the pool, loses interest, and climbs out to prod under the benches for clues.

Rose picks up February's abandoned broom. The glossy square tiles mesmerize her, appealing to her fondness for straight lines. Too bad the missing tiles leave blanks in the pattern. *Brush-brush. Brush-brush.* It is satisfying and hypnotic. A chess piece moves in a predictable way along a grid of squares, like the tiles she brushes. If only human life came with more instructions. An orderly structure.

On second thought, is a defined fate better or worse than the random one we are given?

"You're enjoying all the straight lines and right angles, huh?" February teases from the far corner on her tiptoes, twisting a showerhead in hopes of a clue. "You're so fascinating, you know."

"Monotonous. Task. Commencing," Rose responds in her best mechanical voice.

"A pool-cleaning robot. That's exactly what we need." Feeby grabs a dustpan and hops back in next to Rose. "I thought about what you said about Robbie. I'm going to tell him I like him."

"Ooh, exciting. What then?" Rose has never been in a boy situation like that.

"Well, hopefully, you're right, and he likes me back."

"He does. I promise he likes you."

"I never thought about how I felt about him. We've been going to school together since we were little. It's a small town. There's never anyone new, except during holidays, like you."

"Do you have lots of school friends, then?" Rose asks. What is it like to be as outgoing, as beautiful, as February? She must have tons of friends. Is she only coming over to be a good host?

"Well, I'm kinda unusual. I do my own thing. Since my dad disappeared, some kids gossiped behind my back that he ran away because I'm weird. That he left my mom and me. I help with this place during the school year, too. It keeps me busy, so I don't do school activities or dances and stuff."

"You're not missing much," Rose says, still sweeping. "I don't like dances."

"Why? I imagine they'd be fun."

"I'm not like you. You've seen how I am. No one's been my friend like you have."

"Well, if we went to the same school, I'd go with you. We'd have a good time."

"We would."

They feel like ants under a magnifying glass with the blistering sun pouring through the glass roofing as they sweep and scrub. Their cheeks bloom red and their bodies dribble sweat. Meat Bones has wriggled into a shadowy spot under a bench, and slumbers there belly up, his front paws folded into his chest.

"Clean enough. Maybe there's a clue when it's filled with water," February says. She springs up the pool steps and ducks to a far corner of the room.

There, she spins two valves, one with each hand, and water sloshes out of the spigots.

They dangle their legs over the edge of the pool with Meat Bones between them, watching for the next clue that could appear at any moment.

"Why do dogs' lives have to be shorter than ours?" Rose asks, covering Meat Bones' ears to shield him from the conversation.

"They're so loyal and love us so much, they wouldn't understand why we left them. It'd be much sadder for them if they outlived us, don't you think?"

"So sad. But so wise." Rose sighs.

"Hug?" February offers.

"Hug."

February always understands her.

Another hour of idle chatter passes and the water laps their shins near the top edge of the pool. "You better shut off the water," Rose says.

When the spigots are spun, the last of the water sputters out several small dark objects that sink rapidly to the bottom of the deep end.

"Feebs! What came out of the faucets at the end there?!"

"A clue?"

"They look like purple stones. Wait. Pool tiles?"

"The missing tiles at the bottom!"

"Are we supposed to replace them?"

"Oh! Did you bring a swimsuit?" February asks.

"I have one, but…" Rose doesn't want to admit it. "We never—I never—"

"You can't swim?"

"I can doggy paddle around, sort of."

"Well, we need to fix this. I'll teach you right now."

Rose hesitates. "That's okay, I'm fine."

"Why, are you scared?"

She is, but she can't explain it.

February presses her. "Suit up! I'll go in my underwear. We can replace the tiles at the bottom together."

Minutes later, Rose is standing by the water's edge, uncertain and frowning.

"Polar bear plunge!" February shrieks. She springs up into the air and windmills her pale arms before splattering into the water. She clearly doesn't care what she looks like.

Her petite frame is well-proportioned. The kind of proportions boys notice.

Feeby surfaces with one of the dark purple squares in her hand. "I counted nine of these down there. Looks like a normal tile."

She dives back under, reaches the bottom, and presses the tile into one of the white spaces. She resurfaces, flipping the water out from her bangs. "They lock in place, like they're magnetic."

Rose, feeling slouchy and scrawny, dips a toe into the cold water before quickly retracting it.

"Get in. Help me with these tiles. You'd be mad-sad if I had all the fun solving this by myself," February encourages, waving her over. She kicks her legs, splashing Rose, and dives under the surface for another tile. Meat Bones launches himself over the edge, showing off his natural swimming skills.

"Mad-sad, huh." Rose chuckles. "Doesn't look fun," she mutters.

Less like a polar bear, more like a baby elephant, she flops in. It is the exact opposite of the relaxing, warm bubble bath she loves so much. The cold water siphons the air out of her body and replaces it with needles and dense rocks. Medieval torture!

She finds herself sinking to the bottom like a— what is the heaviest sinking thing?

The *Titanic*.

Or a vessel sucked into a whirlpool. *A Descent into the Maelstrom*, Edgar Allan Poe.

Rose, focus. No time for Poe. Get one of those tiles.

Her mind and body flail wildly. The water pulls her downward.

Kick more. My lungs are bursting. She can't see the tiles anymore.

Sinking ship, the bottom of the sea, corpses—

No, no—dead bodies float. They look like gray narwhals, February said.

She continues to sink, heavy and helpless.

It is very quiet underwater.

****

In an instant, the water forces her to remember. It stirs deep memories, dredging and lifting them like silt from the depths of a sandy bottom.

One particular memory emerges—plucked from where she shoved it and looked the other way and hoped it would never surface.

The day at the lake.

She and Amber row madly across the lake.

A silvery figure on the far shore.

The Lady of the Lake—a ghost—they exclaim, eager to encounter the tourist legend. They steer toward it. The figure glows brighter. It is definitely a spirit, faded and wispy and tentacled.

Is it helping them or hurting them? Do evil spirits exist?

Before she can get close enough, Rose blacks out, and somebody takes her back to the dock, but her sister doesn't make it.

Amber drowns.

Rose gasps at the devastating memory but gulps water instead. Trapped. She can't breathe, as if her lungs have been cut out. Is this what Amber felt in her last moments? The thought sickens her.

Her eyes burn as if she were crying, but she has no idea if it's possible to cry underwater or not. Panic paralyzes her until her foot hits the hard bottom. She pushes off weakly (the surface looks so far away), clawing upward while forcing her horrible memory to continue sinking down and away from her.

Finally, a solid grasp on her upper arm—February is beside her, towing her up and up.

Rose chokes, and with a lot of splashing, breaks the surface. February yanks her forward, depositing her in the shallow end.

Numbly, Rose clings to the edge, coughing and spitting. Meat Bones swims over and offers up a ball, sniffing her head to see if she is okay.

"All right, first you must learn to hold your breath," February determines.

"I'm not coordinated. I can tell you which of Newton's Three Laws of Motion applies most to swimming efficiently," Rose babbles to disguise her humiliation and shock as she spews water from her nose. She hopes February isn't watching her.

"You can't learn how to swim from a book, my dear." February thumps her on the back.

"Let's *never* speak of this," Rose says, alternating between gagging and gasping.

"I got you. I'll bring my suit tomorrow and we'll do this again."

"I don't ever want to do *that* again." She side-eyes the deep end.

"We'll practice. You're okay?"

"I'm okay," Rose lies. She doesn't want to think about her lack of coordination or the catastrophic memory.

"Here," February says, dropping a few tiles into Rose's hand.

"You want me to hand them to you from the edge while you dive down?"

"No. You're going to do it. At least the ones in the shallow end."

Rose practices holding her breath underwater, slipping the tiles in place with her big toe, while Feeby covers the deep end. Focusing on the task calms her, and her heart no longer thunders in her chest.

Once all nine tiles are in place, she pauses scanning the Iris Room. "Nothing happened. They don't match the main tiles. Does it spell out something? A map?"

They stand in the shallow end surveying their work.

"They look random to me. We fixed the pool, though," February says.

"Does nine mean anything to the Peacocks? Number nine, nine squares—"

"Cats have nine lives. Tic-tac-toe has nine squares. Baseball has nine innings—Robbie's on the baseball team." February shrugs.

"Nine o'clock, nine months, the ninth month— September. Aunt September? Could the book be buried with your aunt and all her gold?"

"Yeah! Totally possible. Grandpa Jules took his statue, remember? Cousin March has his mirror collection with him, lining his coffin. Great-Gram Jan has Robert—" She shoots Rose a knowing look. "—her teapot."

February bobs up and down in the water, continuing her chatter. "What would I take with me? Thinking of my dead body all cold and alone in the ground…we have the coldest winters, and if I'm to be buried here, I'd want all the clothes I own, all layered on me."

"So, your one white dress," Rose says dryly.

"HA! It *is* my favorite. Layer number one in my burial outfit."

"This conversation went somewhere morbid."

"I guess if I were hiding the book, I'd make sure to bring it with me when I died."

"Who has it, then?" Rose asks. "It's too vague of a clue."

"I'm going to take a look from a different angle."

Meat Bones joins in what he thinks is February's made-up water game, while she gets in and out of different corners of the pool to study the tile pattern. Her shrieks echo off the glass walls as he splashes in with her, following her with his ball held above water.

He is good at diving. He can kick his back legs fast enough to propel himself down, down, down like a little submarine to retrieve his ball.

"That's the cutest thing ever!" February squeals at him.

The entire day passes so quickly.

They have a new clue. She is going to learn to swim.

Rose can't shake the nagging feeling that her friendship with February will alter the course of her life in unimaginable ways.

Despite the disastrous start, she's…lighter. Happier.

She can almost feel joy without the pain. Almost.

She hasn't felt this way in so long.

It suddenly dawns on her that maybe she hasn't wanted to.

Chapter 28

Dark Shadows

Rose has never worked harder on anything in her entire life. With February coaching her daily, it's only a week until Rose miraculously swims from one end of the pool to the other, and back again. February jumps up and down, cheering wildly. "I'm so proud of you!" she screeches.

Only her sister ever applauded her like that. Meat Bones races alongside the pool, a little wolf lifeguard ready to jump in at any sign of trouble.

They drag themselves out to eat lunch. Mom baked wild truffle and potato galettes that morning. Dad left his desk to search for mushrooms every few chapters— he foraged those wild truffles himself and was quite proud of his valuable find.

Rose hopes his hobby won't poison them all.

"I have gossip," February says. "I talked to Robbie."

"And!?"

"He asked why we haven't been over again and joked that Jelly wanted cute girl visitors. He admitted that he wished he could see more of me this summer. That he'd liked me for a long time."

"Uh huh…"

"I told him I liked him too. I like how he accepts

me for who I am—you know, all my wacky ways. He said there was nothing to accept; that he adores it all."

"Whoa, exciting," Rose says.

"It was. He held my hand—his hand was sweaty because he was nervous—and leaned in close and kissed me once. I kissed him back. Then…we kissed and touched more until I—Well, he's a very good kisser."

"Ooh." Rose finds herself leaning inward, wanting to hear more. Her heart melts a little. It makes her happy. A little jealous, but mostly happy.

"He has this weekend off. Can he come over and swim with us?"

"Of course, yes." Being a good friend.

"Woohoo!" February hugs her.

Rose is curious what first love looks like, feels like, sounds like.

She can only imagine. A secondhand view is the best she can do for now.

Is it like the movies? Or is it different in real life?

They cram their mouths full with the rest of the galettes—a bit soggy and chewy by now—and they begin gathering up towels when Meat Bones leaps up to attention and snarls, ferocious and predatory. The muscles in his haunches are so taut they quiver, and his brownish-gray fur bristles.

Rose whips her head around the Iris Room. A figure streaks across the side of the building in a blur: a shadowy smudge. It drags across the glass panels, writhing ink and cloud, twisting and squirming before vanishing into the bushes.

Rose drops the towels and staggers back. "Feebs, did you see that? That shadowy figure again!"

"I thought I saw someone, but it was moving so fast." February's face is rigid, and she nervously grasps her pocketwatch.

"Who else would be here right now?"

"The gardener? The cleaners?" February asks, a wobble in her voice betraying her uncertainty. "It didn't look like either, though."

It didn't look *human*, she means.

"I couldn't see a face," Rose says.

"Otherwise, only Mom and I come here, and she's at the hospital with my dad."

Meat Bones barks. And barks. *BARK BARK, WOOF WOOF.*

The figure outside the glass moves unnaturally—too fast, too fluid, to be human. It reverses, stalking one more blurred lap around the building before pausing outside the window closest to them.

Rose recoils, instinct steering her away from the unknown—from danger.

But not February.

February strides forward. She stands in front of Rose, motionless and ready, and though her nails dig into her palms, she blocks and protects her friend.

The form shifts, mutating in place into twisting branches of shadow and smoke. Rose cranes her neck to focus through the Iris Room's old glass. The panes rattle as the shadow presses against it. Cool? Terrifying? Cool?

Terrifying.

Rose blinks once, hoping the shadow is a dust cloud or a floater in her eye. This has to be another vision.

But even Meat Bones has gone silent, cowering

behind Rose.

The shadowy form solidifies. Rose makes out an outline of a skeletal bird through thick, smoky branches of purple and black shadow. Where its head should be, there's a horned beak and hollow skull. Below that, about midway down its body, a large bloody mouth—ripped at the corners—gnashes from within the dark tatters of night around it.

Rose presses back against the rising horror crushing the breath out of her.

In between the shadows, passing through the veil of its darkest parts, a woman's face with gold teeth presses forth. Part of her lower jaw is missing, and a large wooden spoon threads through her eye sockets.

The cook from the passageway?!

The depraved face vanishes back into volatile, twisting darkness. In its place, a small child with wormy skin and bleeding ears presses through. He stretches a hand with missing fingers toward them but is sucked back into shadow.

For an instant, her sister's face appears. Amber's eyes are hollow and depthless. Her mouth opens to speak—

"Help us," Amber rasps, but before more words are formed, her face dissolves back into night and ash.

Those two small words rip Rose apart.

Amber is not okay.

Rose is certain of this. The beaked monster turns to her, cocking its head from side to side, searching her with its empty eye sockets.

Then…she *feels* the dark creature, clawing into the very core of her.

Living shadow and death incarnate. It shreds her

insides with icy terror.

In this moment, Rose knows that she will not make it out of this summer whole.

Chapter 29

Anything is Possible, in the Worst Way Possible

The demonic phantasm rattles the pane of glass where it festers. It violates the physical boundary, slowly seeping in like oil dripping through a screen.

"Oh no, oh no!" February cries. She surges forward and throws her hands up, slamming her palms against the glass to repel the figure through the pane.

Her small body strains as she wills the monstrosity back outside, and she mutters words Rose cannot discern.

How does she know what to do?

What is she saying to the thing? Yet, the dark, rotting figure bulldozes forth as if driven by an unexplained gust of wind.

Now half inside, half outside, it screeches like the clawing of a metal pan with a fork, setting Rose's teeth on edge. She shrinks back and covers her ears.

February's hair and dress whip around her as she tumbles onto the tile floor, but she recovers instantly and rolls back up, digging her heels down to stand her ground. Her hands reach into the dark cloud around the torn mouth, now gnashing at her palms.

The monster has made it through the glass, but February's invisible power shoves it back through the window. A spectacular determination rises in her as she stands facing the unknown fiend.

She is forcing the monster spirit away—with nothing but her bare hands and her words!

February finishes whispering and slams the window once more with both palms. Her arms drop, going limp. One soundless, frozen moment passes. Then, as if with the chime of a thousand tiny bells, the glass of the window splinters outward in a perilous explosion of glittering shards.

The rotten shadow blows backward, uttering a piercing wail that penetrates Rose's guts.

Rose can't help but scream, too. She is certain that now, with the glass broken, the monstrosity will enter and take them all. She snatches Meat Bones, throws herself onto the floor curled into a ball, and tries to shield him inside her shirt. He squirms into her, and she clutches him tighter.

The smoke and bones hover at the edge of the shattered window, as if savoring the ease with which it can now enter to reap whatever it wants—her life, her death, her body, her soul?

"The room has been warded. You are unable to enter. Leave *now*!" February commands. The monster holds its ground, refusing to depart, so she repeats, "Leave us, Scraythe!"

Scraythe? She knows its name.

It's one of the words on the burnt lab notes.

"Go!" February hollers.

To Rose's amazement, the writhing darkness rises like lifting fog, spiraling away toward the woods and does not return.

February teeters backward, bracing herself against a bench before falling onto it. She studies her injured palms, burnt red and painfully blistered, and folds over, her breath heavy and strained.

All Rose can do is press Meat Bones into her chest.

"What—was—?" Rose stammers, her voice wavering. Cold sweat forms in odd places. She's going to be sick.

"There's something you need to know," February says, her voice raw. She remains hunched over.

"Need to know…?" Rose can't finish any of her sentences. Everything is too bright. Her head tenses and strains like a balloon about to pop.

"That wasn't exactly a ghost. It was something evil that doesn't belong here. A Scraythe. They're not supposed to be here. They don't have souls anymore." February finally uprights herself. Her green eyes fix on Rose's, and they stare at each other, horrified. Rose has never seen such deep worry lines creasing her friend's forehead.

"*They*? Where are they *supposed* to be? Is it coming back? Are there more?"

"I sent it away. I'll protect you. I conjured a warding of the building. The Manor is already warded."

"How do you know all this?"

"They've always been here. Since the Manor was built." It is all February offers.

Rose's mouth opens, but she gags on her words, suffocated by fear. She grasps for reason or comprehension but is left with impossibility.

Has her life fallen into one of her dad's paranormal thrillers?

Is that—is that *thing* what killed her sister?

February holds out her blistered, bloodied hand. "Don't squeeze Meat Bones too hard. Let's go back to the Manor."

Rose refuses. No! No, thanks. She isn't planning on going anywhere. This building is now warded, Feeby said, but does that mean the property outside is not?

"C'mon, Rose. Let's go," February says, more firmly.

Rose faintly registers the words, as if coming from a great distance. Feeby gently unhooks one of Rose's arms clamped around Meat Bones and hauls her up.

Rose doesn't blink as she shuffles along the tiles of the Iris Room.

Scraythe, for all she knows, could exist in the split second of darkness during a blink.

She has no idea, but it sounds possible.

Anything is possible now.

****

Rose feels the warmth of February's arm around her waist. But she can't hear the exact words, can't focus, or make sense of what is happening. She numbly follows her friend's steady voice.

February marches her back to the Manor, ushering her into bed like a sickly child. She stays until it is time for her to go home. Rose remains silent, refusing to speak.

Rose can't come up with what to say, what to think, or how to feel. Before, the existence of the supernatural seemed entirely feasible, but mostly at the boundaries of her mind, where reality blurred with possibility. But today, the boundaries disintegrated— destroyed by the absoluteness of the Scraythe.

How can she continue trying to summon a spirit— her sister's—if this is what's possible?

She doesn't remember Feeby leaving. Her friend just faded into the darkness.

Chapter 30

Peacock Manor
Day 146,630

It was only a matter of time. I detest those monsters! They have taken more than one Peacock. Those pests are becoming more desperate, more powerful in their misery, to come out during the day.

February was terrified and got the incantations wrong. She has never had to use them before and recited the words incorrectly. Poor little thing. She bungled it.

They would have perished had I not whispered the correct incantation and warded the Iris Room for them. I feel helpful.

Chapter 31

What Is Real?

February returns the next day, but Rose doesn't answer the door. In fact, she refuses to get out of bed all day, except to feed Meat Bones and to let him outside.

The dreary blue morning glory vines around the Manor have completely covered her window overnight. Or have they been slithering up all summer?

It's difficult to tell what is real anymore.

Rose pulls the sheets over her head, blocking what little light trickles through, and squeezes her eyes shut. She takes refuge in the dark, though now, *both* the shadows and the light terrify her.

Chapter 32

Three Incantations

February tries again the following day. Her hands
are bandaged, but she's carrying a large turquoise
clamshell bag she found in the attic. She snakes her
head around behind the bedpost and rattles her beaded
bag noisily. "Cock-a-doodle-doo! Are you waking up
today? I have something to show you." A few teal
sequins and faux gems fly off onto the bedspread, but
she doesn't notice.

Rose remains deathly still, her eyes barely open,
hoping Feeby will think she's asleep and leave her
alone.

February persists, peeling the covers off her.

"Meet me in the library when you're ready," she
says, flapping the sheets as if trying to waft Rose out of
bed. "I highly recommend a bath or shower," she adds
tactfully.

Rose showers off the last two days, then takes the
East Wing stairs to the library, stopping to adjust the
paintings.

Someone has to parallel the lines and square off the
edges.

As she enters the library, February fishes out a
leather notebook from her bag and opens it to a page
she's bookmarked with a pencil.

She uses her take-charge voice to rally Rose.

"This is from Grammy's diary. You're good at remembering things, so I want you to memorize these three incantations. They'll protect you in case I'm not here. Scraythe consume souls—the essence of who you are—to ease their own pain. They don't know who they are anymore. It makes them feel whole for a while, to feel like someone else for a bit."

"Did it only…want mine?"

"Not necessarily. They take young souls. Like Meat Bones'. He has a soul."

"Oh. Yeah. What about my parents?"

"They like newer souls. Easier to extract," February says plainly.

"Are you sure they're safe?"

"Younger souls are easier, like separating an egg yolk from the white. Older folk—adult souls—are more like scrambled eggs. That bony beak, it's ready to peck out your egg yolk. Yes, it was real," February explains patiently.

"How do you know so much?!" Fear morphs into anger, as it often does. "Is it witchcraft!? You're a witch?"

"I'm not a witch. They usually don't come out during the day. I don't know why it was out during broad daylight."

Rose remains frozen, speechless, and sick.

Not usually in daylight? Is she in more danger at night?

Finally, she says, "Is it the Manor? Why didn't you warn me from the start?"

"Would you have believed me? They aren't always around, but yes, they are attracted to the Manor,"

February says, restrained.

"Why?"

"Memorize these to protect yourself and Meat Bones. The first incantation is the one I used the other day."

Rose narrows her eyes at the notebook.

February goes on. "The second incantation is for if you're outside, if you're not in a building you can ward, and you need time to get inside. The third one is if there is more than one Scraythe. Only use it as a last resort," February warns.

"Why a last resort?"

"It damages them, but it can damage you, too. It's best if you don't use it alone. It affects the darkness in them, which is what they're mostly made of, but we all have some darkness in us. It's a part of who we are, right? But you can't damage one part without affecting the other. The strength of others will help you, though. Does that make sense?"

"I think so. Last resort only." With all the despair Rose feels, whatever happens to the Scraythe during the use of the third incantation will surely happen to her too.

A violent shudder rips through her gut.

February reads her mind. "You're *not* made up of darkness, no more than any other person is. You're also not alone. You have me!" She captures Rose in her signature hug and wrings out a smidgen of the terror in the pit of Rose's stomach. "The Scraythe have always been there. Nothing has changed, except you can protect yourself now," she says gently.

Rose's nerves still rattle inside her clammy shell of a body. She presses her face into the book and focuses on memorizing the first…the second…and the third passage. The three incantations that can save her life.

She repeats them to herself.

The incantations bear a hypnotic rhythm that renders them unforgettable, as if they have a heartbeat, as if they are alive.

Among the notes scrawled into the margins, she reads "Death Spirit," "Souls of the Dead," and "The Beyond." There are sketches of deformed, dismal creatures on the pages she turns.

Is this the kind of spirit she and Amber encountered at the lake?

Her skin crawls.

Asking questions gives life to those horrendous possibilities. She isn't ready to be slapped in the face with the truth. What had she expected to find? Not this.

Should she warn her parents? Would they believe her? February says they're safe.

Why does she know such things?

Rose decides to stick to the Green family motto: don't talk about unsavory topics.

Maybe it *is* the best way. If she told her parents about Scraythe, they'd think she was crazy, or on drugs. Her mom would weep silent tears about Rose's "drug use" and go bake a cherry almond layer cake.

More perilous than lies are the truths that are too hard to bear.

She can't tell them.

Rose trembles as she peels back the pages of the notebook, mortally afraid of the answers she may find.

Chapter 33

Get Me Out of Here

Rose can't sleep that night, and based on the chimes of the clock downstairs, it's past the midnight hour. She clicks open her suitcase, gathers up books and shovels in clothes from off the floor and the desk chair. Tomorrow, she will be long gone from Peacock Manor, *if* she can convince her parents to cut their summer stay a month short.

She creeps down the dark hallway to her parents' room, seizing the chance to address them both at the same time; between her dad's work and her mom's constant church activities, they are rarely together during the day.

They need to know they must return home as soon as possible.

"Dad?" Rose rasps.

Dad and Mom are both asleep, facing away from her. Her mom coughs.

"Mom, are you awake?" Rose hisses, more loudly than before.

Her mom has a small, framed photo of Amber on her nightstand. It pains Rose to see it, so she tips it over face down and accidentally bumps the table, knocking Mom's Bible to the floor.

"Amb...Rose?" her mother murmurs, as if her

tongue were too big for her mouth. "Cakes will be ready in five," she says, without waking. She snores and rolls over toward Rose, remaining asleep.

Neither of her parents stir again, and she feels silly standing there watching them sleep. Ridiculous even, for trying to wake them in the middle of the night to ask to go home. For a minute, she is a little girl again, running to her parents' room after a nightmare. Her shoulders drop and she turns away, feeling sheepish.

But instead of returning to her bedroom, she slips deeper into the west hall, masking the sound of her steps and avoiding any creaking floorboards. To the locked mystery room.

That worn, faded door. That frickin' door plucks at her curiosity.

After that first night, she'd gone outside again and counted the windows. *If* she counted correctly, the window where she'd first seen the figure of light belongs to the room of the locked door.

She jerks the doorknob with all her might, as if hoping to surprise it into opening, or perhaps to splinter and split the old wood, but it refuses to yield. She leans her forehead against the doorframe.

The door smells faintly of the sea.

Water gurgles behind it. At first, she wonders if she's hearing the octopus fountain in the courtyard, but the bubbling stops when she lifts her cheek away from the door.

Her pulse thrums in her head in uneven beats, and she thinks of Feeby's pocketwatch as she presses her ear against the wood again.

"Rose," a voice curls around her ear like a wisp of wind seeping through the tarred cracks of the door—

from inside the room.

A female voice. A familiar voice. "We belong together."

The door rattles in its frame.

"Ah!" She staggers back. "Am...ber? Is that you?"

"Rose, we saw a ghost. Eight minutes later, I died. Remember..." the voice wheezes.

She is taken aback. "Of-of course," she stammers. "Was it a Scraythe? Are-are you okay now?"

"No. Find me, help me. Join me."

"I want to help. How do I find you?" she asks, desperate for answers.

"*The Book of Lost Spirits*. Only you know the truth of how. The truth. Tell the truth."

"I can't do that, you know I can't." Her voice trembles.

"But you're so close. You must, Rose. For me? We belong together. There's no way back. Wake up."

"But then—No. I don't want to," Rose says, stiffening. "I want...I wanna go home."

She strains against the door, but there is no response. Her dad's snores rumble from down the hall.

"Amber! Are you still there?" she asks. "Come back to me."

Rose hesitates, pinching her forearm before smacking herself on the cheek. Both sting. She is awake. What is real anymore? Did someone know she was about to give up on her search? Did Amber know? Someone wants her to stay.

Amber wants me to stay.

To be with her. *We belong together*.

The voice doesn't sound like a Scraythe—it sounds like her sister.

Rose stumbles back to her room, her shoulder bumping along the wall as if sleepwalking through a dream from which she cannot wake.

****

Places, like people, can become riddled with disease. Has the Manor become such a place?

Then the Scraythe are a symptom, not the cause.

What has Peacock Manor become over the centuries, or was it always like this?

She shivers at her own startling revelations.

The Manor has ensnared her with its mysteries, its riddles, its unspoken promises of seeing her sister again. *There is more, Rose.* If she resists, she will never cease to wonder. If she leaves now, she will never know the truth, and nothing will change.

The Manor whispers to her to continue, and she has no choice but to obey.

Chapter 34

Peacock Manor
Day 146,633

Pixie Cakes has been through a lot for a young one. She is clever and quiet and curious. Like me. And like me, she is lonely. She's quite perceptive. The quiet ones always are. If only she would open her eyes to the situation around her.

At least she's trying to change herself. But I believe she focuses on the wrong things. I've tried to help her. Is it better or worse to show people what they want to see and hear, or deny them their deepest desires? Am I helping or hurting?

Chapter 35

The Boys and Another Clue

Armed with new knowledge and new resolve, Rose reminds herself that at least one incantation works; it repelled a Scraythe right before her eyes. She forbids herself from thinking about what would have happened otherwise.

She returns to the warded Iris Room, despite the twisting in her gut. They must figure out the next clue as quickly as possible.

August is right around the corner and the end of their vacation looms. Her stay at Peacock Manor will be over.

She scolds herself. In the tiny moments when she was enjoying the swimming, the friendship, the fun, she allowed herself to forget about the pain and—to her regret—her goals, if only for an instant.

An instant in which she forgot about her sister.

But then—the Scraythe! And last night. That familiar voice. The Scraythe are real, spirits exist, and she has to be close to finding *The Book of Lost Spirits*.

She is too close to give up.

The thought burns her with desperation, as though her life somehow depended on finding it. *Be brave*, she tells herself. As February's friend, Rose wants to help her family. If they find the book, the Peacocks could sell the place before anyone else finds out about the Scraythe infestation.

This morning, Rose keeps quiet her reasons for continuing on as she and February scour the building once more.

She climbs the narrow spiral stairs that take her up to the viewing balcony with the thin metal railing overlooking the pool, all of it painted powder white. Nothing is out of place, not a single oddity or blemish indicating a hidden clue.

Disappointed, she rejoins February, circling the edge of the pool.

"What if, um, *something* shows up when Robbie is here?" Rose lowers her voice, as if she could take back the words—in case Feeby doesn't want her to bring the subject up.

"Every last inch of the Manor is warded now. The Iris Room was left forgotten. It hadn't been used in so long."

"Hmmm."

"Oof. I feel like a steamed meat dumpling," February says, wiping away the sweat running down her cheeks.

"Dumplings, yum," Rose mutters.

"Let's get in the water. We aren't getting anywhere and I'm frustrated."

Rose gives Feeby a thumbs-up. She pries her gaze away from the shiny new window where the Scraythe launched its attack. The pane is cleaner and brighter than those around it, but it is still an unwelcome reminder of the dirty, dark thing. A repairman had arrived the very next day, February told her.

While Rose was shamefully sulking and hiding,

Feeby took care of it.

Why can't she be fierce and reliable like Feeby?

"Are you sure my parents aren't in danger?" Rose asks again.

"Yes. The Scraythe want newer souls, remember? Plus, your dad never leaves the Manor and your mom is at church all the time. Both are protected."

With no one else to worry about, no other friends or family, Rose leaves it at that, despite the gnawing dread she's forgetting something.

"What's in the locked room upstairs in the West Wing?" she blurts out.

February skids to a stop on their way to the towel bin. "Oh, did you try to open it?" she asks. Nice and casual.

"No. I was only…curious." Rose doesn't mention the voices. She gauges February's reaction with a sideways glance.

"That was, um, Grammy's room. We don't have people stay in there." Feeby pales, looking strained and uneasy.

Ah. Did Grammy die in there or something?

"Feebs, do you think the book can contact spirits?" Rose turns away, flips open the storage bin, extracts two towels, and shuts it again—as if her question were no big deal.

February eagerly switches topics. "Gramms said it was filled with a collection of knowledge about non-corporeal beings. History and first-hand accounts of contact. That could include conjuring and communicating with them."

"I mean, the Scraythe was repelled by the incantation, so the opposite could be possible—

attracting a specific spirit, right?"

"Rose, is there a spirit you want to talk to?" Feeby's bottle-green eyes are fixed upon her, unblinking.

There it is. February knows there is more—more in the spaces between the questions Rose asks. And Rose has asked one question too many.

"It would be nice to talk to those we've…lost. Wouldn't you want to talk to your grammy?" she asks evasively.

"Of course. But we have to let the dead go. Would you keep summoning them over and over again to chat whenever you want? Glom onto their spirit as if they were still alive? It would be horribly sad for both sides!"

It would be sad, but Rose is already sad, and she needs answers.

"What if there's information on how to destroy Scraythe entirely? Not just repel them. Then you'd be safe," Rose says, regretting how she almost mentioned Amber and her own hidden motive.

"There could be," Feeby says, studying Rose.

"That'd be useful, then," Rose says quietly.

She whirls away from Feeby's uncomfortable scrutiny, staring at the dark tiles in the pool floor in chagrinned silence.

****

Rose shows off her new swimming skills by diving to pluck out the new tiles before replacing them in a different order, hoping this will somehow reveal a clue.

"It's almost a clothes hanger shape, if you connect the dots," she says, emerging from the deep end.

A shadow appears at the doorway.

"Robinson!" February hollers, paddling toward the entrance.

Kamdyn strides in behind him, beautiful and elegant.

"And Kam?! Are you gonna swim, too?"

"Hey, Feebs. Hello, Rose. You know I'm a skier, not a swimmer. Swimming is a lot of splashing and gasping for air. It's not dignified." He indicates his dress shirt, belted slacks, and suede loafers. "I'm heading up to my dad's office, anyway. Got an errand to run." He throws February a meaningful glance.

He is about to turn away, but before Rose can stop herself—

"Too fancy to swim, huh?" she blurts.

He breaks into a grin, the biggest one from him yet. He has protruding canines—the kind of teeth that stick out a bit on the sides but aren't worth correcting with braces. Though his brilliant smile is sincere, his eyes betray starker feelings just below the surface.

There is always a weight to his being, a sadness behind those eyes.

For a brief moment, a cloud drifts across the sun over the Iris Room, and a shadow emerges.

Rose sucks in a breath.

She swears that Kamdyn's veins darken along his neck, spreading to his face, almost as if he were unshaven.

She kicks forward to get a better look, her eyes rounding in disbelief as the dark purple bruises branch into his cheeks, his ears, around his eyes, and down into his hands. His fists clench.

What's happening to him?

But as she rubs away the pool water dripping into

her eyes from her drenched hair, all returns to normal within the span of two blinks.

"In another life. Maybe I'd like swimming then." He flicks his wrist to check his watch. "I'm going to try to catch the shuttle from here. Have fun, all of you," Kamdyn says, stealing another glance at Rose.

She wonders if the reflection of the pool water colors his irises a silvery purple, or if they glow from something else, like they did in Robbie's car.

The shifting lights in the room must be playing tricks on her vision.

Before she can say more, he spins away, striding purposefully out of the Iris Room.

February catches the long moment between Rose and Kamdyn, and whispers, "Kam must've stopped by just to say hello to you. Why else did he come if he didn't want to swim?"

"Nope, not possible," Rose replies, turning away to hide the idiotic smile she's fighting back.

Robbie sets up his towel on one of the loungers and peels off his T-shirt before kicking off his flip-flops.

February waves him in. "Robbie, get in here! Rose and I are seeing who can hold our breaths longer underwater."

"Well, prepare to lose, girls. Look at this lung capacity," he jokes, as he thuds his wide, shirtless chest with his fist. February pretends to vomit into her hands by spitting pool water.

Rose snorts, laughing. She can't think of anything to say, so she dunks back into the water to avoid both conversation and gawking. Even underwater, she can see Robbie's tanned skin gleaming as cords of muscle flex with his movement. Functional. Natural, like a mountain lion. *Stop your depraved thoughts, Rose Green.* What does Kamdyn look like in swim shorts? *Whoops.* She can't help wondering in both embarrassment and desire.

And what were the shadows creeping up his skin?

A ripple of water carries her backward; Robbie has jumped in, so Rose surfaces and blinks away the water. Robbie and February gaze at each other, intense and adoring as the newly in love do.

Robbie clasps his arm around Feeby's waist, keeping them afloat in the deep end. Her small body presses into his wall of a torso, skin on skin. Cozy and intimate.

Their beautiful faces, noses touching and foreheads tilting into each other's, form a heart shape.

In another life, as Kamdyn said; Rose imagines herself as one of them. She swims to the far side, crawls out on her hands and knees over the edge and rolls herself in a large fluffy towel. She lies on her belly on the warm, smooth tiles. The sun radiates through the glass roof. Not a shadow to be seen. No Scraythe. How can they be real? *Today is real.* Swimming. Sunshine. February-Robbie-Kamdyn. Cookies.

Meat Bones waggles over to share her towel. She reaches for another peanut butter cookie on a tray next to her, crumbles half into her mouth, and lobs the other half to Meat Bones, who catches it in mid-air. She flattens a cheek to the floor and eyeballs her gorgeous friends across the Iris Room. Lost in their own happiness. Floating, splashing, laughing. It's like watching a sappy, romantic movie.

She sighs and looks away, wishing for a turn to star in her own movie.

After a while, February and Robbie wriggle out of the water. He holds open a towel for her, folding her into it, and then they share a plastic chaise, melding into each other's bodies. February giggles and makes faces at him while he gathers her in his arms and pulls her closer, kissing her brow. She curves over him, swinging a leg over his hard thigh, her wet swimsuit pressing into his torso. They are kissing again. His hand slides down her backside, around the front of her thigh and between. His other hand slips higher, stroking her ribcage, pushing upward until his fingers disappear under her swimsuit top.

Rose's face flushes, warmth seeping into her ears even as she turns away. She does a floppy pushup to press herself up and invites Meat Bones to take a walk.

They hurry down the path out of the Iris Room toward the Manor. Still unsure how safe it is in the spaces between warded buildings, she tries not to make eye contact with any shadows except her own.

Light-headed from too much sun, she craves something cold to drink and rushes into the kitchen.

She stands in front of the open fridge, the frosty air wafting through her as she surveys the selection: the cold brew, bottled cappuccino, and iced mocha that fill her dad's mug day and night. Coconut water and pineapple juice, her mom's beverages of choice. An assortment of fizzy waters in fake fruit flavors.

The refrigerator door slams shut in front of her, hitting her hand.

"Hey!" she scolds. "Dad?!"

They've avoided each other since their fight.

Her absentminded dad wheels back around. "Oh, oops, I didn't see you there, sorry! Coming through to check for snacks."

"Hi, Mr. Green!" February has come in search of Rose through the banquet room entrance behind her. She smiles, her coral red lips swollen and her pink cheeks aglow from basking in the sun and certain other activities. Robbie-type activities.

"Take a look at these." Dad offers a basket of mushrooms he's foraged from the forest nearby.

February sidesteps past Rose and hovers over his assortment of mushrooms.

"How do you tell the poisonous ones from the edible ones?" Dad asks.

"How?" February asks.

Rose senses a set-up for a regrettable joke.

"Give them to someone *else* to eat first," Dad replies, arching a brow.

February cackles and says she'll write that down.

My dad, everyone. Rose pretends to laugh. After all, he is trying to be normal after their awkward fight, and normal for the Greens is to act like nothing is wrong. She figures this is better than angry or sad, and enough time has passed that she decides to forgive him.

"Do you know any others?" February asks.

"I know many because I'm a fungi. Right? A *fun guy*?" he says, delighting himself.

"Do not encourage him," Rose warns February, expressionless.

He thanks his audience, takes a deep bow, and pedals backward out of the kitchen, disappearing back to his office.

"Your dad is funny."

"*He* thinks he is. Want anything to drink? Does Robbie?" Rose opens the fridge again.

They collect a few more snacks before returning to the Iris Room.

Robbie is floating on his back, gazing up at his enviable reflection in the sloping glass roof. When he sees them, he says, "Hey, take a look at this. The darker purple tiles at the bottom of the pool reflecting on the glass. There are nine of them. They remind me of something."

Rose leans over the edge. Is it possible he's found a clue they've missed?

Robbie narrows his eyes, tipping his head. "I think it's...a constellation? It's inverted, flipped around on the bottom of the pool, but in the reflection in the glass above, it's the right orientation for the nine stars in Leo, the Lion."

The girls exchange animated glances before running to the library to confirm his find. They ransack the shelves for a book on constellations and race back with it to the pool to compare the pattern.

Robbie climbs out of the pool and dries himself off. He shakes out his light brown hair before pulling his shirt over his head.

"Robbie, you were right!" February exclaims. "The tiles form Leo the Lion, one of the larger constellations in the sky. Nine stars, one constellation."

"What's it mean?" Rose whispers beside her.

"You should be an astronomer, Robbs!" February regards him with admiration. "How the heck did you know that?"

"We're so far from city lights—when it's too hot to sleep, I sneak out to our fields and search for meteors and constellations," Robbie confesses. "Does this have anything to do with the puzzle games you're playing?"

He checks his watch as he slips his feet into his flip-flops. "I better take off soon anyway—I gotta make dinner for my brother."

"Games, yep. Fun puzzles to stave off summer boredom," February replies. "We'll walk you to your car." She levels a knowing look at Rose.

A lion, huh. Rose can't recall any statues or paintings of lions around the Manor.

"Bye, Rose. You and Feebs need to come over and ride horses sometime."

"That sounds fun. Bye, Robbie." Rose gives him a quick, vanishing grin.

"We will for sure," February agrees.

February leans against Robbie's car. He grips her waist to pull her in and rests his chin on top of her head, holding her as if he might never see her again. She presses her cheek onto his chest as he curves his head down and turns his mouth to hers. More kissing. *Kiss. Kiss. Kiss.* Like their lives depend on it.

Yuck. But sweet. But yuck.

Rose impatiently pitches the ball for Meat Bones while observing them from the corner of her eye.

Finally, the two peel away from each other, reluctant to break apart into two humans.

It feels odd to Rose that while they are all the same age, they seem so separate from her at this moment.

She longs to know what it's like.

Chapter 36

The Last One

Once Robbie's car turns out the gate, they dash up the hill and into the Manor, searching for a lion.

"Where's there a lion? I don't remember seeing any among the garden statues," Rose comments, closing the door behind February.

"There has to be one somewhere in the Manor," February says from inside the hallway closet. "Nothing here. Lab has no décor—it can't be there." She stares vacantly at the floral ceiling, her tongue pressing the inside of her cheek in thought.

"Sometimes they're in paintings, or, oh—lions guarding the entryway stairs. Hmmm, only sea dragons here," Rose says, opening and closing the front door again.

"You try upstairs, and I'll search downstairs," February calls out, already hurtling into the sitting room.

"Mo-o-o-om! Have you seen any lions anywhere in the house?" Rose yells into the kitchen where her mother is rolling dough, not proud of the whiny voice she employs, but desperate for answers.

Without waiting for a reply, Rose races upstairs into the bedrooms—except for the locked one—while February whizzes around downstairs in the West Wing, the kitchen and dining areas.

Rose ends her search after the six bedrooms in the East Wing, then heads downstairs to the library, but stops abruptly in front of the grand entrance to the ballroom.

"Feebs! February!" She's swung open the tall golden doors and discovered an extraordinary possibility.

The seal fountain in the middle of the ballroom floor.

February rushes in.

"What do you see there, Feebs? Do you see it?"

"It's a seal."

"No, it's a sea lion, with its little ear flaps. Seals don't have ear flaps, only ear holes! Sea *lion. Lion*," Rose emphasizes.

"Whoa," February says, impressed. "How do you know these things?"

"You know I like animals. And I memorize pointless facts."

They skid across the sleek ballroom tiles to the fountain.

It isn't in use, so Rose hops into the dry basin next to the golden sea lion.

Etched inside it are the words:

The truth lies within you.

"What secrets are you keeping, sea lion?" Rose murmurs as she studies the statue.

Like the narwhal's rowboat, her childhood furniture in the thirteenth bedroom, the lantern in the octopus fountain—the sea lion feels strangely familiar and scratches at her memories.

Why does Peacock Manor do this to her? Forces

her to remember. She feels herself pale, the blood draining from her face as she unwillingly recalls yet another gruesome detail.

That day. The sweatshirt she wore on the rowboat had a golden sea lion on the front. One of the animal conservation groups she and Amber donated to had sent them a sweatshirt with their logo, a sea lion.

But why is it *here*?

What the hell is this place?

Rose's chilling thoughts are interrupted when February grips her arm for balance as she steps into the fountain next to her.

"Does this seem unusual to you?" February crouches down, picking at one of the sea lion's flippers.

She looks up at Rose. "This screw here—it's not rusty like the others."

A gold bolt secures the flipper to the base of the fountain. The bolt is newer and larger than the others, so Rose bends forward, unscrews it with a few quick turns, and yanks it out.

Attached to it is a small ampoule—smaller than the vial they found on Amaryllis' headstone—containing a rolled note.

Rose unfurls the brittle paper, the color of old lace:

Great Ones Bring Appreciation,

Changing King's Thoughts Over Time.

Here, Enter Friends In Realms Seeking Truth.

3,2,4,8

p.s. this is the end.

****

"This is the last one!?" February jabs at the postscript.

"Sounds like it. *Great Ones Bring Appreciation,*

199

Changing King's Thoughts Over Time, …that could be books," Rose says, eagerly. "Great books are appreciated and change minds."

"You would know that one. It fits well," February says. "And then the third line, *Here, Enter Friends In Realms Seeking Truth.* What realms seek truth?"

"I think it means somewhere you go when you're looking for the truth, the facts. The…library?" Rose suggests.

"Ooh! A perfect hiding place for a book. Maybe too good." February mumbles. "There's like a million books in there."

They rush next door to the library.

"A secret shelf?" Rose asks.

"Hmm…what about the numbers?" February re-reads the riddle.

"A numerical sequence?" Rose asks, darting across the library from corner to corner, searching, scanning for any abnormal detail. "A code for a safe?"

After two hours of climbing ladders, flipping page after page, scouring shelves—they pause to reassess what they are missing. A secret lever? A hidden passage or door? A fake book?

Rose sinks into a plush ruby-red armchair near the fireplace and swings her high-tops onto the matching ottoman. Her eyes ache.

She rubs her face. "Feebs. I see something. It's haunting me. I can't look at it anymore, and I know I won't be able to sleep tonight. It's gonna give me nightmares," Rose says.

"What, what is it? I can help. I want to help you," February says, alarmed.

"That thing on your neck. What's Robbie doing,

chewing you when he kisses you?"

"Gah! You're so awful!" February's hands fly up to her neck, covering the red marks. "Speaking of Robbie, he invited us to ride horses tomorrow. Wanna go?"

"You go, the two of you…"

"C'mon, Rose. You can't turn down riding horses! Robbie and I can't kiss while horseback riding. I promise. It will be fun!"

She's right: Rose wants to go. *Horses.*

"Fine, I'll go. I'm happy for you, though. It's nice you like each other so much."

"So…Robbie told me that he loves me. Have you ever been in love?"

"Nope. You?" She has no idea what it feels like, but based on how her classmates act when they like someone, she suspects it is like being under a dark magic spell.

"I'm not sure if I have either, but Robbie is worth risking heartbreak for."

"You're worried he'll break your heart?" Rose asks. February doesn't seem like the type who spends her free time worrying about boys.

"I wouldn't want to lose his friendship, but sometimes, you know, you have to go for it. Right? What do you think?"

"I dunno, I guess I'm not a '*go for it!*' kind of person, especially when it comes to boys."

"Why not?" Feeby presses.

Rose sighs. "It's not worth it? I guess? I'm not…I'm not worth the trouble? Anyone's trouble. It's better to stick to myself."

"You're worth it." Feeby's eyes lock on her.

"You're worth it, Rose. I'd go to any length of trouble for you."

Rose fights her quivering chin. "Well, you're one of a kind, Feebs. I mean it." Her feelings are raw. With February, she knows she truly belongs somewhere.

Before, Rose could only belong to the memory of her sister. Amber is in her own shadow, in the fiery flickering of a campfire, in the stillness of the air after a thundershower, and in the unspoken flashes of grief in her parents' eyes. Amber inhabits the spaces between moments and thoughts, but Rose…Rose can't really be in any of those places.

She never dared to dream of finding anyone else who makes her feel like she is exactly where she is supposed to be—exactly as she is in the moment—and nothing more.

****

"I've gotta go home now, but I'll come back tomorrow morning. Early. Wakey wakey!" February says, glancing at her pocketwatch. "Heya, look, it's telling the right time today," she says proudly, holding it up to the grandfather clock in the hallway.

"I'll wake up before noon if you promise not to say *wakey wakey*," Rose says.

Chapter 37

Vale Green, The Hidden Valley

The next morning, Rose opens her eyes and...doesn't cry. She still snaps awake with an audible gasp, but after a few rattling breaths, she waits for the teardrops, but none come.

She aches for her sister, the same as yesterday—minus the tears. Meat Bones is still in bed beside her, and he rolls up onto his four round paws, stretching his rump into the air. He lifts his ears, focusing on his leader for what to do next. His dry-eyed (!) leader slides out of bed, brushes her teeth, spikes her hair, and plods downstairs in search of pastries.

He follows like the loyal pup he aims to be every day.

****

February wears cowboy boots over brown riding pants and a white blouse. They've promised to meet Robbie at noon at the Skyler family farm.

"Okay, be normal, have fun, be norm—" Rose mumbles under her breath.

"I'll try, but you know me..." February says.

"Hah! I was talking to myself."

"You're fine the way you are, Rose."

A tall, slender boy stands in the barn next to a slightly shorter and heftier Robbie. Both silhouettes wave at Rose and Feeby as they stride across the yard, down a worn dirt pathway cut by generations of hooves, tractors, and Skylers.

Rose slows her steps, idling a little, and scowls.

"I thought it was just the three of us? As in, I'm the third wheel, no room for a fourth wheel?" She condemns February to her best look of disapproval—slack jaw, rolled-back eyes, and all.

"Don't give me that dead face!" February screeches. "Kamdyn's good company. I *know* you two like each other. You don't have to be any wheel at all. You can just be a nice, normal person who gets to know a new friend today."

"I'd rather be a wheel," Rose mutters, now recognizing Kamdyn's distinctive profile as they enter the barn. His white collared shirt is pristine and ironed, tucked neatly into dark pants, his paddock boots polished.

"Or it could be a double date—" February whispers.

"Don't you dare say it!"

"Horses who resist leaving the comfort of their stable are called *barn sour*." February purses her lips in a knowing look.

"I'm barn sour when it comes to people."

February laughs and tips her head his way. "Well, his horse likes him at least."

Kamdyn bows forward, inclining into his horse. Forehead to forehead, he rubs the cheek of his blue roan, whose long-lashed, drooping eyelids are half-closed in contentment.

February nudges Rose toward him. "Heya, Kam. Rose is coming with us today."

"Feeby! Oh good. Rose, I'm glad you're here—I thought they only invited me to have an extra horse to carry the food for our picnic." His mood is brighter than she's ever seen it—unrestrained, and even...cheerful? What has changed?

"Hi, Kamdyn," Rose says, keeping her promise to be normal.

His lashes sweep up when he meets her gaze, and he smiles—doing so with only a slight part of his lips. She likes the way his pointy incisors jut out onto his bottom lip. Disturbingly attractive. *Ugh.* Always handsome and charming when he wants to be, but *he knows it.* She judges, of course. She desperately wants to, but can't control where her brain decides to roam, like a mole tunneling in the dirt. She is the randomly tunneling mole of social situations. *Burrow toward decent conversation, please,* she scolds herself.

"Not too fancy for picnics and horses?" she asks.

A toothy grin. "Just the right level, really. Rose, meet ASH, my horse. I board him with Robbie's horses so he isn't lonely."

"Oh, your own horse—fancy after all. His name is cute."

"ASH for his coloring, but also it stands for A Spectacular Horse." Kamdyn continues stroking the horse's dark muzzle. "I was ten when I named him." He laughs mildly at his younger self.

"Right now he's more of A Sleepy Horse."

"Ha-ha, one hundred percent. A'napping Soundly Here."

"Admiral Snoozy Hooves."

"Perfect. Have you ridden before?" Kamdyn asks.

"I won't fall off."

"Half a pear for your horse, if you want it?" His arm stretches out toward her. There is a coiled energy to him, calm but ready to spring. The way an arrow drawn back in its bow is ready to fly—fly far, far away. It pulls her in.

"Sure, thanks." Rose holds out her hand as he drops the bisected pear into her palm.

February steps in. "The white one with the silver mane is yours today, Rose. Her name is Moonstone." She steers Rose two stalls over.

"Sweet." Rose side-shuffles and ducks into Moonstone's stall. Moonstone flares her nostrils and snuffles her, requesting the fruit in her hand.

Whew. At least I didn't snort, Rose congratulates herself.

****

February skips over to Robbie, her dark hair and skirt swishing together.

He's wearing a faded red and beige flannel and jeans. They give each other the longest hug ever, eyes shut as though they've fallen asleep standing up. With his body draped around hers possessively, Robbie breathes in the top of her head as if inhaling preciousness, like a baby bunny or a handful of buttercups.

Kamdyn yells, "I'm dying from the mushiness! *Dying*."

February beckons Robbie to lower his head by tugging on the collar of his shirt, and whispers into his ear. She finishes whatever she is saying and brushes her lips across his jaw in a soft kiss. Robbie keeps one arm tight around her as he sticks out a finger of choice at Kamdyn. Both boys break into laughter.

Robbie swings February onto a tan and cream Morgan horse and checks the girth on her saddle, before slipping on his worn leather hat and yellow rancher gloves to mount his own large chestnut mare. He clucks his tongue twice and his horse lopes ahead, leading the way. Robbie is as agile a rider as his horse is nimble—both of them buoyant in movement and spirit. February quickly catches up to him.

Kamdyn kicks off, his slender figure upright and graceful and steady, trailing them in an effortless rising trot.

Luckily, Rose recalls the riding lessons Amber begged for as a pony-obsessed child and knows what she's doing—or rather, her gentle horse knows what she's supposed to do, and shifts into a wonderfully smooth canter. Rose relaxes and moves with her mare, feeling like she's floating on a cloud.

Amethystine peaks rise all around them, shielding them from any known city.

Robbie promises a secret scenic spot with a once-in-a-lifetime view. He says to keep their expectations high because it won't disappoint.

Clip clop, clip clop. Plop plop. They slow to a walk uphill, pass through a meadow lined with pencil-straight trees, and trek over a precarious wooden bridge spanning a ravine where the earth has split in two.

Moonstone drops her head to yank up grass along the trail. Rose loosens the reins; they aren't in a hurry.

Except, it allows Kamdyn and ASH to catch up alongside her.

Her stomach drops like the nuggets falling out of Moonstone's behind.

****

"So, February tells me you're reserved and introspective. I respect that," he says casually.

"I guess so?"

"Good. I like it," he insists.

"Why?" *Ugh, his smarminess is revolting. So, why do I like it?*

"You don't like being the center of attention. You're quieter. More attention for me."

"Pfft, ha-ha. Figures."

"Figures? Hmm. You'd only say that if you assumed I loved attention. And since we don't know each other well, you must be basing it off of how I look. So you must think I'm confident and handsome. Those are the people who love attention. Right? Thanks for the compliment then."

"What? Um. No? Hah, you're ridiculous." *He's not completely wrong, though.*

He shrugs unapologetically. "Well, I've made you laugh twice already."

It is impossible to ruffle him.

"It's nervous laughter."

"Because I'm so intimidatingly charming?"

"Because I'm a nervous person."

"You seem cool to me."

"Like you said, we don't know each other well. Plenty of time to change your mind."

"Nah. Robbie and Feeby said I'd like you and they are both great judges of character," he says, grinning recklessly.

The midday sun radiates above, glinting off the dark strands of his hair. His skin is dewy from the warm day.

He goes on. "So…what book did you bring to

entertain yourself while those two kiss all afternoon? I have an extra one if you forgot."

"Hah! I'm reading *In a Hundred Dreams* right now."

"Wow, no way! That was the last book I read before…" he abruptly trails off, as if he's mentioned something he hasn't meant to bring up.

But he pivots effortlessly. "Good choice—top ten favorite."

"It's totally pretentious, I know. But I'd love a week in the Land of Purple. So amazing. What did you bring?"

"I'm re-reading *The Imp's House*."

"Kids' book? Couldn't understand it the first time?"

"Oomph, harsh. Ha-ha, you want that kind of relationship, huh?"

"Any port in a storm."

"I'm starting to get a perverse thrill from your insults."

She bursts into laughter, surprising herself.

His lips curl up into his high cheekbones—a charming, lopsided smile. "The story is like comfort food for my brain."

"That's the best." Rose nods, in sync with Moonstone's gait.

"I know you're leaving at the end of summer, but I need more nervous friends who can discuss literature. Robbie's busy working, and then spends the rest of his time thinking about February. Plus, he's awesome in so many ways, but he doesn't know a book from a brick."

This time, she laughs so hard she snorts. *Oops, gross, Rose.*

Kamdyn's head whips around. "Did you just snort?" His gray eyes reflect bits of blue from the endless sapphire sky around them. "Don't deny it! The Wild Snort of Vale Green."

"Thank you for the title to my humiliation."

"Makes you less intimidating."

"I'm intimidating?"

"Intelligent, beautiful, and morose is intimidating. Yes."

"Morose." She chuckles. "I suppose I am."

"C'mon, let's catch up with them and ruin their romantic ride." He motions ahead at February and Robbie. "I see them trying to hold hands right now, while riding. Ridiculously adorable and nauseating at the same time. You be morose, and I'll be confidently attention-seeking."

"Sounds fun." And it is. She doesn't have to explain herself or overthink. It is…easy.

****

The four of them twist around one last hairpin bend. February sucks in a breath and squeals, "Wow, Robinson, you weren't kidding."

Robbie grins, pleased he's impressed her. He extends his arm toward a small crater of a valley scooped out between two peaks of lush greenery.

"This is Vale Green. It's the greenest little glen in the entire mountain range. The grass here doesn't dry up and turn yellow in the summer like everywhere else."

Sunbeams pour into the sloping vale dotted with pink and tangerine wildflowers.

"Magical, right? Like I promised," Robbie says. He removes his hat to ruffle his hair.

Rose hinges forward at her hips to rake her fingers through Moonstone's silvery mane.

"A place lost to time,
that's been here a thousand years,
existing unmarred."

She whispers her haiku to Moonstone, who smells of hay and sunshine. Rose can't help her eternal fascination with the everlasting and the constant. Her thoughts weigh heavy for a moment, as she wonders why humans and pets can't also exist forever.

Robbie signals downhill with a gloved hand toward a lazy stream carving through the secret valley. "We'll stop there for lunch. The horses will have water to drink." He pats his mare on her coppery shoulder, and the four of them adjust their course down into Vale Green.

The flowing brook hypnotizes Rose. Slow and winding and musical, the water ripples over perfectly round rocks, sloshing softly. Rose imagines in the springtime the stream would flood and rush with melting snow from the mountaintops.

As the thought enters her head, the stream quickens and the waterline rises onto the dry banks, stiff white peaks churning over rocks.

She stifles a gasp. Moonstone's pointy white ears swing forward at the new sound of surging water. Rose whirls back, searching the faces behind her, but no one else has noticed the stream. When she returns her attention to the water, it is back to its languid state. "You saw that too, right, Moonstone?" The others ride past, so Rose urges Moonstone on with a squeeze of her calves.

"Maitake mushrooms!" February halts her horse at

a hen-sized clump of ivory and copper fungi growing at the base of a beech tree. "It means 'dancing mushroom.' Legend says Buddhist nuns and woodsmen traveling through the mountains were the first to discover these. They ate them and couldn't help dancing, not because they were hallucinogenic, but because they were delicious."

"My dad would love that legend," Rose says.

"He totally would!" February cackles. Her voice echoes off the hillside. "Helloooo! Did you hear that?" she says of her delayed echo.

"Echoes are mountain spirits answering," Rose chimes in, quoting her "research" on nature spirits. "They live in valleys and forests and mimic your voice."

"Or...have we fallen into the spirit realm and we are *their* echo?" Kamdyn suggests.

"We fell through!" February gallops at full speed down into their hidden world for the afternoon, shrieking so loudly with laughter that she startles a flock of tiny birds from the trees. Robbie pursues her, riding alongside the flank of her horse.

Here, Enter Friends In Realms Seeking Truth. Rose drifts into the riddle. Enter friends. She has friends now, more or less. She's still seeking the truth. Will she ever find it?

Another hundred feet downstream ahead of Rose, Feeby stops and dismounts, her arms encircling her horse's neck for her signature hug before draping the reins over him.

Rose slides off of Moonstone to walk the rest of the way, wanting to savor the scenery. From afar, she watches February thread her pocketwatch over her head and slip it into her saddlebag. She tumbles toward the water, kicking off her cowboy boots and socks before dipping her bare feet into the stream.

Robbie dismounts, watching in adoration as February twirls and spins, kicking up water. She calls him over, and when he approaches, she scoops water with both palms, takes a sip, and launches the rest at him—splashing his pants so that he looks as if he peed on himself.

He swears and laughs, then peels off his boots.

"You're a tiny little demon," he snarls. He rolls up his pants and sloshes in after her as she scrambles away screeching. His long reach catches her by the waist, tackling her, but pulls her to him before she topples into the water.

He lifts her in his arms and threatens to drop her back in.

She kicks and screams. Instead, he kisses her brow and sets her back down on her feet, but she flings her entire body at him, wrestling him off balance, and they both crash into the deepest part of the stream.

The frigid water calms them both, and sopping wet, they clamber back up the bank hand in hand.

February slips out of her soaked blouse and pants before draping them over a low tree branch. Robbie offers an extra T-shirt from his bag, and she throws it on.

His shirt covers her like a short dress. She reaches under, wriggles a bit, and off come her undergarments to dry on a flat rock in the sun.

Robbie—seemingly tantalized knowing she has on nothing underneath *his* T-shirt—can't contain himself and, with an apparent flare of desire, sweeps his broad arms around her from behind, bending in to nuzzle his face into her neck. He kisses her ear, her throat, her collarbone.

February lifts one of his large tanned hands to her mouth and grazes his fingers against her lips, sucking on one before pressing his palm to her chest. Her eyes close tightly when his thumb circles the peak of her breast. Robbie's face flushes as he slides a hand down her thigh, curling under the edge of the T-shirt—

A light hand brushes Rose's shoulder and she leaps out of her skin.

"Do you want to go exploring the valley with me? Those two. Summer love. We can leave the horses. Robbie says they'll stay near each other," Kamdyn says.

Gah. He's caught her staring her eyes off. She couldn't help her curiosity, and now her ears are blazing hot.

"Uh, good idea," Rose mutters, mortified.

"Unless…you want to do *that*?" Kamdyn turns back to gesture at February and Robbie, now lying tangled on the picnic blanket in the grass. Their bodies spiral around each other. February's fingers drag through Robbie's wavy hair, and his hands are underneath her shirt.

"Um. No. Not with you," she sputters, flustered. "Absolutely not."

"Ha-ha! With *whom*, then?" He isn't bothered. He's *never* bothered.

"No one. Let's walk." She hurries away from the soft sighs and purrs coming from the blanket of the attractive pair.

He glances sideways at her and aims a slender

finger at a group of giant boulders. "Let's go see what's going on at Stonehenge there. Who doesn't like rocks?" He beams a beautiful smile at her.

She shoves her hands into her pockets and follows silently, face still warm.

"I've lived here my entire life—this town, this mountain—and it never stops surprising me. The mountain can be treacherous, but also hauntingly beautiful. Even I had no idea this little valley was here. Robbie doesn't share his romantic date tricks."

"Why treacherous?"

"You haven't seen this area in a winter storm, have you?"

She shakes her head. "Nope."

"Everything has a dark side. A shadow side," he says, rubbing his neck, serious for the first time all day.

She almost allows herself to ask what lurks in his shadow side but is certain he would ask about her in return, and she doesn't want to answer her own question.

"True," is all she says.

The shadow passes. "Do you ever make up songs in your head?" he asks. "I've already made up one for today on the ride here. I call it, 'Vale Green at Seventeen.' It sounds angsty, but the best songs always are, aren't they? Want to hear a verse?"

"Sure," she says, relieved he has enough ideas to keep the walk from awkward silence.

He sings off-tune about his horse ASH and a valley evergreen,

how they trekked across a bridge hanging over a ravine,

to a gleaming stream,

sky aquamarine…at seventeen,
to a place in between…
the beginning and end of all things, and a dying dream.

He laughs—his laugh is raspy and deep—at his own singing. "At least it rhymes. Nobody's good at everything," he says, lifting his shoulders, "and you can't trust someone who is perfect."

"That wasn't horrible. It started off light and went somewhere. There's a haiku in there, you know—

"A place in between
The start and end of all things
And a dying dream."

"Whoa. That's talent right there. You, out-thinking me at every turn. I'll let you know if I think of more verses."

"I'll be in the front row. Time will be standing still until then." She can't hide her large grin.

"Ha! That bad, huh?" He takes it in stride—the silvery specks in his eyes gleam. "Well, here we are. Do you know what these rocks are called?" He slaps his hand against the nearest towering boulder, elephantine in size and color.

She nods. "Glacial erratics. They differ from the surrounding rocks because they were carried here by a glacier."

"Exactly. You have all the answers. I'm impressed."

She shrugs. She wishes she could turn all the useless facts in her head into good conversation. "I like the permanence, the survivability, of rocks." *Wow. Did I just say, "I like rocks?"*

"Ah, everlasting, huh."

He reaches around for his back pocket and extracts a small paperback.

"Next question: Do you want me to read to you? You were too busy gawking and forgot your book," he says.

"Hmph." She braces against the embarrassment writhing in her again as she crumples her nose.

"Comfort food, like I said." He flaps his tattered copy of *The Imp's House* at her. "I'll read; you bask in the sun."

"I'd love that." *Amazing.* When was the last time anyone read to her? She arches back against the nearest boulder and slides down, settling into the grass. She lifts her cheeks to the sun and closes her eyes, seeing flashes of light on the back of her eyelids.

"Don't fall asleep, though. I'm going to start with my favorite chapter. When all the River Imp wants to do is eat his water fungus and grilled bread with fern-moss jam, but his Water Sprite friends insist on him trying new foods."

"Hilarious scene. Willow bark candy!"

"When I was little, I ate bark off a tree because of that," he says with a long-suffering sigh.

"No way! That's hilarious. Ooh, after that chapter, can you skip to the quest for the treasure—the magic forest of jewels? Where you can pluck gemstones like fruit off trees?"

He nods. "Of course. Got to get the quest in."

"A quest is when everyone's strengths and weaknesses come into play. It makes me love the characters more."

"Exactly! When I was little, I liked that the real treasure in the story was accepting who you are and finding where you're supposed to be. Even if you're not the same as everyone else, not like all the other Water Sprites."

"Who wouldn't want to be a Sprite, though?" she asks.

"Their ears are weird. And living forever is sadder than most people realize." He looks away, surveying the columns of trees lining the ridges of the valley.

"Why?"

"Nothing is sweet if there's no such thing as bitter," he says.

"An end point—an expiration—makes life sweeter?"

"Perhaps? Or a struggle, a difficult quest, even?"

"Don't you sometimes wish you were someone else?" she asks.

"I dunno. Who's to say their fate would be better or worse? You'd want to be someone else?" he asks.

"Yes. I'd want to be an immortal Sprite." She slumps into the rock. Kamdyn stands in front of her, scrutinizing her with his head cocked.

She wants to brush his dark hair out of his eyes.

He looks right into her, unwavering in his hard stare.

In a flare of panic, she wonders if she said something weird.

"Immortal? Do you, really?" he asks, each word with a gravitas that sinks through her, like blood in water. He stalks her with those celestial eyes, trying to figure her out.

Is he fascinated or disgusted? She wrenches her gaze away and picks at the clumpy grass next to her. She doesn't think she's said anything surprising.

"Yeah, of course. Stop looking at me like that," she replies.

"You wouldn't miss your family and friends when they get old and die?"

His question strikes her where it hurts the most. She fumbles for words. She doesn't have friends at home to miss, and her parents, lately, aren't around—and Amber...she'll never have a chance to get old...

The reminder rips her insides to shreds.

But then, all the more reason to find *The Book of Lost Spirits*. Plus, if February's family could keep the Manor, maybe she'd invite Rose to return next summer to visit and help her run it...

"Better to be the last one standing than the first to go?" She musters a lame shrug.

His red lips crack into a smile. "Well. You certainly know what you want! You have it all figured out."

"You have it together more than me. You're so sure of yourself," she says.

"I thought I did, but people have other plans for me; my family had different plans for me. Most of my life, my parents prepared me to take over the Charbon family business and continue the legacy. One day, I realized there was more to life than this mountain. I wanted to leave. They wouldn't allow it, and we had a terrible fight." A shadow of torment stains his handsome face. "They never accept the decisions I make for myself or acknowledge I have goals besides making money for the Charbon empire."

"What decisions? You mean, like, skiing professionally? Feebs told me."

"Something like that. I only want it to be my

choice."

"Why won't they let you choose?"

"They think theirs is the only right way. They aren't proud of my accomplishments outside of what they want me to do."

"It's comfortable and safer to not see too many options."

"Right," he says, running his finger along a fissure in the boulder next to her, his dark eyebrows knit together in thought.

There is kindness in his solemn face, but it's marred by a deeper sadness she recognizes as pain similar to her own.

She nods quietly.

"You're a good listener, Rose, but enough of my entitled whining. Bitterness corrodes the soul, right?" Kamdyn's fingers drum the cover of the book in his palm. The storm clouds pass from his eyes and they are vibrant and roguish again.

He flips the pages of *The Imp's House*, locates the chapter he wants, and begins reading to her.

His captivating tone peaks to a crescendo at tense action, and purrs low and hypnotic when narrating description—transporting her far away, to a land where magical creatures and fantastical treasure thrive.

She swears she holds her breath the entire time—there's no disguising her delight. The heart-shattering intimacy of someone reading aloud their favorite book may be lost to most people, but not to her.

It alights every dark recess of her soul in a wildfire of bliss.

That afternoon, the story whisks her imagination away, but his voice—his voice melts her sorrow.

****

"You're not what I expected," Kamdyn says as the two of them walk back.

"What did you expect?" Rose asks.

"Nothing. That's the problem. I don't expect things anymore."

"Wow, I exceeded your expectation of 'nothing.' I'm terribly flattered," she snarks.

He whirls around, frowning. "What? That's not what I meant at all!" he blurts.

He's flustered!

She laughs. "I know. Seen it all, though, huh? You need one of Feeby's hugs."

"Hah. Truth. That girl can bring out the best in anyone." He inclines his chin to the two small figures by the stream.

By the time they reach Robbie and February, Robbie has laid out a picnic lunch for the four of them.

"Where'd you go?" February shouts, spraying crackers and cheese from her mouth, as Rose and Kamdyn approach. Her voice echoes off the jagged walls of Vale Green.

Rose points a finger across the valley at the group of boulders.

"You guys went that far? Robbs, they went all the way to those rocks!" She jabs an elbow at Robbie, who is rooting through their picnic basket.

Feeby raises an eyebrow, asking *how'd it go?*

Rose grins shamelessly. Kamdyn had been easy to talk to and the time passed all too quickly.

February crams another water cracker spread with goat cheese and fresh fig into her mouth. She circles her arm in the air, inviting them to sit and eat.

"Robbie made all of this amazing food!" she says.

Rosemary chicken, macaroni pie, grape salad, and blueberry corn muffins. Who knew he was such a good cook?

Rose sniffs the delectable spread, suddenly famished.

"My grandpa's old recipes," Robbie says, spraying chocolate crumbs out of his overstuffed mouth. "But Rose's mom's honeycomb-fudge pixie cake things are...*the best*," he adds, shoveling another cake into his handsome face.

Everyone is less intimidating with chocolate dotting their faces, Rose chuckles to herself, reaching for a corn muffin.

"You not only defiled our picnic blanket, but started on all the food?" Kamdyn smirks.

"They're hungry after all the lust," Rose blurts, surprising herself with her boldness.

February chokes on her cracker and giggles.

Rose and Kamdyn snicker at their expense as February steals a glance at Robbie. A smile crosses his face as he catches her loving gaze. They beam at each other—as only the young, the newly in love, the truly alive do—re-living the memory of their time by the stream.

****

Rose, Kamdyn, February, and Robbie gorge themselves on scrumptious food from the Skyler farm and grocery, dip half-naked in their underwear in the icy stream, banter and laugh and read and nap amongst the swaying pink buttercups—basking in the most exquisite daydream sprung to life. Rose could never have imagined such a day, and delights in every sensation.

The cornbread, grainy and sweet on her tongue.

The glacial spring numbing her toes, feet, and ankles.

The faraway screeching of hawks circling the cottony clouds and azure skies above.

The itch of grass and warmth of sunbaked dirt below her.

Their laughter. And friendship. And love.

Today, they are the only four humans in the world, hidden away in an ancient valley where heartache does not exist.

Rose never wants it to end.

She finally feels in control of where her life is going.

Chapter 38

Mr. Peacock

Rose and her friends ride back to the Skyler farm. Robbie hauls out a crate of root vegetables and herbs that February's mom ordered. Beets, radishes, chives, shiso, tarragon—*yum*, carrots, leeks, kale—*yuck*. Robbie says root vegetables and herbs grow best in this mountain region.

"Let me drive you guys home," he says, but February prefers walking. She will drop off the groceries at her house before accompanying Rose back to the Manor.

Rose and February each carry one end of the crate, swinging it between them all the way to February's house.

"You're a good rider," February says.

"Moonstone did all the work. I've had horseback riding lessons, though."

"Grammy said a good rider has *hips like a whore, shoulders like a queen*," she snickers.

"What? That's so embarrassing!"

Feeby insists on hearing what Kamdyn and Rose talked about. "You're both tall and look good together," she comments.

Rose scoffs at the idea.

"Well, I'm proud of you for trying something new,

out of the ordinary," February says.

"Ordinary Rose is a thing of the past, we hope?"

The Peacock home, unlike the Manor, is modest and bright and inviting. Sunlight streams through a row of bleached birch trees onto the white wood siding of the two-story house. Laundry that smells like February hangs from clotheslines, idly flapping its apple and blossom scent into the breeze. White lilies trim the wrap-around porch.

"Mom's favorite scent," February says of the creamy florals. "She re-plants them every year so they bloom in the summer."

Rose helps February deposit the crate onto the kitchen table.

They turn to leave, and she reminds Feeby of the riddle.

"During the ride, I was thinking—we have to focus on the numbers. There are four numbers, but only three lines of the riddle. It's got to mean something."

The end, the riddle promised. *The end* of my old life, Rose promises herself.

"When we get back to the Manor—" she starts to say but stops short.

February's dad totters out from his bedroom, in rumpled striped pajamas. Tufts of dark hair stick out sideways around his ears.

"Hi, Dad," February says quietly. She tenses but remains calm.

He hesitates when he sees February with a guest and slumps his shoulders to shuffle back to his bedroom, when Rose shifts beside her to say hello. His drooping eyes meet her gaze and flit open, the black pools of his pupils expanding into utter darkness.

Something in him snaps.

He screams. His wail pierces through Rose's ears, shredding her mind, a grown man screaming off the rails.

Rose throws her arms around her head, shielding herself, but the unmerciful metallic screech scrapes the inside of her skull. She desperately wants to claw it out.

He's screaming at something he sees *in her.*

She curls into herself and sinks to the ground, her knees hitting the floor as wave after wave—of his gasping scream, and her nausea—assaults her. He is the little boy from the library shrieking at her again.

February rushes toward him, shushing him. She cups his stubbly, horror-stricken face in her hands, begging him to look at her, to only look at her.

"It's okay, Dad, it's okay."

Except, it's clear that *nothing* is okay. And worse, he doesn't stop. He continues gesturing at Rose with both hands, his voice stuck in an unceasing screech.

"Mom! Dad needs help!" February hollers. Quick footsteps pound from upstairs. Inaudible words follow.

February whirls back to Rose, grips her arm, and hauls her up off of her knees.

"Let's go, Rose. I'm so sorry. I didn't know he would be like this right now. Let's go. It'll be okay. My mom will take care of him." Fingers interlaced, she tows Rose forward, and they run.

Out of the house—Feeby's dad still wailing—
down the dusty lane back to the Manor,
their fear prevailing,
running for their lives but not knowing why,
until they collapse onto the front steps,
wheezing, mouths bone-dry.

Rose slumps deeper into the stone stairway. A stitch stabs into her side with each inhale.

February drops her head between her knees. "I'm sorry. He hasn't spoken since he was found, and he freaks out once in a while over nothing. Over nothing. Are you listening to me?"

Rose isn't listening. Her bones quiver like jelly. She looks down at her dirty shoes but can't remember running through mud on the way back. Her socks have slid down, but she doesn't bother to fix them.

Instead, she counts the flecks of dirt until her vision blurs, needing to shut out the world around her.

Feeby drapes her arm around Rose's shoulder and pulls her in close. "Will you be okay? I have to help my mom." She clasps her pocketwatch in her free hand.

"Don't leave," Rose pleads.

"It's all right, I'm here. I'll stay."

"Just for a little bit. Let's talk about something else. What's your pocketwatch doing today?"

"It's, uh…strange. It's going backward. I've never seen it do that." She taps it gently with a fingernail.

"That's weird."

"Let's find Meat Bones. We can all hang out and relax."

Rose closes her eyes and takes her time, slowly sipping a breath, holding it for as long as she can, focusing on the flashing colors inside her eyelids. Finally, she blubbers, "It's okay. You go home, help your mom. I'll be fine," she lies.

February grips her tighter.

There is nothing else to say. There's already a silent agreement not to bring it up. They both know, under no circumstances was Mr. Peacock screaming *over nothing.*

They both know, without a doubt, he was screaming at Rose.

She begins to tremble again.

Something is wrong…wrong with *her.*

Chapter 39

A Surprise Visitor

February warns Rose that she will likely have to stay home to help with her dad the next few days, so Rose resigns herself to reading in her hidden chamber in the library, folded into a velvety blanket. No matter the season outside, the Manor is frigid and raw like the northern windward side of the mountain.

Her search for the answer to the last riddle has stalled, and she makes no headway on her own. For a quick second, she wonders if there even is a solution; "p.s. this is the end" might only mean there isn't more.

That can't be right. The book has to be real.

They only need to find the right room. "Here, enter friends…"

On the second day, late in the afternoon, the doorbell announces an unexpected visitor.

She expects dark bangs and a single emerald earring.

Instead, she swings the door open to find the elegant figure of Kamdyn in a crisp button-up, smelling of lavender and soap and a hint of something she can't define, fresh and sweet at the same time.

His brilliant smile lights up the dark entryway.

Rose tries to conceal the surprise twisting her face into a god-knows-what expression.

"*All we see or seem is but a dream within a dream,*" he says, as devious as he can muster.

She knows this poem!

And she's thrilled she can play his game. "*I stand amid the roar, Of a surf-tormented shore…*" she quotes back effortlessly, as smug as he.

"Beguiling, Rose. Morose and beguiling," he says, curling his lips into a wicked grin.

"Did you come over to test me on old poems and remind me of what a grouch I am?" she asks, proving her grouchiness.

"Nope. I came over to borrow books. February said you wouldn't mind."

"There's a children's section in the library if you need a chapter book."

"Ha-ha! Right. Can you sound out the words for me? No one's ever used books as an insult as well as you, Rose. If you're busy, I can go bother Robbie again. He dropped me off because he has deliveries to do today, and I thought you would be finer company."

"I'm not busy. Come on in." She grins to herself once she's turned away from him.

Meat Bones investigates the new guest, sniffing his shoes, and receives an ear-scratching in return. "What a cute little buddy you have here," Kamdyn says, bent over.

"He likes to think of himself as big and fierce."

"Yes, I see it now. Your oversized paws and ears say adorable, but the way you attack that ball says you're a dangerous, ferocious wolf," Kamdyn corrects himself, rubbing Meat Bones' drooly jowls.

Meat Bones leans into him and waggles his rump furiously.

They spend the rest of the daylight hours reading; then they discuss their all-time favorite characters.

When the sun disappears over the mountains, the old lanterns dangling above them illuminate the room with a thrilling glow, like candlelight on Halloween.

Their stomachs rumble at this twilight hour, so they raid the kitchen. Rose's mom baked mini steak-and-cheese potpies for her church event and prepared a saffron and chanterelle chowder from the mushrooms Dad gathered on one of his breaks. She's left some potpie, soup, and an apple cheesecake behind for the non-religious Green family members.

"How many radians—or degrees—of cheesecake do you want?" Rose asks, plate in hand.

"Let's share one radian."

"Glorious."

"It's important to describe the precise amount of dessert you want." He picks up two napkins and organizes the rest of the stack into a neat pile.

"Glorious," she repeats, impressed. "Here is your almost-sixty degrees of cake."

"Thank you. Let's eat outside. There's nothing like a balmy midsummer night on this mountain," Kamdyn suggests.

Meat Bones trails them, hoping for a taste of steak potpie.

Rose gives him a whole portion in a glass bowl.

A growing pup needs his own potpie.

****

The purply-blues and dirty yellows of an old bruise stain the sky at this hour of the evening, reminding her of the gloom within her. Rose retreats into an unforgiving corner of her own psyche.

Yun Johnson

"What's on your mind?" Kamdyn asks.

She recounts the incident with Mr. Peacock, jabbing at the last of the shortbread crust with her fork. She can't look Kamdyn in the eye when she describes February's dad screaming at her.

Kamdyn listens, intent on understanding.

When she glances up, his expression is kind and sympathetic, but not pitying. Thank goodness. Pity would be as welcome as open disgust.

He considers his response. "You know, it doesn't matter what other people think of you. In the end, it only matters what you think of yourself. He could have been screaming at you. But that's his issue, it's in his mind. Your mind is your own, and you can make decisions about yourself rather than letting others fill your thoughts."

"It's difficult to do. It's true, though—you're right. That's insightful."

"Rose doles out a compliment? Should I capture this momentous occasion with a photograph? Will you autograph it so I can remember this forever?" he teases.

"Enjoy it. There might not be another one if you keep mocking me." She grins.

The pair recline on the back lawn, shoulders touching, propping their backs against the gnarled roots of the old cypress outside the library, underneath a brilliant night sky.

Deep in the unknown universe, someone has carelessly scattered gemstones of aquamarine and opal; then as a second thought, thrown golden sapphire and carnelian into the mix across an ebony velvet curtain.

Kamdyn settles back on his hands and tilts his face upward.

"The night sky is as vast and infinite as the imagination," he says with a tight sigh.

"Makes you wonder what exists that we haven't imagined yet."

"Definitely. Do you know any constellations?" Kamdyn asks, kicking his legs out to stretch.

Rose wants to lean toward him—his low voice, his warm body, his pleasing scent all draw her in.

As he shifts beside her, she smells his clean soapy lavender scent, with just a bit of...sugar cookie? Yum.

"Leo the Lion," she snorts, laughing.

He grins. "Robbie mentioned that."

"Do you know any?"

"I have a great story about those three bright stars in a row. There. The locals say it's a bamboo pole." He gestures with two fingers, angling his head into Rose's for a moment to confirm she is seeing the same stars. She feels the heat from his face before he moves away again.

He goes on. "There were two sisters—the second one carried water buckets on a bamboo pole. On their way home, they were chased by a demon, and to escape, they climbed a rope to the stars—but the second sister had her foot bitten off by the demon. She kept going, following her sister, and made it to the stars. *That* area is her remaining foot, and she still carries water with that bamboo pole." He traces a shape in front of them with a finger. "It's a story of endurance, and the will to continue."

"Whoa. Good backstory, the second sister."

"Right? Everyone should have one that good."

She thinks of her own story, how she's arrived at this moment in time, sitting here with Kamdyn, closer to the stars than she's ever been.

Do the stars, in all their eons of existence, ever count the multitudes of souls who stare upward upon them in astonishment? And, how many friendships are found...

lost...

broken...

reunited...

beneath their twinkling gaze?

Kamdyn senses her mind has wandered, so he asks—and she describes—what she's thinking.

"How many souls, do you think, then?" she reiterates.

"Probably as many as there are stars?" he suggests.

"That sounds right," she says, seeing that no one would ever know.

"Rose..." He pauses on her name, making sure she isn't lost in thought again.

"Hmm?"

"I wish I'd met you sooner," he says with such deep yearning in his words that Rose can't help but turn to look at him.

The sadness across his face softens as she studies him.

As always, there's an awful faraway look in his eyes that says his heart is already there, wherever *there* may be.

"You'd have regretted it. February helped me be less anxious this summer. I'd have choked on my own saliva and not talked to you like a normal person before."

He laughs. "Well, I'm glad you can talk to me now."

"Me too," she says.

He shifts his body toward her, pressing closer, and then...

She feels a thrill surge in her when he reaches out tentatively, grazing her hand with his, before finding her fingers and holding them in his palm.

She doesn't flinch or pull away, but slowly curls a few fingers around his.

Confident now that she isn't offended, he grasps tighter and idly strokes the back of her palm with his thumb. Her hand liquefies.

His skin is smooth and hot, and she steadies her breath so as to not appear flustered.

No big deal, right? Her spine tingles.

She can no longer see the stars in front of them.

The only sensation she registers is their hands clasping, their fingers tangled, and her loneliness breaking—

Her loneliness breaking as it has been doing little by little this summer, ever since she met February.

And now, *this*.

Her loneliness breaking because she belongs somewhere, and that is here and now.

Together, they gaze up at the never-ending expanse of night sky, black as ravens' wings protectively cloaking them in blissful silence.

Chapter 40

Peacock Manor
Day 146,637

I see why Pixie Cakes and the solemn boy get along—both are so brainy, and as melancholy as the moon.

A good poem, though—the one they were quoting. Is Edgar Allan Poe back in fashion?

I too, can recite it from memory:
"A Dream Within a Dream"
By Edgar Allan Poe
Take this kiss upon the brow!
And, in parting from you now,
Thus much let me avow—
You are not wrong, who deem
That my days have been a dream;
Yet if hope has flown away
In a night, or in a day,
In a vision, or in none,
Is it therefore the less *gone*?
All that we see or seem
Is but a dream within a dream.
I stand amid the roar
Of a surf-tormented shore,
And I hold within my hand
Grains of the golden sand—

How few! yet how they creep
Through my fingers to the deep,
While I weep—while I weep!
O God! can I not grasp
Them with a tighter clasp?
O God! can I not save
One from the pitiless wave?
Is *all* that we see or seem
But a dream within a dream?

Chapter 41

The Missing Key

The next day, instead of the library, Rose sets up in the sitting room so she can see February from the front window if she comes over. Or anyone else who might decide to make an unannounced visit.

Last night was unexpected. And fun.

She contemplates the last riddle, collects a large pile of books to research and—out of desperation—randomly searches the tea room and the music room.

Failing to find anything, she blows through a couple of older novels. The old-leaves scent of aged paper transports her. She consumes books, and pastries. Both, eagerly. New flavors for her mind and her taste buds.

The sitting room's beetle-black ceiling and walls, adorned with hundreds of brass-framed portraits, whisper to her of melancholy parlor days of pipe smoke, snifters of tawny port and guests who required impressing. Melancholy, because she knows a sitting room was once called a *death room*, where the deceased were laid out and mourned before burial. Eventually, the room was re-branded, given the more upbeat designation of *living room*. By then, rooms in the house were for the living, and the dead went off to the morgue.

Milky daylight filters into the parlor through thick-paned windows. She sees her mother load the car for her day of worship and waves at her. The old, viscous glass in the lower portion of the windows is warped and thickened, so Mom doesn't notice Rose in her rush to her meeting with Jesus.

Rose sprawls sideways on a velvet turquoise chaise, half-seeing the riddle in her mind. After the events of the last week, the riddle seems less real, less tangible. More like a madwoman's taunt, to Rose's chagrin. Why couldn't Grammy hand down the book like a normal person?

Her attention veers upward to the portraits lining every inch of the black walls. Each frame houses an oil-painted subject, not one of whom is smiling. A man in a ceremonial robe; a woman with such an elaborate hairstyle that it has to be a wig; a teenage boy in a suit—modern. His features resemble February's small nose, round cheekbones and honest eyes. He must be a relative. Twin infants above him, side by side. The frames are perfectly level, mounted on the dark wall.

Only one portrait hangs slightly off-center, with an almost imperceptible tilt to the left.

The crooked painting is the only one depicting two subjects. Rose climbs onto a wingback chair underneath the portrait to examine it.

A handsome naval captain with a sword, posing next to a half-woman, half-fish, naked. Her perky breasts with their salmon-hued nipples peek out from under her long seaweed hair. Rose immediately feels the need to compare her own in size, shape, and color. Slightly smaller, rounder, pinker, maybe.

She wonders how she would fare as a mer-creature.

At the very least, she can now swim, thanks to February.

A large key hangs at the mermaid's neck. Like the teenage boy in the suit, the mermaid watches her from the brass frame with the same sea-green eyes and heart-shaped face as February, minus her perpetual smile.

Rose needs to fix the tilt. She taps the bottom right corner of the picture with one finger. It doesn't budge. However, she discovers it can be moved from the left. The frame swings easily to the right, resulting in more tilt. She keeps going, and the whole portrait spins counterclockwise around the exact center of the picture.

On the third rotation, the painting and the wall behind it open, revealing a small cavity carved into the wall.

Rose reaches in and scoops out a single item: a brass skeleton key, eerily similar to the one on the mermaid's neck.

One key.

One mysteriously locked bedroom upstairs.

Two puzzle pieces. She leaps off the chair and races upstairs to the West Wing, her feet pounding the hallway parquet, stopping only at the driftwood door.

Rose studies the antique key. Her hand hovers—trembling—at the keyhole in the mystery door.

This is wrong. She should wait for February. Is this another clue she's unearthed—has she skipped ahead and discovered one out of order? She should wait. It would be unfair not to.

The brass in her hand stays cold, even as she grips it tight.

She turns away from the colorless door. Why is it so worn? What's behind it?

No, she needs to know.

After wrestling with her conscience for another quick minute, the lure of discovering answers overcomes any guilt.

She shoves the key into the lock and twists until it clicks.

She draws the doorknob toward her, crouching lower into the crack of the doorway. Clamping her elbows tight to her body on instinct, she plunges headfirst into the darkness.

A darkness devours her with its hollowness.

There are no windows.

No light.

Nothing.

At first, she assumes her eyes aren't adjusting to the darkness—that she's discovered another secret bedroom like the thirteenth bedroom in the attic, except without furnishings. However, the room isn't just empty. There is no floor, nor ceiling, nor wall containing the emptiness as she leans her head further inwards.

She can't breathe in here. The darkness startles her. It is a moonless night, where even shadows do not dwell.

The nothingness bleeds into a heavy silence that only ends when she retreats to gasp a breath of air. It isn't a room at all, but an expanse of nothingness, a vacuum of space! A void.

It's as if someone erased reality and replaced it with infinite space.

Could it be? Is it possible she's at the edge of the universe where stars and the fabric of the cosmos end, or have yet to reach in its perpetual expansion?

This isn't possible.

She blinks, but she barely has time to make sense of what is before her because—

The emptiness—it wants her. It plucks at her, an invisible net towing her through the doorway. She lurches backward, straining against the pull of the room, fighting a void wishing her to be the same as it: non-existent.

A voice begs from somewhere beyond the nothingness, a whisper at first, but increases in volume until it ends in a rasping shout. "You cannot return home, please, please—PLEASE DON'T GO!"

It sounds like her sister, but Amber would never whine like that.

Rose grasps the doorframe and fights against the pull by digging her heels into the floorboards. "Let me go!" The soles of her high-tops squeak as she slips.

"You can't leave. I won't let you. You belong to me," the voice whooshes.

It doesn't sound like Amber at all.

"Who are you? What do you want?"

"I want you to stay here. You will NEVER leave here. That's the truth," the voice says.

"Let me go, and I'll find you. I promise. I'll help you."

Her fingers tremble. As she fumbles the key, a rush of phantom wind slams the door violently. She snatches the key off of the floorboards, her hand clammy. What just happened?

She needs another look, despite the frightening voice. The other side of the door tugs at her. Before she can change her mind, she reinserts the key and grips the doorknob so tightly that her fingernails are white. She cracks the door open again, standing behind it to steady herself, not wanting to fall into nothingness.

She strains, listening through the crack of the door.

No voice speaks. No wind blows.

No void draws her in.

Gathering up her courage, she counts three breaths, and opens the door the rest of the way.

Chapter 42

Peacock Manor
Day 146,638

I suggested that Rose see what is behind the door.
After much debate, February and I decided it was the
right thing to do. So, I made sure she saw the key's
secret hiding place behind Captain Peacock's painting.
After all, he was the first to use the key.

Chapter 43

Darkness and Nothing More

Impossible. What is before her simply can't be.

A wall of round, black stones. The entire doorway is blocked off. She traces the solid wall tentatively with her fingertips before smacking it with her palm. The impact hurts her hand. The rocks are cold and smooth and...real. She raps her knuckles against them but draws no echoes—the wall isn't hollow.

How did the room transform into this, then? She can't trust her senses anymore.

The Manor blurs the lines between the real and the imagined.

She stands there, immobilized, unable to look away. She is bewitched by this door, yet it isn't real. It isn't a real door if it doesn't lead anywhere. It was stupid of her to hope for a magic door to a different realm, like in the stories she loves. Still. She wants things to be not as they are, but as she wishes.

She wants something more than reality. Because in reality, she isn't any closer to any real answers about her sister now than at the beginning of the summer.

Despair flares through her.

The grandfather clock clangs just as the doorbell chimes, startling her out of her skin.

February is back.

Chapter 44

Kamdyn

"Feebs, is that you?" Rose calls out as she dashes down the stairs. Her voice echoes through the otherwise soundless, empty halls. Her dad must've needed a break from his writing: his hat, basket, and handbook are missing from the entryway table. He's gone foraging. And Mom is—well, where Mom is all the time these days.

Rose deposits the key into a drawer of the hallway table; she will replace it behind the portrait later. She's decided not to tell February that she's been nosy, poking around where she probably shouldn't be.

"It's me," replies a male voice from the other side of the door, "Kamdyn."

Oh!

Right before Rose pulls back on the handle of the large wooden door, she has a conversation with her face and hopes it can comply with her plan of unconcerned calm and composure.

She creaks open the door.

"Hello," she says, as flatly as possible.

"*Here I opened wide the door—Darkness there and nothing more*," Kamdyn quotes, his slate-and-stone eyes never breaking from hers. Somber at first, but at the sight of her, a grin plays across his lips.

Her breath catches at his words. Does he know what she's seen upstairs? The door, the empty darkness? She holds his gaze, attempting to decipher his greeting.

He stands before her, as certain and unflinching as the solid marble statues of the Manor.

Her face struggles to resist—scrunching in an attempt to frown—but loses the battle and cracks into a smile so absurdly wide, she suspects it's borderline creepy.

She recovers. "Appropriate. You. Rapping at my chamber door, dressed all in black like The Raven."

She can definitely get on board with another evening with Edgar Allan Poe.

His throat bobs as he laughs.

"So, Rose, do you want to…" He pauses for effect. "…see me slow down time? Even *rewind* it?" he asks. "For you, I'll rewind time. Tempting enough? You'll need a sweater, though."

"Time travel is cold, huh?" she asks, dying to know more but not wanting to appear too eager. No need to fuel his overconfidence.

"My kind is," he replies slyly.

It's entirely enticing.

Willing herself not to stare, she glances at him once more before answering.

If someone could swagger while standing, it would be Kamdyn.

His reckless stance suits his mysterious invitation. One well-manicured hand hangs casually off his dark gray pants pocket while his other arm—with its black shirt sleeve rolled halfway up—props him lazily against the doorframe as if the only reason the frame exists is to emphasize his good looks.

His mouth curves up ever so slightly, revealing the triangles of his canines on his bottom lip. The low slant of the late-afternoon sunlight throws long shadows on his angular face, illuminating his strikingly straight nose. A small scar across one eyebrow leaves a hairless slash.

She's never noticed that before.

He appears wilder, a little less human...a little more like...an untamed lethal creature of some sort—a dark faery or a vampire. But there are no such beings, and she is only seeing what she wants to see because she just finished a book about them this morning. *Be cool, Rose.*

"I'll grab a sweater, then," she says coolly. *Good job.*

"I'll wait here, then," he offers, imitating her flat tone, though he draws his lips together, suppressing a smile.

****

They walk down the grassy knoll, cross the red garden bridge that stretches over the tiniest stream, and out the driveway toward the main road.

"You're not going to ask me where we're going?" Kamdyn glances sideways at her.

"Do you hear that?" Rose holds out a hand to silence him, staring straight ahead.

"No, nothing. What?"

"That's the sound of me not asking."

"Hah! You're so grumpy and hilarious."

"All right. Yes. I'm curious. Curious why you smell like lavender and sugar cookies."

"Herbal soap and sugar scrub."

She lifts a brow. "Sugar scrub?"

"Soft skin. That's all I'm saying."

"Hah!" *Adorable*. "Where *are* we going?" Rose asks.

"Shuttle stop."

"Where does the shuttle go?"

"Up. We're heading to the top."

"Then?"

"Then, I rewind time," Kamdyn says dramatically, inflating his chest as he tips an imaginary top hat like a magician enthralling his audience. He commands attention with his every word.

"Humph. How far back in time do you want to go?"

"The...other night at the Manor, under the stars with you?" he suggests nonchalantly.

Ugh. Rose bites her bottom lip. His words melt her into a useless puddle of mush. She may never be solid again. What's she supposed to say to that? She's afraid she might sputter something mortifying, but instead, he says—

"Oops, there's the shuttle. We might have to run." He holds out a hand to her, palm up, as if expecting her to give him something.

For a moment, Rose hesitates, wondering if she needs a ticket, or—

He grins and grabs her hand, lacing his fingers in hers. They dash toward the stop, as a group of gray-haired tourists disembark for a scenic overlook, cameras ready.

The two of them slide between the closing doors and shuffle to the rear of the bus.

"Our stop is the last one," he informs her.

He hasn't let go of her hand, and she's reciprocated, so here they are. She's holding hands with a boy, on a bus, going somewhere. Calm and unruffled, at least on the outside.

She can see what all the fuss is about now—why the girls at the sleepovers make a big deal over such things.

He's lived here all his life, he says, pointing out how the trees change with the elevation, and how the redwoods are gravitropic. Even on the steepest slope of a mountain, they always grow straight up and down, not out to the side. When a branch gets too heavy, it will skewer itself into the ground and grow new roots.

"Survival. Doing whatever it takes to survive," Rose observes.

"Aren't we all?" He squeezes her hand. "Last stop, here we are."

Charbon Lodge and Ski. There's no snow at this time of year, and the slopes are a patchy yellow and flat green, as if a child had used a crayon to carelessly fill in the colors.

Her eyes narrow at him accusingly. "You've kidnapped me to a hotel. How is this time travel?"

Did watching February and Robbie together in the grass at Vale Green give him *ideas*?

"It's my family's business. Don't worry, we aren't going inside."

He leads her around the back of the building and up the hill to the ski lifts.

"Where are we going, then?" She wants to know why his plans are so secret, so intriguing. *I'll rewind time*, he'd promised.

He clamps both hands on her shoulders and spins

her around, to face away from him. "The sun—it's about to set. The colors are incredible up here."

Gold and dusty rose ribbons of light purl together across the sky around them. Kamdyn's strong hands remain clasped on her shoulders from behind. He leans into her, his warm breath on the curve of her ear, and whispers—

"Tell me the exact moment when you see the last of the sun over that hill."

The crimson ball of fire, muted in its descent, finally drops over the edge of the earth.

A phenomenal sunset. Breathtaking. The beauty and constancy of the world captivate her.

"There. It's gone," she says. "Sun has set."

He dashes over to the operator booth for the ski lift, ducks inside, and presses several buttons. The lifts sputter to life with metallic whirring and cranking.

"Okay, let's go," he says, as the hanging chairs begin to pass by them.

The next seat scoops them up, and they swing back and forth as they ascend high into the dimming heavens. The ground drops away rapidly and Rose jolts backward, scrambling to pull down the safety bar, straining to stop herself from trembling.

Kamdyn steadies her arm. "Don't look down. Look to your left—west, Rose. Here's where I rewind time."

The upper peak of the sun appears again! Like a sunrise.

They are getting a second sunset!

The sun holds its place above the horizon—an eternal sunset—as they climb higher and higher. The upper portion of the sun bares itself once again. The lift carries them up the highest, longest run on the mountain. They hover in the sky, legs dangling, while the last of the sunlight bathes them in its coral glow, filling the spaces between the peaks and crevices below them.

At the summit, they hop off, landing on ragged grass. Right on time, the top of the sun explodes out beneath them, flaring one last ray of light before it bows out and plunges below the horizon for a second time.

"A never-ending sunset. Almost! If we could climb higher and westward..." Rose whispers, stunned at the incredible beauty, and that Kamdyn delivered on his extraordinary promise. He definitely didn't oversell himself.

They stand hand in hand as the light disappears and shadow falls over the valleys below them.

"A second sunset. That's the end of my magic trick," he says, satisfied at her reaction.

"You said the other day—everything has a dark side. The sun doesn't have a shadow."

"Huh, clever. That's true. It makes up for it by creating all the shadows, though." He throws her a wry smile.

"We can't escape them then—our shadows."

"Facing them or turning away from them is a choice."

"Turning away is hard," she retorts.

"Turning away is not always the answer," he murmurs.

She can't guess what is on his mind, but his words carry a burden, as hers do.

"There is an end to everything. A final goodbye," he says, the cadence of his voice like the night itself—

quiet, edged with peril.

He's referring to something in his life.

"There's always a goodbye?" she asks.

"You can trick fate for a quick minute and get two sunsets, but ultimately the sun will set every day, for eternity." He lets loose a heavy sigh.

Her heart cleaves in two at the devastating sorrow in his words.

She can't help stealing a glance at him.

A gust of wind draws jagged bits of broken leaves around him before spinning away.

Kamdyn is a shooting star falling unnoticed,

a final step before dropping off the edge of a windy cliff,

Chopin's Nocturnes, 9 and a little of 19.

She aches to reply, if only to relieve her own anguish, but finds no words to follow his heart-rending remark, his certainty of an end to all things.

They lean into each other in silence and ease, shoulders touching, overlooking the deep violet and forest greens of the sloping mountainside. The night wind coils around them once more, and Rose huffs warm air into her hands.

Taking notice, Kamdyn curves his arm around her and pulls her gently into him, planting his foot between hers.

He holds her steady, anchoring her to this soaring mountaintop, as close to the heavens as possible while remaining on earth. Heat blooms through her core as he shelters her with his solid embrace. His arms drift around her waist, moving with her, until they find comfort in each other's warmth and finally—a stillness within themselves.

"Do you bring all the girls up here for your magic sunset trick?" she asks.

"Ha! When I was little, I used to ride up here by myself all the time, to see the double sunset. But no, I didn't want to share it with anyone else. I wouldn't want to use something so beautiful and magical as a cheap date trick."

"Honorable."

"Also, I don't need romantic scenery to get girls."

"Less honorable. Are you even physically capable of being modest? I was reading this psychology textbook this summer—"

"Dork."

"For sure. But did you know that the more confident you are, the more likely you're *overestimating* your skills?" She catches herself in her dad's habit of did-you-knows and stops abruptly.

"You're intelligent and attractive, and I couldn't trick you into liking me if I tried. You may not see yourself that way, but you must know you're captivating."

"Amber was the pretty one…" Rose mumbles, but pauses. "Thank…you," she says.

She shivers.

He draws her tighter into him. "Let's get back down the mountain before someone shuts off the lift. It's getting too cold and windy here, but we can light one of the firepits behind the lodge."

****

The crackling flames devour another smoky log, sparking crimson and gold. Rose holds her fingers up to the soothing heat of the fire and sinks deeper into the bench beside Kamdyn.

He snakes his arm around her shoulders, so she leans into his musculature, feeling the heat of his body and the steady rise and fall of his chest. He sweeps his fingertips along her arm in a slow caress.

She almost forgets to breathe.

He angles his head to hers, his hot breath on her ear, her neck.

Rose knows if she turns toward him, he will kiss her.

And she wants him to.

So she turns toward him, her heart thundering, because she's never kissed anyone before.

Her first kiss.

Gazing up at him, outlined against the dark sky of jewels behind him, she feels the need to close her eyes. This can't be real.

She last glimpses the silvery-gold rings flashing in his eyes, reflecting the flickering flames in front of them before he closes in and brushes his soft lips on hers.

Warmth seeps into her cheeks, her ears, her breasts.

She is lost in the moment when he takes her mouth with his, parting her lips—his touch quiet and yielding.

All else around her blurs into spiraling, shimmering starlight.

His kiss is slow and reverent and delicate, first with the feathery strokes of his tongue.

Then deeper and fiercer when she places a hand on his firm chest.

When she touches him, his breathing snags.

He must find this as exhilarating as she. Her stomach tumbles.

There is no other place in time or space. She

doesn't dare open her eyes, doesn't dare risk waking up, doesn't dare question if she is daydreaming in the car again.

Rose wonders how long this kind of kissing lasts. She doesn't want it to stop, and apparently neither does he—but she stops thinking altogether when his fingers rake across the back of her head, grasping a handful of hair to pull her in.

She tenses as her breath hitches and plays her tongue along his teeth. Is she doing this right?

His free hand weaves tightly into hers. Yes, she must be.

He tugs her bottom lip, rougher this time, nipping it lightly as he withdraws, skimming his hot mouth and cold nose along her cheekbone. He buries his face in the hollow of her neck, kissing coarsely—and the wildness of it thrills her.

He's unrestrained. He's usually so proper, and when she secretly imagined kissing him—*yes, there were daydreams about it*, she embarrassingly admits to herself—she figured he'd shake her hand or offer some other formal gesture before kissing like a robot for two seconds because that's all he would want from her.

Nothing like this.

He devours her with his desire, his soft noises, his firm hands, and she's surprised at his reaction to her every movement. When she pauses, he yields and waits. When she presses into him, he gives her more. And she wants more.

He's hot and clever, and he thinks *she's* hot and clever. It's intoxicating.

He drags his lips on her earlobe, pausing right below her ear.

"*Rose,*" he exhales her name softly into her exposed neck, his voice fiery and low—devastating her with his longing—fragmenting the world she knows into a million shiny pieces.

It feels ridiculous. It feels right.

And nothing else matters.

Chapter 45

It's Time to Go Home, Rose

"You did what? He what? What else?!" February shrieks the next day when she arrives at the Manor. "I missed so much!"

Her dad is back in the hospital, delirious and tormented, but the doctors sent her home to rest after she stayed by his side for days.

"That's it, there's nothing more to tell."

"I want to hear about the sunset and the firepit again."

"Sheesh. It's innocent, compared to you and Robbie."

"Oh, Rose, it's all natural, you know, expressions of love and affection, nothing to be ashamed about. I love kissing. Smoochies!" she shouts, launching herself on Rose and giving her cheek a wet dog kiss.

"Yuck. So yuck."

February loses it, laughing like a maniac.

Rose retreats and wipes her face with the back of her hand. "The kissing was good. There. I admit it. I liked it. That's all I'm going to say. What's going on with you and Robbie these days?"

"Well, I'm glad you enjoyed it. I was about to tell you, Robbie says he thinks I'm his soulmate—we've known each other all our lives so he thinks it's meant to be, but I'm not sure if I believe in soulmates. I believe we meet who we need to—across different lifetimes. Sometimes it's at the beginning or middle, and other times, it's right at the very end."

"That's deep."

"But I love him, and he loves me. And, Rose, guess what?" She pauses for effect. "We did *it* on one of the lifts—in the gondola—it was…very romantic and fun. On that next run over from where you went."

"Whoa. That's…advanced." Many curious and shameful questions form in her head, but Rose stalls, unsure what she wants to discuss without getting *too* much information. She suspects Feeby would be an over-sharer if she allowed it. Yet, she wants to know…

"Hah! It was an unforgettable night. Is this embarrassing you? You're ruby red. We can talk about something else."

"Hmm. Yes, I'm always embarrassed. You know that." She covers the flush of her cheeks with her palms. "Should we work on the riddle, then? The end of summer is coming up and your family wants to make a decision on the Manor, right?"

"My mom said my uncles are accepting offers! It makes me sad." She passes Rose the last clue.

"No! You can't give up the Manor. What do *you* want to happen if you find the book?"

"If it were up to me, I'd keep the Manor forever. Finding the book would allow that. I'd pay off my uncles, stay here, and run this place. It's been in the family for so long. I would *never* sell it," she says.

"We must be close to finding the book, right?" A strange sensation creeps through Rose. So close to finding Amb—

"I hope so!"

"Why are some of the letters capitalized?" Rose asks. She hasn't looked at the written riddle in a while, only seeing the words in her head. Their library search was a failure. *Books* and *library* are not the answers. "Why is the *'p.s. this is the end'* all in lowercase?"

She examines the capital letters, and words form in front of her. "Feebs! I see the message we missed before!" she exclaims.

Great Ones Bring Appreciation,
Changing King's Thoughts Over Time.
Here, Enter Friends In Realms Seeking Truth.
3,2,4,8
p.s. this is the end.

The first letter of each word in the riddle spells out: GOBACKTOTHEFIRST

Go back to the first.

"Go back to the first—*what*?" Rose asks.

"The first, the first…clue?" February wonders.

They shoot each other knowing glances. This is it. They're about to find the book.

"Yes! Those answers from each line of the first riddle. We haven't used them yet," Rose says.

Rudder. Meteor. Mirage. Arachnid.

"What do we do with the numbers?" February asks.

"Let's see. There are four numbers, and four words we haven't used for anything. Is it a code we have to spell out? The three refers to the third letter of the first word, two is the second letter of the second word, and so on?" Rose suggests.

Rudder. Meteor. Mirage. Arachnid.

3, 2, 4, 8.

"Rudder, 3, that's a D."

"Then Meteor, 2, that's an E," February says.

"Mirage, 4, an A, and Arachnid, 8..." Rose begins.

Something strikes her as wrong. A prickling sensation runs up her spine.

She chokes on the next letter and can't continue. Icy horror threads through her veins, and her voice breaks when she finally says, "...D."

What the hell is the meaning of this? What kind of sick game...

D-E-A-D.

"What does this mean? D-E-A-D? A dead end?" Rose demands.

The pocketwatch at February's neck chimes abruptly and the alarm springs a high-pitched wail as though a tiny demonic creature shackled inside were wild to break free of its little glass prison.

"Why's your watch doing that? I've never heard it go off before. Where is the book?"

Feeby returns her stare with wide, frightened eyes.

Rose shakes the tiny piece of paper at her. "Feebs, is this...the end? Where is *The Book of Lost Spirits*? *What's dead*?" She spits out the words venomously.

February's pocketwatch continues to peal, violent and demanding, vibrating the chain around her neck. She drops her chin, lifting the pulsating watch. "Rose, *it's time*."

"WHAT?" Rose says.

"It's time to go home, Rose."

The words from the attic. The creepy note.

"That's not funny at all. What are you talking about? You're not making sense. Can you turn off that frickin' alarm? What does this clue mean, February?!" Her pulse throbs inside her head, as if it's about to burst out of her ears.

"WHAT IS DEAD!?" Rose shrieks, desperate and wounded.

February flinches as Rose yells at her.

Rose demands an answer because the one she comes up with on her own is unacceptable in the most sickening way imaginable. Hot tears burn her eyes, and she drops the paper clue.

Her most dreadful secret, the one she's thoroughly concealed, is fighting hard to emerge from the deepest, darkest corner of her mind where she abandoned it long ago.

This is the end. They both know it.

February's round, innocent eyes flood with tears and she lifts a slow finger to point at Rose. Her hand shakes.

Color snakes into her cheeks, blotting red as if she'd been slapped.

"*You are*. You're dead," February says, the sureness of her words masking her fear.

Chapter 46

Nothingness

Rose stops breathing. Something has changed, and she doesn't need air anymore. She presses her palm against her sternum. Numbness. Her fingertips tingle, growing thick and heavy as if her hand has fallen asleep.

She can't feel a heartbeat.

She presses harder. No pulse.

How can this be? She glances down, hitting her chest with a fist. Beat! The world around her convulses, and a brightness flares upon her, the harshest white light she's ever seen.

Except, she can't actually see—no hand, no ballroom, no February.

Then, colorless shadow and nothingness engulf her.

Chapter 47

February's World, A Prologue

Dear Peacock Manor,

We would like to rent your property for the summer season. You came highly recommended by our unconventional therapist, who specializes in grief counseling. We lost our only daughter, Ambrose (sometimes she goes by Rose) last summer. She has been haunting us ever since. Our therapist explained that Mr. Peacock assists in paranormal manifestations and apparitions who are unable to depart our realm, whether unwillingly or unwittingly. We are unable to communicate effectively with Rose in her spirit form— we cannot see our beloved daughter but can sense her presence in telltale signs such as disappearing or moving objects (clothing, food, keys), mysterious weeping and laughter, unexplained temperature changes, lights flickering on and off, doors slamming or locking, odd shadows, water and plumbing incidents, etc. We've read that a spirit who stays too long may become frustrated, angry, and dangerous. My wife is distraught with worry and hides at church all day, in fear we will be haunted forever.

We love and miss our daughter beyond comprehension, and only want her to find peace. Our therapist said Rose may be afraid of leaving or needs to complete certain experiences she never had or may not even realize that she's passed. We wish to help her move on.

Please help us as you have helped countless others in our heartbreaking situation. We will be eternally grateful for any assistance.

Sincerely,

Mr. and Mrs. Green

Chapter 48

The Lies Keeping Me Alive

Time is infinite. So why was I given so little of it?

How can this be my fate? I tried to take control of it, to make it all go away. Rose's thoughts flail.

To make it all okay. Dreams. Lies. Dreams becoming lies. The thin, fragile border in our minds separating the two, like the twilight veil between the spirits and the living. Easily passable at certain times when the light is weak. Or when hearts are weak.

When there is not enough courage to face the truth.

I wasn't brave.

Who is, though? It is Death, after all.

The comfort, the sweetness of lies. The world as she wishes it to be.

Lie to me. Keep my dream alive. Keep me alive.

The stories she told herself were the only possible way she could go on. To survive. In whatever form that had to be.

I wanted to be in charge of my own fate. It's my life, after all. Is that too much to ask?

Isn't it what everyone wants?

To survive.

To live.

****

"Wake up. It's me, February. You blacked out,"

says a feathery voice, familiar and unknowable all at once.

The voice Rose trusted all summer. The one that helped her find happiness again.

"Hmmph?" Her eyelids are heavy. She can't open her eyes all the way.

"Rose. It's not a dream. You need to remember."

"What happened?" She blinks but can't focus.

"Don't black out again, but I need you—your family needs you—to remember how you died," February pleads.

"My sister died. Amber died." Her own voice comes out toneless and tight. Why is February doing this? Nothing makes sense, but Rose doesn't want to feel. If she allows feelings in, she will feel betrayed. Cheated. Furious. Because of February.

"You don't have a sister. Please remember." February wrings her hands in her lap, then tries to wrap an arm around Rose.

Rose shrinks away from her touch.

"I have a twin. Twins run in my family. My mom has a twin, my grandma has a twin..." Rose shakes with indignation as she struggles to contain her fury.

"Your mom and grandma have twins, yes. Not you, though. You passed away that day." February's hands keep trembling, so she interlaces her fingers to still them. Because she is nervous—*because she is a liar*.

"My sister, not me. Amber died at the lake house last summer. She drowned. Everyone was sad. Everyone is *still* sad." Why does she have to explain all this? It's none of February's business. She doesn't know anything.

"You said you saw a spirit before. When was

that?"

"We saw a ghost, the Lady of the Lake. My sister and I took the rowboat out, and at the end of the day—at dusk—we saw a silvery presence on the other side. We rowed closer. I think the spirit attacked us."

"Rose, listen—"

"I stood up, and the boat toppled over. My sea lion sweatshirt caught on a nail on the boat. I struggled and hit my head on the rudder underneath the boat. Somehow, I made it back to shore, but I couldn't save Amber."

"I'm sorry, but that isn't—"

Rose cuts her off. "Was it a Scraythe? It killed Amber, drowned her. She inhaled too much water. We couldn't swim. You knew that; you taught me. The ghost drowned her. Stole her from me."

Time was stolen from us. She sweats hot and cold all at once, ensnared in a feverish nightmare.

February presses a sheet of paper into her hand.

"This is the letter your parents wrote my dad. Don't you see? You don't have a twin—you never did. Your name is Ambrose Green. *You* drowned that day."

Rose recognizes her dad's handwriting.

"Wrong. I saw a spirit, and it caused Amber's death."

"You must've seen a Death Spirit. You were dying and it invited you to go with it, right? A Scraythe takes your soul against your will, but a Death Spirit *asks* you to go with it."

"It was a Scraythe—"

"Your soul got back on that boat, but your body was in the lake. Your parents found you in the lake. I'm so sorry. You drowned. But you kept on going, and you've haunted them for a year."

"No."

"They finally found Peacock Manor and asked for help, to help you move on. This is what my dad does, what the Peacocks do. We—I can see and communicate with Lost Spirits."

"NO!"

"I'm trying to help you. This is hard for me too. Please don't be mad. It's what the Manor does. The key you found opens the door to The Beyond. You saw it. You're Ambrose."

Amber. Rose. *Ambrose*. The name she and her twin sister came up with together. The one her parents and friends and everyone else who knew them called them, as one unit, instead of referring to them separately, instead of saying "the twins," or—if someone couldn't tell them apart. Her heart wrenches. She hasn't used that name because it was for both of them and there is only her now.

Ambrose. Both their names together, because they loved each other so much and wanted to be one, as best friends are wont to do.

Ambrose. Amber and Rose. Her better half died, leaving her alone and sad.

Now she's left to deal with this lunatic changing the story of her grief, her life.

Nothing February said sounds right. All Rose knows in the moment is that she can't trust her anymore. An infantile part of her wants her parents, so—still shaking—she heaves herself out of bed, tripping past February toward the doorway.

"You're a creepy liar and you make things up because you're completely insane!" Rose yells. Rage pulses through her, sickening her.

Deadlier than poison, the betrayal of a friend.

Lights flicker in the old house as she continues. "You want the book for yourself! You're using me to help you solve the riddles—"

"The riddles are real, passed down the generations. But no one has ever found the book. I'm not sure if there *is* a book."

"LIAR! Why are you doing this to me?"

"Rose…let me help you." February moves closer with her arms outstretched.

Rose's blood simmers and she needs out, out of the Manor. "Don't you dare hug me! You help people DIE? You're sick. Get away from me!" she snarls, throwing February a menacing look, daring her to go on, to take one more step.

February stiffens as if she's been hit. "No! I'm scared too. It's been tearing me apart. I haven't helped a lost soul by myself before, but my dad can't anymore. You saw him. I did what I had to do."

Rose pauses, not having considered what this must be like for February. "You're scared too?" Part of her wants to hug her friend. Another part may also want to strike her. Her feelings boil.

"This is something I'm meant to do—no one else can help lost spirits. I'm trying to figure it out as I go. I wanted to help *you*. We're friends."

Rose's anger rises at the word. *Friends*. "You're tricking me. End of friendship. We will never be friends again! You're out of your mind, like your dad, and I'll never trust you again."

She instantly regrets her words. She didn't mean them, but it's too late now.

The crushed expression on February's face pains her. They've been close all summer. Best friends, she thought.

February allows herself to recover but refuses to let Rose leave.

"LET ME OUT!" Rose barely recognizes her own voice. It seethes with tremendous rage, hot and bubbling with a dangerous force that yearns to destroy something, everything.

This isn't her. She's never like this—never loses her temper.

February fixes her with a long, unreadable look before finally stepping aside. "I didn't know what else to do. I couldn't let you turn into a Scraythe," she says quietly.

Rose lunges for the door but stops just outside the room. *Turn into a Scraythe?*

"Please, let's talk…" February says, sensing hesitation and jumping on it. She sidles up next to Rose and steps out front to face her. The sight of February's concerned expression—fake or real, Rose doesn't know anymore—annoys her, because either way, February only pretended to be her friend all this time.

"Get out of my way," Rose snarls.

She doesn't wait for February to move.

She shoves her aside and races down the stairs, the disastrous storm of anger still surging in her chest.

February's footsteps slap behind her.

Water spurts and whooshes from one of the bedrooms. Not the hissing of a small burst pipe, but the fury and might of swift, wild rapids. Rose swings back briefly, glancing behind her. A great murky waterfall crashes down the stairs, cracking and splintering the railing, sweeping around February.

February screams as she grips the banister, fighting her way back upstairs. Somehow, the water doesn't affect Rose. She is neither wet nor cold. She'd seen the waterfall in her mind—wished she could stop February from following her, maybe even hoped to wash away the entire night—right before it manifested.

But Rose can't stop to wonder what happened.

"Stay away from me!" she warns February from halfway down the stairs.

February obeys, retreating into one of the bedrooms. Rose hears footsteps, and, as she arrives on the last step of the east stairway, February emerges before her, blocking her escape again.

"Aah! How'd you do that? You're the frickin' ghost!" Rose says.

"Rose, listen to me. I used another secret passageway," she says as she presses on a wall panel, revealing an inner set of stairs. "It connects to a closet upstairs. I heard you snort the night you arrived and couldn't help laughing. You must've smelled my mom's lily perfume I wore for good luck. I'd stayed too late setting up the riddles and had to spend the night in the passageway to avoid the Scraythe. You saw me through the window when you pulled up the driveway—that was my flashlight."

"You're making this up."

"Why do you think you want to find a ghost so badly?"

"I'm normal. The therapist said searching for ghosts was a coping mechanism. A stage of grief."

"That therapist was addressing your parents when they asked whether you might be haunting them. He didn't believe them. They found someone else, who referred them here—"

"Stop. You don't know anything about my family!" Rose dodges sideways, leaving February behind. She races toward her parents' voices in the sitting room.

Rose slows, creeping around the corner, hearing her mom say her name. What are they saying about her? She peers into the sitting room, concealing herself behind the doorjamb.

Mom sits on the turquoise chaise, hugging herself, leaning her shoulder into Dad next to her. The grim-faced portraits glare down at them, illuminated by the monumental chandelier weighing heavily overhead.

"What was all that, Obsidian?" Mom asks, fingering the cross around her neck. "The lights are going again. The plumbing has been better for a while, though." *Mom and her plumbing. Gah.*

Rose fights back the horrifying thought that *if* she *were* a poltergeist, then *she* would be the one affecting the water and plumbing.

No. Stop it. It can't be.

"It's been quieter over the last week. And I haven't heard the crying in a while," Dad says. His eyebrows lift, creasing his forehead.

"Rose is gone, then? She's moved on?"

"February says she is still here, but she's close to the end."

"We can't have a spirit haunting us, especially if a new baby arrives. That doesn't seem right."

"It's not just any spirit, dear. It's Ambrose. Our only daughter." He edges closer to hold her hand. "February believes Rose doesn't realize she died. It hurts my heart, Opaline. It's been four hundred and six days, but I'll never get over losing my little girl." He presses a palm over his face.

Rose has never seen her dad cry. Her stomach drops.

Her mom's stony face is silent, but she glances down at her fingernails before shutting her eyes. One heartbeat. Two heartbeats. Her bottom lip quivers.

The feelings have been sealed tight in her heart jar, but they are worming, squirming their way out.

"I pray for her every day at church. I wish I could tell her how much I miss her. And that I love her. I didn't tell her enough," Mom whispers, as the tears finally spill out of her closed eyes. Her fragile shoulders droop.

Mr. Green gathers her in his arms.

"February said when Ambrose is ready, we can talk to her one last time, before she departs. You'll tell her then."

Her mom weeps and weeps in punctuated high-octave squeaks.

It pierces Rose's insides. She can't take any more.

What an elaborate ruse. A new therapy to help her snap out of her grief for her sister.

She steps into the doorway, furious.

"I'm right here!" she screams at the two of them.

Neither of them shows any sign of surprise at her outburst, even though Rose has *never* thrown tantrums, not even when she was little. She finds it strange that there is no furrowing of eyebrows, no cringing or gasping, no reaction at all, as expected by her extravagant display of emotion. It should've shocked the Greens, who do not discuss disagreeable feelings.

The crystal droplets of the sitting room chandelier ripple and clink against each other; the lights flicker. An earthquake?

"Rose?" her dad says. "Ambrose? Are you here, sweetheart?" He stands up.

She runs to him and waves her hand in front of his perplexed, agonized face. No response. *Good acting, Dad.*

"This isn't funny anymore!" she cries, and flings her arms around him, trying to hug her dad as a small child would, expecting to bury her face into his shoulder, but instead…instead, she passes right through him.

Is she inside a simulation, a replication of a manor? Virtual reality? No, that can't be right.

A hologram. A fake image of her dad.

Dad?!

He flinches and shivers. "I think she's here, Opaline." His tired eyes flick sideways.

Rose stumbles over her own feet, shocked at passing through her dad, and scrambles to recover her balance. She swivels over her shoulder, seeing past the back of Dad's head.

February lingers in the doorway with her hands on her hips, soaking wet. Her damp dress clings limply to her legs and her hair is pasted to her forehead. She faces the adults, but her eyes skim over to Rose.

"What's happening, Feeby?" Dad asks. "Are you okay?"

"Mr. and Mrs. Green, Rose's confusion and anger is manifesting itself as…" February begins, pausing to catch her breath and steady her voice. She wrings out water from her dress.

Rose can't take anymore tonight.

Everyone she trusts is talking about her as if she isn't there. February has already betrayed her in the worst way possible.

And now, her parents.

She doesn't want to hear the rest of February's lies, so she sprints toward the front door to get out of this haunted manor. She doesn't care where.

Anywhere but here.

One minute, the house is still and dark, as it always is.

The next, it's rippling, its wooden beams splintering.

The walls jolt and crack as water bursts from the walls, plaster crumbles to dust, and paintings tumble to the floor. The octopus fountain in the courtyard behind her is overflowing with dark water, filled with shiny bubbles she knows are *not* bubbles.

She saw this the first night! What poltergeist is influencing her now?

She hurtles out the front door of Peacock Manor. Without opening it.

Careening down the stairs outside, she loses her balance, slips and lurches into an iron lantern illuminating the stairway. Blinded by searing pain on her right side, she must have fallen, though she no longer sees the front drive of the Manor; she's landed near an evergreen tree that wasn't there before. Here, the trees grow very close to each other, unlike near the Vale or along the highway. A thicket of old-growth trees. The air is cooler here. This is wrong.

This isn't the front yard of the Manor.

Rolling onto her side, she pushes off the ground,

not even bothering to brush off the dry pine needles sticking to her palms. She doesn't care. She intends to get as far away as she can from this nightmare.

Except—when the one place you don't want to be is with yourself, there's no place far enough.

She staggers across the soft ground, disoriented, but picks up her pace and runs with all her might, forcing herself to keep moving forward. In her burning misery and rage, she sprints faster than ever before without tiring.

Starry sky and mist blur by her in the most unnatural dream.

The strangest feeling overtakes her. That feeling when somebody is stalking, creeping, staring? That finally slows her. When she stops at last, her head whips around in bewilderment.

Where the hell is she? The sound of her own breath draws her attention to how quiet it is. The trees are so thick here, she can't see the stars anymore.

She's never seen this forest before, but something ghastly in the forest has seen her. And that ghastly, beaked creature stalks her silently, before gliding and slithering its tattered existence over her as she screams and screams.

Chapter 49

Peacock Manor
Day 146,641

Well, that was dramatic. For the record, there is nothing wrong with my plumbing. Pixie Cakes can manipulate water. It is going to take forever to dry my interior—I'm made of cypress wood! I wonder who will repair me if February's father is still unable to function? I suppose February will figure it out. She always does. She will help me. I've grown quite attached to the girls. They are entertaining and work so hard for something so futile. I suppose that is human life.

I have offered to transfer some of my powers to February. She is going after Pixie Cakes. "You'll need me," I said. She reluctantly agreed. The littlest Peacock believes she has to do it all herself, like everyone before her. I didn't want to be crass and point out what happened to her father, and his father before him, but I did.

She accepted my help.

I will transport February and Kamdyn to Pixie Cakes so they can rescue her. It is dangerous. I know what gathers in the woods at night. I have given February more of my knowledge. She has new incantations that cannot be forgotten.

Humans say giving makes them feel good, but after giving away my powers, I have begun to feel unwell. I am not human, so giving comes at a price and saps my spirit.

Chapter 50

The Haunted Forest

Rose folds over her knees, breathless, after running away from the Scraythe. She scans the deep forest and fights the panic slamming into her.

In daylight, the Scraythe is smoke and shadow, but at night—illuminated by moonlight—it casts a disembodied indigo glow, like a deep-sea jellyfish distorted through layers of tide. Its light is ever so faint, almost imperceptible—though a bit brighter if she doesn't look at it directly—for it is not a creature of light, but of darkness and torment.

It looms like mist, drifting wretchedly toward her in short bursts, followed by another. And then another. From all four directions, the beaked monstrosities gather. At times, they manifest faces of the dead. But mostly, they haunt as moving streaks of night, indistinct shards of bones, and glimpses of nightmares.

Bloody mouths appear on some, but not others, but all have beaks.

She pries her eyes off of their lethally sharp beaks and struggles to remember the incantations. Will they work? February told one lie after another. Are the incantations a lie? Maybe February controls the Scraythe.

Or are they hallucinations? Has she been drugged?

Have her dad's poisonous mushrooms consumed her mind?

The Scraythe have voices. Voices that tear at her with an ancient wickedness, promising suffering. "Take us with you, Rose," they gasp. "Take us, or we take you." She isn't sure how the creatures speak. Their words do not come from their torn mouths, for their lips hang open and lifeless around spiked fangs, and their sharp beaks clack, ready to pull flesh and pluck souls.

The blood drains from her face so quickly it leaves her unsteady and she sways, willing herself not to black out.

The phantasms stalk her, predatory but cautious. She closes her eyes to see February's notebook in her head and recites the first incantation. *No, wait.* The first is for indoors only.

From the deep forests they come, swarming to her like scarab beetles to dung.

When they hear her incantation, most of the horde of Scraythe pause behind the trees. They linger to allow the braver, more desperate monsters to sift through first.

She shouts out the second incantation—the one for outdoor use. It repels the monster closest to her. Others advance. They want souls and will peck and tear hers to shreds.

There are so many, and they will have to share. The idea repulses her.

Leaves rustle behind her, and she expects more Scraythe, but then—familiar barking. Meat Bones? He's followed her here. He lunges at a Scraythe as he backs into her, protecting her with his howl-bark, his angriest noise. They are a wolf pack of two, defending themselves.

She gathers him up and holds him tightly to her chest, murmuring into his frizzled coat. She doesn't care that his fur smells like eggs.

Thank you for coming, little buddy. I will protect you, too. I promise.

She repeats the second incantation and, as the next wave is repelled, a small opening appears in the mass of Scraythe. She dashes between them, even as they peck at Meat Bones in her arms, and sprints toward the mountainside.

If she can find a cave, then she can ward it.

It might be her only hope.

The Scraythe are greedy. Delighted there are two souls to consume, they give chase.

She reaches the rocky mountainside and squeezes into a crevasse, panting, out of breath. It's almost a cave, but it will have to work. Etched into the stones beside her are symbols like those on the puzzle box. She recalls Robbie's description of old caves with glyphs in the mountains.

She crams herself in deeper with Meat Bones still clamped in her arms, but after a few more feet, the passage is blocked.

Will the warding work? She spins around, wedging her back against the rocks.

It's too late. They've caught up. The Scraythe tracked them and now form an impenetrable semicircle in front of her.

There's no way out.

She can feel them pulling at her, like someone tugging at your clothing, except from the inside of her being.

Then, they are upon her. Meat Bones snarls

menacingly from under her arm.

One bloody mouth, two ripped lips, three Scraythe jabbing their beaks, ready to peck and gorge. The one who attacked the Iris Room carrying a wooden spoon—the murderous cook from the passageway-turned-Scraythe, opens a mouth on its belly containing three gold teeth. Their mouths can form anywhere on their bodies, February warned. Their beaks peck out the essence of who you are, then their mouths consume it. Wooden Spoon Scraythe slips to the front of the pack. She stirs her spoon in the air. Stirring, stirring.

Rose shrieks but manages to shout out the third incantation. She's shaking. Her fear devours her and she can't finish. She stutters, petering out into a useless babble. She needs to save Meat Bones, at least, so she starts over from the beginning.

As she speaks the last line a second voice joins her from the darkness behind the Scraythe.

Familiar, sure, and strong. February.

And then a third voice, calm and low and steady.

Rose squints through the indigo fog swelling around her. Despite the swirling chaos, she recognizes February's small form.

Rose stretches out a grateful, unsteady hand.

"Keep repeating it!" February tells her. "There's no room for mistakes!"

The third voice continues as Rose begins, and on the second repetition, with the three of them chanting, the Scraythe shift their attention to February. Cautious and greedy, they drift, surrounding her.

It's too dark for Rose to see the face of the mysterious third voice, but after another repetition, February shouts in her clear little voice, a different spell—one Rose does not recognize—and the symbols in the rocks begin to radiate a pale blue. The aquamarine blue of the glowing glyphs in the lab…

The Scraythe hesitate, uncertain of what they are up against.

What little luminescence they have diminishes to shadow.

The glyphs beam brighter for an instant before their light bursts from inside the rocks like a fragment of day rupturing the darkness.

The Scraythe are blown backward—scattering chaotically like rats whose dark hiding place has been laid bare.

"The Impenetrable Glyphs of the East Ridge!" February exclaims in surprise. "They were put up by the first Peacocks, but the effects are temporary. The Scraythe will be back." She squints into the darkness beyond the trees. "Yep. They're coming. Run!" she yells. "They're here!"

A hand reaches out to Rose and grasps her firmly by her arm. Once on her feet, she finds herself staring into a pair of hypnotic, glinting eyes, steely with resolve. *Kamdyn.*

"We have to go, Rose. Hold my hand and move fast! It's the only way to survive this. There are too many of them. We need to get inside—there's a ranger cabin halfway out of the forest we can ward from the Scraythe. C'mon, you can do this." He masks his distress, but the worry in his voice wills her to quicken her pace.

February leads them at first, but she falls behind. She can't keep up, and Kamdyn says that her human legs are exhausted. Rose's legs aren't tired, perhaps because of the adrenaline coursing through her, but she doesn't have time to question if that's true—or if, as a spirit, she doesn't tire if she doesn't believe she will.

They switch their formation as they escape, and she and Kamdyn each hold one of February's hands and tow her through the trees, sprinting ever faster. Rose doesn't dare turn her head away from what lies in front of her. She needs to get out of the thicket of Scraythe.

She does what she has to do. To survive.

"Faster! They're here!" February shrieks.

So she speeds up, and her feet no longer touch the ground. She doesn't want to know how it's possible.

Meat Bones is still tucked under Rose's arm like a loaf of bread, his back legs dangling.

Rose doesn't fully grasp it in the moment, but the thought occurs to her that if someone could see them right now, they would be flying across the mountaintop, soaring through the depths of the midnight forest, haunting and beautiful.

Not a single footprint behind them; only the sparkling star-studded night sky ahead of them.

Chapter 51

That Day

February slams the cabin door, scrambling to ward the small room with the first incantation.

Part of Rose admires the sheer nerve February displays, but the other part is certain they wouldn't be in this situation if February hadn't betrayed her.

February turns to her and Kamdyn. "We'll have to wait until morning. There are too many right now, and Scraythe are stronger at night. They're attracted to me more than they are to you three. Partly because I will not help them go Beyond. They cannot go Beyond as Scraythe—they'll terrorize that dimension as they terrorize ours. It's too late for them, in all realms and possibilities, for eternity."

Her words sting. Rose sees in February a shadow of a small but powerful creature, like a majestic owl swooping noiselessly on its nighttime prey. Her eyes seem to glow green. Strong and unafraid. Feeby can see through the depths of the darkness, seeing what others cannot—through the hollow lies.

Something is very different about her tonight.

"Their own souls have decayed and disintegrated. I told you before they want *new souls* to feed their emptiness. Newly *dead* souls. They are scavengers. Your parents, and Robbie—they can't see or sense them like we can, so the Scraythe can't scare them. Scraythe do not normally prey on the living; their souls are bound too tightly. Your soul is already separated from your body, so it's…easy.

"I can see them, because I can see spirits, and they haunt me because they want me to let them into The Beyond. There's so much anger, they've become sadistic, and they want to torture and hurt me. They want to inflict their own pain on others, on me especially, to wreak psychological damage," she explains as she checks the windows.

Kamdyn nods gravely but doesn't say a thing. He's tensely organizing the papers and books on the ranger desk into neat piles.

February continues, "It sustains them more than say, taking your soul. It gives them *something to do*. It's what they did to my dad, Rose. They tore at his soul. They can't take it completely, so they tear bits and pieces. He doesn't seem whole because he's not. Do you believe me now?"

A chill goes over Rose. She's seen the delirious terror in Mr. Peacock's face. His demonic cries still reverberate within her own being whenever she closes her eyes.

She doesn't answer February, though.

"Dad was caught off-guard outside at twilight after he risked his life to try to help a spirit like you, and the Scraythe got to him—got to them *both*. It's why I can't go outside after dusk. They know me. I'm still learning how to do all this. My dad was teaching me, even though he hoped I'd leave the Manor, leave the mountain and live a different life." Her voice breaks and she looks as if she might cry, but she presses her lips into a firm line, refusing to give in.

Kamdyn winces and abandons his nervous cleaning to lay a reassuring hand on February's shoulder. "Why are there so many in this forest?" he asks.

"They've collected here over time, trying to get into The Beyond, and live in dead trees and stumps, sometimes dead animals. They thrive in rot," February says.

Rose finally speaks up, glowering at Kamdyn. "You, what are *you*, then? Do you help February?" Her words tear from her lips. Another vile betrayal.

"Rose, I wanted to tell you, but you weren't ready." He is infuriatingly controlled.

"Tell me *what*. What do you mean?" she says coldly.

"I died in a ski accident last winter. I broke my neck and died up here. The mountain, I told you—the mountain is both beautiful and treacherous."

His words hit her like a knife stab to the gut. This can't be real.

"You're a...ghost?" Rose tries not to retch. The subject that once stirred excitement now induces disgust.

"My family won't let me go, won't say goodbye. They've refused to acknowledge that I'm dead. They didn't follow my wishes to scatter my ashes from this mountain. My urn has been hidden, moved from place to place. I knocked it over a few times when I first came back, trying to free myself, so they believe someone is trying to steal it. For a couple of days, it was on my dad's nightstand; he talked to me like I was still here, training me to take over the family business. I can't go to The Beyond—not when they didn't complete my final rites." He scowls, pausing to regain his composure.

He goes on. "I don't have a choice like you do, and I'm terrified that I'll become a Scraythe if I stay too long. They are lost spirits, once like us, but have stayed on this plane of existence too long. Their souls have collapsed in on themselves. Disintegrated, like February said. It will happen to us. You've seen me—when I feel regret and anger and loneliness, shadows branch all over my skin. I'm becoming like them. Soon, I will be Scraythe."

Kam is turning into a Scraythe? This plane of existence? He doesn't belong.

"What are you doing here, then? And at the Manor?" Rose demands, furious that everyone lied to her. She doesn't care that she's yelling, that she's losing it.

"I've been haunting Robbie, while I look for my ashes. I miss my best friend." His voice wavers for a moment. "And, like the Scraythe, I'm attracted to the Manor. It pulls at me. I'm drawn to that damn door, and I need to depart. That door is for lost souls. It's all true, what February said."

She chokes on his words, unable to take a full breath, as if an invisible hand strangles her. "We don't look like them. Like Scraythe. I'm still me," she rasps.

"The smoky chicken skeleton? Scraythe don't have souls anymore, they can't control what they look like. We still can, until our souls corrupt. You and I. We don't belong here, Rose."

We don't belong here. His words sting. She's seen him beginning to turn.

He couldn't fake that. So, it isn't a lie. He is a Lost

Spirit…and she is too.

She's the ghost she's been looking for. *She* is a ghost. The clues, the Manor, February—they have all been trying to show her. Whispering all summer, pleading with her to remember. The water visions, the voices murmuring the truth, the single bed in the thirteenth bedroom that she and Amber had—except Amber's was missing because she never existed, the rowboat with the narwhal (a corpse whale, a drowned body, Feeby said), the rudder she hit her head on, the sea lion from her sweatshirt…

Those were the *real* clues.

Extraordinary and horrendous. Her soul wants to scream.

All at once, in one wretched flash, she remembers.

She remembers not being able to breathe.

She remembers panic and fear, and water in her lungs, being trapped under that rowboat.

She remembers yanking and pulling at her shirt, held by the boat, needing to rip it off to save her life. Her head hits the rudder, and her world spins. Her outstretched arms churn the water, a broken windmill. Her thigh muscles burn, cramping from kicking away death.

Screaming into liquid. All sounds are devoured by the heavy dark water around her.

Muted screaming. Screaming in silence.

She screams into the inky lake as it engulfs her.

It tastes like rotten eggs and dark green things and mud. Thickness fills her lungs. A half-eaten fish head floats by, its still-shiny eyeball leering at her.

Then, giving up hope,

she sinks,

deeper
and darker
and dying,
away from the light.

To the world beneath. The underworld. The surface is so, so far away.

Silence. Cold. Numbness.

But then! A wisp of light comes to her. A lantern. Followed by…a tentacle.

Another tentacle unfurls, forming itself into a soft hand.

The spirit seeks out Rose's hand, snaking around it, beseeching her to go with her.

"No, please," Rose begs. "I don't belong where you want me to go. I don't belong in the realm of the dead. I want to belong…to the living. I want to be in charge of my own fate."

"Take my hand," the spirit offers. "Come with me and be at peace," she implores. Her other tentacle drags her lantern over their heads, illuminating their faces with its aquarium-green glow. Her face resembles that of a fish.

"I can't. I don't belong there, wherever it is you want me to go. I can't belong."

"You belong," the spirit says, tentacles coiling eager and tight.

"No. No! I do not. I don't want to belong *to you*. Never!"

The spirit lingers. Swaying like seaweed.

NO!

The Death Spirit rises upward, propelling itself away from her in spurts, as an octopus retreats after squirting ink, and spirals effortlessly to the surface—

without Rose.

The lake absorbs her tears, absorbs her body, her life.

She died that day.

Chapter 52

Kamdyn Needs Help

February and Kamdyn draw closely around her, understanding the brimming tears of recognition in her eyes.

But Rose is empty, and the tears retreat. If you're not in charge of your own fate, what is the point? What is the frickin' point?

Fury fills the emptiness.

There is always something waiting in the dark to fill the emptiness inside.

A churning flood from a torrential storm invades her mind, and as she slams her eyes shut, envisioning a raging wall of water surging, the ground beneath her rumbles—

"We love you. We need you," February says quietly, attempting to fill the emptiness with light instead.

Rose's eyes snap open. The rumbling subsides.

"Please, Rose, I need your help," Kamdyn says, tender and mild, as if gently waking her up from a deep sleep. "I want to depart, and I need my ashes freed from my family so they can let me go. So I can go. I need them scattered across the mountain, as I requested. The day the four of us went to Vale Green was supposed to be my very last day here. I was ready to depart, but wanted one last look at this world's beauty, in that valley, with my favorite friends, with my favorite book. Then I found something even more beautiful. You, Rose."

His voice is hoarse. "February was supposed to steal my ashes that night, but I asked for a few more days to spend with you. But in those few days, my family moved my ashes into my dad's office safe. February needs help getting into it. Robbie can't help her and risk his family's business ties with mine. We have a quest. Right? When your strengths and weaknesses are tested? Just like you said. Can you be strong for me? I'm not asking you to depart, but I need your help. Please?"

His words burn away the agony and weariness consuming her. She softens.

This is real. Rose is certain now, with absolute humiliation, that she has been lying to herself. Grasping onto a lie when the truth was too hard to accept. Now, Kamdyn's family is doing the same thing to him, and he has no choice. *That* was what he meant at Vale Green when he said, "*I only want it to be my choice.*"

"Yes. I can...I will help you," she stammers. She presses her lips together, willing herself not to fall apart again.

He cups her chin with a palm and strokes her cheek affectionately, tracing her jaw with his thumb, and then as his arm falls, he gives Meat Bones an ear rub.

Rose glances down at her dog nestled in her arms, before glaring at February, resentful and lost.

"How does Meat Bones know I'm here? What is he, then?" He perks up at his name and swishes his tail, ready to follow his pack leader's commands. Rose still loves him. She doesn't care what he is, dog or wolf or ghost.

"Meat Bones was hit by a car in the spring. I buried him. He never had a family and never felt love. Nobody to care for him. He was so lost and confused when he died, and I tried to catch him—his spirit—to help him into The Beyond, but he was afraid of me. He'd never trusted anyone before. I think he sensed you when you arrived, came to Peacock Manor and found you, and you loved him. He would follow you anywhere. He'll go with you to The Beyond when you decide, so he can finally be at peace, too." She angles her head attempting to capture Rose's eyes.

But Rose refuses to meet her gaze. Instead, she scowls at the faded maroon rug in the ranger cabin, strewn with browned pine needles.

The rug needs adjusting. It isn't lined up with the wall.

She says nothing and shuts her eyes, not wanting to see what is before her anymore. *Any of it.*

The stupid red off-centered rug. February. The truth.

And she definitely, certainly, isn't going to any Beyond.

Chapter 53

Sunrise, Take Me Instead

Rose hasn't seen a sunrise in years. Not since her dad took her camping and the wild birds whistled and chirped so loudly before first light, she was wide awake by the time the sun appeared. Today, the peach and lavender dawn seeps into the spaces between the trees surrounding the wood cabin, and the cold air smells of piney morning mist.

"We need to leave; the forest isn't safe, even in daylight." February cracks the door open and surveys the area for any sign of Scraythe before whispering the fourth incantation. "Okay, *now*. Stick together."

Not a hundred feet from the cabin, the Scraythe— faded back to camouflage gray in the light of dawn— ambush them from behind a cluster of fallen boulders the same shade of dingy gloom.

"Rooose. Come with us. They don't want you— you're just a burden. You don't belong with them," they say. "Join us, and we'll let them go. This is your fate. You're different. *We know*."

The last two words, they chant together in eerie harmony, sending chilling shivers up her spine.

"Join us. We know," they repeat.

She stiffens. "They only want me?"

"Don't listen to them, Rose," February warns. She

turns, guiding them left, but skids to a stop when another cluster of Scraythe slinks toward them.

Their voices thunder in Rose's ears. There are too many. The incantations barely held back the smaller group last night, and the glyphs had amplified the effects.

What chance of escape do they have now?

"They'll leave you alone if I go with them?" Rose bites her lips to stop her voice from trembling. *They know.*

She feels naked. She feels shame. The shame twists and snakes inside her until her worst thoughts surface—regret and worthlessness and failure wounding her deeper than a dagger could ever pierce.

Her friends are only in this situation because of her.

If they are captured and tortured by Scraythe, their souls destroyed, it will be because of *her*.

"I don't even belong here. You said so yourself. I'm going to become one eventually, you said," she murmurs.

"Stop it. You're not thinking straight. You don't have to become one. You can depart." February digs her fingers into Rose's forearm, drawing her back.

Depart? Or stay, and be a Scraythe? Or neither—and let one take her and save her only friends. She can't change her destiny, but the others needn't perish.

She isn't thinking straight, like February said, but her feelings overwhelm reason, and she can't stand one more second of it.

A perilous place to be, where feelings are no longer wanted.

"You're with us. Let's go," Kamdyn says, offering

out his hand. His face falls when Rose refuses him. She's never seen him flinch, but in this moment, a flare of alarm and pleading tarnishes his eyes.

She's made up her mind. Her one soul for their three souls.

This is the answer she's come up with.

Nuzzling Meat Bones one more time, she whispers to him, "You've been the best boy ever. I'm going to save you, so you need to go with February. Goodbye, my friend."

Rose turns to Feeby, passing him to her even as he wriggles in protest.

She needs to face reality.

The truth.

February and Kamdyn have places they need to be.

She has no place to be. Tears sting her eyes.

"Protect Meat Bones. I promised him. You guys go—you heard them. They only want—want me," Rose stutters.

She has to be brave, unlike when she was with her sister—no, wait, no more lies. Then it will all be over. They were brave for her, even Meat Bones, and she put them all in danger.

She staggers forward, toward the nearest Scraythe. Its beaked skull juts forward and back, delighted, but impatient. Its smoky wisps solidify into its skeletal form.

"You won't feel lost anymore," it croaks. "We have found you. It is meant to be. Fate."

This has to be the right answer. The answer to her secrets, her lies, her disgust, her confusion, her sorrow.

"Don't!" February pleads. "Don't listen to them! We need to run!" She grabs Rose's hand, but Rose twists away. She lunges for her again. "You're Rose Green. You think of answers. You don't give up. You solve things. Don't do it this way!"

"Rose, this isn't why you're here," Kamdyn growls, edging closer, trying to block her.

"But…we don't have a choice. It's me, or it's all of us," Rose says, her voice wooden as she slowly wobbles toward the writhing darkness. Her mind is fuzzy, and nothing makes sense anymore. She feels sick but sees no other options: Rose Green is dead either way.

At least she can save February and Kamdyn.

To be a good friend, now that she has friends.

Maybe that's all she's destined for.

Her mind spins chaotically, even as the rest of her is petrified.

"No! You're wrong. Please, don't," February cries.

"You do have a choice," Kamdyn says. "Don't let them decide your fate for you."

"My fate is done and gone," Rose reminds him, holding his stare. "*You* of all people should know!"

Kamdyn doesn't respond, but his eyes darken dangerously. She's hit him where it hurts because she's hurting, and it's unfair, but all of this is appallingly unfair. His expression remains inscrutable.

"I know tonight's all been a shock—you're in shock, but—" February shrieks and dodges, falling as a Scraythe strikes and pecks at her from the side.

Rose crosses the small distance between her and the nearest Scraythe. It awaits, swaying in the dark, clicking its hooked beak in anticipation.

Like a blind serpent striking, it snaps at the darkness between them, ever closer…

The beak lunges for her. She shuts her eyes as tight as she can.

****

She's made a horrendous mistake.

This isn't what she wants.

A fate worse than death. Having your soul pecked out is a fate worse than death. Mr. Peacock's screams echo her own now…

She crashes to the ground.

Her knees burn as they slide along the forest floor, but nothing else hurts.

Nothing pecks at her soul.

She only dares to open her eyes when she feels a hand protecting her head.

The hand is covered in dark, shadowy veins.

Kamdyn has thrown himself on her, knocking her away from the beak. As the beaked skull sways, rebalancing for another strike, the bloody mouth at its belly champs at them.

"Watch out!" Rose yells from under him.

Lightning fast, the bird skull stabs at Kamdyn's legs before gnashing into his shoulder. He cries out in pain as he thrashes against the beak, trying to free himself while still shielding Rose with his body.

Meat Bones leaps out of February's arms and rushes forward to bite the Scraythe. It shrieks as he snaps at its skeletal legs and releases its hold on Kamdyn. He and Rose scramble to roll out of the way.

February repels the onslaught of Scraythe with the third incantation, but there are too many to hold back for long.

"Get up! *NOW*. They're trying to separate us!" February drags them up by their arms, but Rose stays on her knees, motionless, her thoughts spinning on those words. "Don't let them do it again!" Feeby pleads, but her voice fades as something clicks in Rose's mind.

Separate us.

The veil that separates the realms is weakened at twilight.

Her pulse thunders wildly through her body. The veil is weakened at twilight.

When light and dark meet.

Dawn is the same thing. *Use The BoLS, dawn and dusk, use 3 on Scrayth*e? said the burnt notes in the laboratory.

She understands now.

It has to work.

"Feeby!" Rose yells. "We have to use all three incantations on the Scraythe. Feebs, say the first one, I'll use the second, Kam—the third. Now!"

"What?" February and Kamdyn shout at the same time, looking at her like she hit her head too hard when Kam knocked her out of the way, and spouts nonsense out of shock.

"The lab notes. Trust me on this. All together. Do it!" Rose hollers as the Scraythe loom over them.

They clasp hands and huddle together as the first light of day seeps between the trees.

Dawn.

"Now!" she bellows, and the three of them recite the words simultaneously.

All three incantations at once. Shouting.

The air vibrates around them as their voices echo into the mountainside.

When they complete their incantations, the

Scraythe halt abruptly, suspended in place.

Then—they fade, slow at first, as if gradually being erased around the edges.

"It's working," Kamdyn says, stepping forward, only to stumble, weakened by his stab wounds. "It's destroying them."

The creatures shriek in frustration as they dissolve into the spaces between realms.

They are the ones who truly belong nowhere.

"Let's go! More will come," February says. "Kam, are you okay? I have an incantation that can help heal you, if you can wait 'til we get outta here."

"You've gained some new skills, huh? It hurts like hell, but it's not like I can die, right?" he says wryly. He checks the punctures in his shoulder and calf—they look like burnt holes—deep, dark stains spreading on his skin. "They didn't get my soul."

He flexes his arm and grimaces. "Rose, you saved us," he says, his grip tightening on her hand as he pulls her up. The forest sways around her, and her vision grays for a second as she stands.

She can't reply. They risked their lives and souls in the first place because of her.

February chimes in. "Rose, you for sure saved us. This is huge. I had no idea they could be destroyed like that. Move, you guys." February clutches Kamdyn's wrist, he clasps Rose's hand, and Meat Bones is gathered under Rose's other arm. Like a chain of cut-out paper dolls, they make their way out of the misty woods in a rush of adrenaline and dread.

Rose can't believe how far she ran last night. How did they find her—Meat Bones first, then February and Kamdyn? She'd ended up deep in the old-growth forest on the dark side of the mountain, the sharp north side. How did she run so steeply uphill? In the descent to the Manor, they'd raced past a ski lift.

It surprises her to think how much effort it was for February to find her. February has been there for her all summer when nobody else was.

But then, she lied.

February betrayed her, worse than anyone else ever. Because Rose trusted and loved her.

That kind of betrayal hurts the most.

But what exactly did February do wrong? She did it all to help Rose accept her real self and discover the truth. *That's what a true friend does, right? Helps you to accept yourself as you are.* When no one else could. When Rose couldn't accept herself.

February pried the secrets and lies out of her—out of her terrified grasp.

She shouldn't be mad at Feeby, who is right, after all. Rose wouldn't have accepted the truth; she didn't even accept the truth when it was finally thrust upon her.

Her disastrous actions had nearly gotten February, Kamdyn, and Meat Bones consumed by Scraythe.

A fate worse than death.

Chapter 54

It's Kamdyn in There

At the Manor, they review their plan to help
Kamdyn while February speaks a healing incantation,
first for his shoulder, and then for his leg. His spirit
form can still feel pain and suffering, she explains,
because your spirit can be damaged. It doesn't make
sense to Rose, but she remembers the pain of falling on
her knee that first night when she was rushing to see
Kam up close, and when she banged her head on the
attic beam. It is a good "did-you-know" fact about
ghosts, she supposes.

Kamdyn explains their goal. "My dad purchased a
seventeenth-century chest as an urn to hold my ashes.
It's made of iron. I can't touch it. Spirits can't touch
iron without being displaced, so, Rose, you won't be
able to handle the box."

Rose winces, but nods in understanding. When she
touched the iron lantern on the front steps at the Manor,
it cast her into the forest. Part of her still doesn't want
to accept that she is a spirit, but there is no escaping the
truth now.

He continues. "I can't be near my ashes. We aren't
supposed to be on the same plane of existence anymore
and being near them does weird things to both me and
the ashes." A muscle in his jaw clenches, but he

continues, his voice restrained.

"The safe may be made of iron, but if you get February into my dad's office, she can open it. I've been haunting my dad's office and finally figured out the code. No one uses the offices on the weekends in the early morning—they're all helping at the restaurant for breakfast, but you never know. It's the *least* busy time, so we have to do it now."

February nods in agreement as she checks that Kam's injuries are mending.

He studies Rose, so she puts on a brave face as he goes on. "Once you retrieve my ashes, I'll turn on the lift, and you two will hop on and go to the top. Scatter my ashes off the steepest side, the north side, and oh—it's probably best to toss the box off the back of the mountain too. Good riddance."

****

The shuttle ride up to Charbon Lodge is marked by nervous silence and jittery feet.

February spins her pocketwatch in her hand but doesn't speak the entire trip.

Rose still has nothing to say to her, so she stares out the window.

Kamdyn mutters under his breath, listing all the ways the plan can go wrong while considering alternatives for each scenario.

She recognizes the ski lift from the night of two sunsets, and glimpses the empty, extinguished firepit. It still glows a fiery orange in her memory.

Her heart stumbles. It may as well have been one of her daydreams.

Onward. And upward.

"Okay, team, good luck," Kamdyn punctuates his

statement with a clap of his hands.

He waits at the ski lift. February sneaks to the back of the lodge, into Mr. Charbon's main office. Rose follows, looking over her shoulder at the scenery one more time. The morning sun transforms the shape of the mountain, illuminating its eastern face. There is no time to mull over whether that sunset with Kamdyn was real life or not.

They leave the lights off in the hallway as she and February creep along slowly, ready to run if someone else enters the building.

"It's this one," February says as she tugs at the doorknob.

Locked.

"It wasn't supposed to be locked, Rose," she whispers.

"What do we do now? Get the keys from Kam?" Rose rasps.

"He wasn't able to get a copy of the key. They changed it once they found it was missing after the first time he stole it. Rose, you'll have to go through the door and unlock it and let me in."

"What? How?!"

"You can. In your spirit form, you have what is called intangibility; you exist in another dimension. So, you can pass through objects and walls. Like how you passed through your dad," February says quietly.

Ah. She had to bring *that* up. So she *did* see the desperate, sad hug Rose tried to give him.

"So...like this..." Rose says, pressing herself toward the door.

Rose smacks into the door and hits her forehead.

"You might have to visualize the other side and

imagine fading away. Try your hand so you don't bang your head again," February suggests.

Rose closes her eyes and recalls how feather-light she was when they were soaring through the woods away from the Scraythe. Desperate, but weightless and airy. She sailed into the night as if she were winged with a draft of celestial wind.

She sticks out her hand, expecting it to slam into the wooden door, but keeps her eyes shut, envisioning herself as vaporous and invisible as wind.

"You're doing it, Rose," Feeby says, almost inaudibly, so as not to break her concentration.

The rest of Rose's body follows her hand through the door. She senses the shadow of the door as she passes, but otherwise presses through as if the wood were made of air—a hologram of a door.

Once her body is through into the office, she opens her eyes and spins around.

The smoky wisps of her hand solidify, becoming corporeal.

No frickin' way. She has passed through a solid object!

She isn't sure if she should celebrate or vomit.

"Are you there?" February whispers from the other side of the door. "Let me in," she reminds her.

Rose unlocks the door with a click, and February pounces into the dark office, excited as ever.

"I'm so proud of you!" She hugs her, but Rose's arms remain slack by her sides. She isn't ready to feel or admit anything, and February's love confuses her.

She doesn't return the hug. She can't. And, she has no idea what to make of her newfound abilities. Feeby still cheers her on, like always, whether her accomplishments are big or small.

No friend ever did that for her before.

Anguish slams into her, and she feels torn in two.

"Where's the safe?" Rose asks, gathering her thoughts to concentrate on the task at hand.

"Kam said it's behind the painting of his dad." February shuffles behind the wide mahogany desk and pries the painting away from the wall, swinging it open. "Hey, Rose, do you feel the need to fix this painting?" she teases.

"Too soon," Rose says. "I'm still mad at you." But she smiles slightly, because yes, she does feel the need to tilt that painting back in place.

"Oh, please don't be mad. We can talk about this as much as you want."

"Okay. But hurry. I hear someone coming down the hall," Rose warns.

Feeby's nimble fingers punch in the code she's scribbled on her hand, and the safe beeps once, loudly, before it opens.

Horrified at the sound, they freeze in place.

The footsteps in the hallway halt. Someone knows they are in the office, and February will be caught stealing.

The footsteps stride right to the office door.

The locked doorknob jiggles, but Rose remains motionless, glancing at February for guidance.

February acts quickly, stretching her arm past a collection of ski trophies and plaques and photographs, and extracts a small ornate box. A miniature pirate's treasure chest, if Rose didn't know better. But no, it is…it is…

Kamdyn.

It's Kamdyn in there. Her stomach twists. It sickens her.

No time to shrivel up in grief, Rose Green.

"Can you see who's at the door?" February rasps. "We need to get out of here."

Keys jingle outside. Rose creeps to the doorway and closes her eyes to imagine that the door isn't there. She hopes for the best but braces for impact before she drives her head through.

Whew.

Her eyes blink open and she finds herself face-to-face with an older man in a suit.

A man with the same refined nose and lips as Kamdyn, but his face is lined with wrinkles.

Kamdyn's father, Mr. Charbon.

He unlocks the door, but Rose quickly spins the lock from the opposite side and secures it. His keys jingle again, thinking he's inserted the wrong key.

Rose remembers something from her research on spirits. "Wait. Can I possess people? Possess him and move him down the hall?"

"You can. Once, my dad helped a boy who possessed his uncle. It doesn't hurt them, necessarily, but you're messing with someone else's free will, and that's not right."

"What else could I do to distract him?"

"I think you might be able to control water. Like when you got scared in the attic, or mad back at the Manor—and I saw you staring at the brook at Vale Green. You changed the flow of the stream. Hydrokinesis. Some spirits whose deaths were related to water—like you—can manipulate it. Have you had flashbacks, visions, or hallucinations that were water-related?"

She is right. The octopus fountain. The underground passageway. The stream at Vale Green. "Hmm. Water. There's a drinking fountain at the end of the hall. I'll cause a distraction while you run outside?"

"That could work." Feeby's voice is barely a whisper.

Rose presses through the door again, passing through Mr. Charbon, who shivers and whirls his head around, searching for the source of the chill. In a few soundless steps, she arrives at the drinking fountain and jabs at the button to turn on the water. She visualizes it gushing like a waterfall.

The water rises out of the faucet, cascading over and darkening the carpet beneath it.

Mr. Charbon doesn't notice.

She needs more.

She envisions a tidal wave, a catastrophic typhoon washing away a beach.

The waterspout hisses, shooting sideways from the fountain, and Mr. Charbon turns his head toward her. His eyes narrow, but he returns his attention to his keys.

She needs more.

Her eyes snap shut, forcing her mind back to *that* day—how black, frigid water had surged into her nose and poured into her mouth and down her throat, filling her chest, choking, and engulfing her. An entire lake, relentless and merciless. She begged it to release its liquid grasp. She remembers the absoluteness of the water's will to overpower her. Water. A source of life. A source of death. For her.

The water fountain erupts with a thunderous crack.

Water spurts everywhere, rushing up the ceiling,

spraying the walls, sparking the lights.

Mr. Charbon curses out loud and rushes toward Rose, toward the fountain, throwing his hands up as if trying to catch the water flooding and destroying his hallway. He dives into the supply closet for a bucket.

Rose runs the other way past him to his office. "Distraction achieved. We're good to go," she informs February.

Kamdyn sprints into the building, stopping at the office doorway before glancing back in a double take at the sight of his dad flailing around the broken water fountain.

"Why's it taking so long? You need to get out of here, Feebs!" His eyes shift to his dad's open safe.

He falls silent, lingering at the sight of the contents: his neatly stacked competition trophies and countless awards and magazine clippings.

When he finally speaks, his voice is husky. "He kept all of it?"

He steps forward, needing a closer look.

His face suddenly seems years younger, and Rose can imagine what he looked like as a child. "Every single trophy is in there. All the articles about me. The score reports. I can't believe it." He blinks rapidly and turns away, his hands absently arranging items on his father's desk to line up with the edges and corners.

"Kam, your dad was very proud of you, even if he didn't say it," February says softly.

Kamdyn's attention switches to the iron box in her hands.

"Ready? I've got it," February says, drawing it closer to her.

As she takes a step toward him, the outline of his

silhouette flickers.

"Uh oh, I can't be this close to the ashes." Kam retreats, displaying his fading arms. "Not supposed to be on the same plane of existence, remember?"

Checking the hallway, Rose raises a palm to silence them. "There's someone else coming down the hall," she whispers.

Kamdyn thrusts his head through the door. "Walter. One of my dad's employees."

"We've gotta get Feeby outta here," says Rose.

Kamdyn slips the rest of the way through the door, and Rose follows, leaving February behind.

Mr. Charbon glances up from the fountain, staring at them—no—through them. "Walter! Can you get into my office and call a plumber? My key isn't working."

Walter nods obediently, pausing in front of the office next to them. He lifts his keys.

Rose thinks fast. "Kam, I know Feeby says it's wrong to possess people, but what if we did it long enough to move Walter, so Feeby can escape?"

"February plays by the book, it's part of her charm. I can try possessing him; I have different morals." A corner of his mouth curls into a devious grin. "But I don't know how—I've never done it before."

"Neither have I," Rose says. "But I read people are more prone to possession when they're scared or distracted."

"Okay, we don't have much choice right now. You try messing with him, and I'll catch him off-guard."

Rose slinks beside Walter and tousles his half-bald head. He jumps back, looking up and around as if something has flown into his hair, flinging his arms around his face.

She jabs him as hard as she can in the side, and he staggers before doubling over as if his stomach were cramping.

"Oof. Chili cheese fries for breakfast was the wrong choice today, Walt," he grumbles to himself.

Kamdyn leans into him, as if stepping into a full-body costume.

Walter lurches sideways, shaking his arms as if he were cold.

Kamdyn pursues him and tries again, matching Walter's stance this time, and successfully shifts into him.

Walter-Kamdyn freezes in place, motionless.

Walter's eyes are glassy, but the voice is Kamdyn's. "I think it's working," he whispers to Rose. "I'll move him away from the office toward my dad. I have something to say to Dad before I leave. You let February know when it's safe to come out, and then meet me at the ski lift."

"Got it. Your dad keeps his cool, same as you." Rose curls a finger at the water fountain.

Mr. Charbon holds a bucket under the largest spray of water while a smaller spray shoots him in the face, dribbling down his expensive suit. He remains stony-faced as he tries to figure out what to do next.

"Right," says Kamdyn, watching him. "Once in the worst thunderstorm ever, he made me check every single window in the resort and take down all the umbrellas at the picnic tables. When I complained of being wet and cold, he said, "You made of cotton candy, Kamdyn Charbon? No? Then you won't melt in the rain.""

"Ha!"

"Remember my dad's favorite saying?" Kamdyn reminds her of one of their first conversations.

"*We are not made of sugar*? He loves reminding you that you're not candy," Rose observes.

Kamdyn pauses. The opportunity to confront his dad floods him with conflicting emotions. Walter's face tenses and the muscles of his jaw pop. Rose isn't sure if it's anger, resentment, or something else.

"Walt, you can't get in there either? Grab some rags and help me sop up this water," Mr. Charbon orders.

Kamdyn-Walter strides over to Mr. Charbon and stands squarely in front of him. "Sir, there's something I need to say to you."

"Yes? What is it?" Mr. Charbon says.

Kamdyn hesitates, and his hands clench into fists at his side.

Rose slips through the office door. "Feeby, get out of here! Kam says to meet him at the lifts."

February nods quickly as Rose retracts back into the hallway.

"Spit it out, Walter," Mr. Charbon demands. "We have a plumbing crisis."

"Sir, I wanted to thank you for everything you've done for me over the years," Kamdyn-Walter says.

"Oh, hiring you? Walt, you're my best employee. Why? Are you quitting?" Mr. Charbon asks, perplexed.

"No, no. I realized after all this time, you wanted the best for me. It means a lot, and I'll always remember—you know—that you…cared."

"Of course. What's the matter? You sure nothing's wrong? You sound like you're going away." Mr. Charbon tilts his head sideways and glances around as if Walter could be talking to the wrong person.

"I'm okay. Yes. I think I'm good now, sir. Thank you." Kamdyn hugs his surprised dad. One second. Two, three, four seconds.

February sneaks out, and escapes through the far door unseen.

Kamdyn finally lets go of his dad and strides back to Rose in Walter's body.

Mr. Charbon remains absolutely still, bewilderment plastered on his face. He opens his mouth, sputtering, "Your voice sounds...Kam—?" but thinks better of it and composes himself. "Stay here and try to clean up as much as you can. I'll call the plumber from the main building. Thanks, Walt."

He turns on his heels before hurrying down the hall. He's clearly had enough of this strange morning.

Kamdyn drifts out from behind Walter, leaving him standing confused next to the damaged water fountain. Walter shakes his head a few times, gawking at the mess in front of him as if he's forgotten what he was doing, but finally decides that picking up a mop is the answer.

Realizing Kamdyn has said his last goodbye to his dad, Rose asks him, "Are you all right?" She will never forget the look on Kamdyn's face when he saw that his dad had saved every single trophy.

"Yep, yep. I never thought I'd have this opportunity, so I'm glad it happened." His voice catches and he clears his throat, but he takes her hand and steers her toward the exit.

She knows deep down that she would *never* be able to do what he just did.

Say goodbye forever to her parents?
No way. Never.

Chapter 55

Ashes to Clouds

They meet Feeby at the operating booth outside.

Kamdyn dives in and flicks on the switch to the ski lift as Rose and February sprint uphill and heave themselves onto the nearest chair.

Feeby holds the iron box. She tucks it into her chest, and curls over it.

February knew Kamdyn well, went to school with him her whole life, and misses him, she says. Rose knows all too well what the tremor in her voice means—although Feeby lowers her eyes to hide her tears, the tip of her nose is red.

Rose doesn't want to see February sad, so she places a hand on her wrist. She wonders now if her touch is cold. Probably, yes.

And yet, Feeby never once flinched from her.

"Are you mad at me?" February asks, sniffing quietly. In the morning sun, her emerald eyes mirror the greenery below them.

"Feebs…" Rose treads carefully, truthfully, so she doesn't lose her temper again. "Yes. I was—at first. I think I understand all that you did. But then, does that mean there's no book? Why would you trick me?"

"I didn't mean to trick you—we think that the first Peacocks hid the book, and no one has found it since.

My dad and Grammy believed the clues were supposed to help lost souls realize they'd died and that it was time to move on. Sometimes the Manor changes the details of the riddles, but the answers are always the same. Grammy was my great-great-grandmother. She lingered for a few generations after she died, and taught Dad the secret abilities of my family: how to help Lost Spirits. Dad's own parents died early—one of illness, the other killed by Scraythe—but the Peacocks all have this power. Grammy departed when I was little, but I remember her. In the end, she felt sad most of the time after being in the mortal realm too long."

"What about the notes on the Scraythe? They referred to The BoLS. The book has to be somewhere."

"You found the lost notes about how to destroy Scraythe! None of us ever knew that. It looked like someone tried to get rid of the lost information, which is a mystery in itself. It could be from The BoLS, or else someone figured it out later."

"It's good you know now. Safety first," Rose says.

"Why did you want The BoLS so badly?"

"I guess if I proved my sister was real, then I hadn't really died. Or, if ghosts existed, then I existed."

"Ah."

"Why didn't you just tell me?"

"No one accepts it at first, and with all the supernatural abilities a spirit can wield, an angry and confused disembodied soul is dangerous, to themselves and other people, even their own family."

"Right." Guilt weighs heavy on her chest. She's destroyed part of the Manor.

"We're supposed to reveal information slowly. You were very resistant, though. I think whenever you were scared, you had flashbacks of drowning. You refused to remember what happened, even when you sank in the pool. You're stubborn as heck, Rose!"

"Ha. I am. That's always been true."

"I've never done this on my own. My dad was the one helping lost souls who came to the Manor. He hoped I'd be able to leave, do something else with my life."

"Wait, what about Robbie? He's not a spirit...is he?"

"No, he's not. He must have thought I was nuts at first. I explained a little of what I do after we started dating. He accepts me for who I am—like I told you. He doesn't see or hear ghosts, but I tell him what you or Kam are saying."

"But pixie cakes. I eat." Rose points dumbly at her mouth.

"You've made food and objects disappear. I think you've spirited them away; you know, transported them to another realm," February explains. "Interesting fact: Spirits are repelled by salt, so maybe that's why you like desserts so much."

"Oh, hah." Rose knows that—she's done the research. "Why...why do Kam's eyes seem to glow sometimes?"

"Rose, yours glow too. Kind of purplish. Oops, we better hop off here or we'll go around again," she says as they approach the top.

Feeby swings her legs off and lands lightly. Rose plunks onto the ground but realizes she could have floated. She glances behind her: there is only one set of footprints on the grass—where February landed and walked on.

They make their way over to the far side of the run, down the back of the peak. February stops over the ledge and kneels, sitting back on her heels. Rose hovers over her, frowning down over the steep, rocky edge.

"Will Kamdyn just disappear after you scatter his ashes?" Rose asks, afraid she won't have another chance to see him again.

"No, he'll have to go Beyond through the door in the Manor. For Lost Spirits," Feeby explains.

February sets the iron chest on her lap, extracts a key from her dress pocket, and carefully turns it in the keyhole. The latch clicks; she lifts the lid. The wind is blowing from behind them, and her short hair flies into her mouth, but she doesn't bother fixing it. She focuses on the chest, slowly tipping it forward.

The ashes cascade over the precarious ledge.

Thousands of feet down.

It is a lifetime to the bottom, a lifetime since Rose journeyed up the mountain, for all that has happened.

February's eyes brim with tears, but her voice remains steady.

"May you find freedom in your choices and peace in your next life, Kam." February continues to pour the contents of the chest into the deep expanse of rock below them.

Kamdyn's ashes sift out and over the mountainside, flurrying in a draft of wind before soaring boundlessly upward. As if he were racing downhill on his skis before launching into a jump.

As he wished.

Rose's heart aches, and her vision blurs. For a brief moment, she morbidly wonders where her own body is, or its ashes, but the idea sickens and confuses and rips her to pieces, so she chokes it back down to the place where nightmares go during waking hours.

Kamdyn, she calls to him softly.

She doesn't know what else to say.

When the chest is completely empty, February rises off her knees, spins on her heel, and lobs the chest over the edge of the precipice. The chest is a cage, a prison that would've held Kamdyn captive, until his soul deteriorated into a hideous and broken creature for eternity. It warrants no respect.

The old iron box bounces off the side of the jagged granite with a *clank* before splitting apart. The metal fragments disappear deep into the crevasse, lost in the abyss of the mountain forever.

Kamdyn is free.

Chapter 56

Not a Third Wheel Anymore

"Were you afraid of getting caught?" Rose asks on the lift back down the mountain.

"Yes. But I had to help Kamdyn—that was all that mattered," February replies, calm and collected.

"I'm sorry I scared you when I was mad," Rose blurts out.

"Oh, Rose, I wasn't scared of you. I could feel your pain, and I don't like feeling helpless—unable to help you or your family."

"I destroyed part of the Manor."

"You wouldn't be the first. My mom and I will fix it, along with Mr. Charbon's contractors."

Ashamed, Rose doesn't know what else to say. She's caused a lot of trouble.

February reads her mind. "You're worth the trouble, remember, Rose? You're worth it."

Rose bites her lip, feeling her face flush. If she says anything, she will cry, so instead, she scrunches her face and closes her eyes.

"Friends create situations to help each other to grow in ways we can't do alone," Feeby says. "Another wise Grammy quote."

"Very true. You've shown me," Rose says gratefully, "that friendships change everything."

Kamdyn greets them at the bottom of the hill.

"We did it!" February hugs him.

He grins, the silver in his eyes sparking.

He turns to Rose. "I can't believe this worked. We make an incredible team, don't we? Thank you for your help, both of you. It means the world to me." He kisses her forehead.

She pulls back. "Well, you're free now. To...to...depart." Rose stumbles over the last part, not wanting to acknowledge the future. "We scattered your ashes and tossed the chest over the steepest side of the mountain." Though her insides twist, her voice emerges flat and listless.

Kamdyn senses her confusion and tightens his grip on her hand.

"I know you don't want to leave, but I hope you change your mind. Come with me. You know I have a thing for not leaving anyone behind. Club Never Forgotten. Did I ever tell you about that? It's ultimately your choice, though; you've given me back the ability to choose. It's the most important thing anyone's ever done for me. I'll forever be grateful."

He leans into Rose, reaching both hands to her face. He almost touches her—

February cuts in. "I better get to the shuttle stop. Meet you guys there—I can see I'm just a third wheel here." Giving Rose a devious wink, she scurries off the Charbon property.

Rose smiles and turns her attention back to Kamdyn.

"Quest successful," Kamdyn says, his outstretched hand offering to shake hers.

"Pleasure to quest with you," Rose replies, clasping

his hand firmly.

He yanks her toward him. As she crashes into his torso, he releases his hold on her hand and captures her in his arms in a tight embrace.

Her face softens, and she presses her nose into his neck. Closing her eyes momentarily, she inhales his sweet lavender scent, trying to commit it to memory—for she knows, deep down, this will be one of the last times they'll be together. She wants to savor the closeness, the comfort—of being wanted, of belonging to the moment, of Kamdyn.

He angles his head toward her, his cold nose nuzzling her cheek, his soft lips finding hers once again—possessive and desiring—filling her with molten sorrow and thrilling delirium all at once.

Chapter 57

Goodbye, Kamdyn

Rose retrieves the portrait key from the drawer of the hallway table where she left it, and the three of them turn right, heading upstairs. They halt, standing shoulder to shoulder partway down the West Hall of Peacock Manor.

The moment February inserts the key, the doorframe glows soft as pearly moonlight, and the door blows open with the same phantom wind that slammed the door on Rose before. Beyond the door, there is no black stone wall, no darkness—only a golden luster, luminous and dense. If fog were made of gold dust instead of water droplets…

Kamdyn turns to February first.

"Thank you, Feebs, for everything, for being you. I couldn't have done it without you. You saved me from becoming a Lost Spirit forever. You truly saved me."

"You're welcome. I'll miss you, Kam. Robbie misses you."

"You gave Robbie my message?"

"I did—he knows. He says to tell you that he'll never stop missing his best friend. You grew up together, and he's very sad he won't get to share the rest of his life with you. *Never Forgotten*, he said to tell you, too."

"Ah, never forgotten, yup," Kamdyn says grimly, then turns to Rose and scoops up her limp hand in his.

She can't meet his eyes; eyes in a striking face she'll never see again.

He presses a small paperback into her palm. She thumbs the dry pages and knows exactly which book he is leaving behind. The one he'd read to her in the Vale. His favorite.

Her heart cracks, and she is forced to shut her eyes, mortally wounded by the finality of his gesture.

"Thank you for helping me. Like I said before, I wish I'd met you sooner. February said you were the girl of my dreams. As usual, she wasn't wrong. You're what my soul has always wanted. Don't look so heartbroken. I wrote a song for you, you know, over the last few days."

She blinks up at him. "What song?"

"Don't laugh. It's called, 'And Into the Darkness, I Belong.'"

"What's it about?" Rose asks. She can't keep the tears from falling. Her nose drips sorrowfully.

"It's about you, of course."

"How's it go?"

"You'll have to find me and find out in the next life."

Even here, at the edge of the end, his devious grin thaws the icy agony in her chest.

He brushes her cheek, tipping her face to meet his, and wipes away her tears. Tears that remind her that she hasn't cried in the longest while, and that she's even found moments of joy. Long moments. The bitter does make the sweet sweeter, as he promised.

"You are my *second sunset*, Rose. You are more

than I could ever ask for."

She gathers up what is left of the shattered fragments of her heart and fixes on his glistening eyes one last time.

He's crying too.

He leans inward and kisses her brow, lingering his lips there, before clasping her head in his hands. He breathes his final words onto her, *"Find me sooner next time, Rose, and we can go on a quest for an Eternal Sunset. I absolutely love you."*

"I will. I love you." Tears spill off their faces as if they stood in a rainstorm.

He grasps her chin and sneaks in one last kiss before turning away.

As he faces the doorway, his fists ball up, but then—he strides through surely and disappears into ancient starlight.

Rose cranes forward, wanting to see what is Beyond—she hears phantom tides lapping distant shores. She is mesmerized by the rhythm, the musical pulse of the energy on the other side of the door. The Beyond is alive. But she doesn't trust it, so she retreats, stepping back into the dark hall.

February grasps her hand, pulling her out of the way, and closes the door softly with a subdued *thump*— the shutting of a book when the story has ended.

The celestial glow of the doorframe surges once more, before fading into the drabness of aged wood—a tired, old bedroom door again.

The starlight is gone.

Kamdyn is gone.

Chapter 58

Beyond

The next morning, a new small brass-framed portrait appears without warning on the sitting room wall, among the hundreds of others already lining the onyx wallpaper. Rose instantly recognizes the familiar face as she passes by on her way to the kitchen.

A stab of recognition pierces her gut as she stares with bewilderment at the somber gray-eyed boy in the portrait.

She's horrified at the sudden alarming realization that *all* the portraits are of those who've passed through the Manor's westward door. She shudders violently as she bolts from the sitting room.

Will *she* end up there?

No frickin' way.

Her throat tightens. A wave of repulsion crashes through her as she runs back upstairs and retreats into bed.

Chapter 59

Peacock Manor
Day 146,643

It is true. Every portrait is of a soul who has passed through The Door. Is it strange that I remember The Door before the Manor was built? Did I come through it?

When someone passes through, I feel heavier.

I slumber a lot these days. I have weakened and am exhausted most of the time. After gifting my knowledge to February, there's not much left to do. Quite like humans, I suppose, I've passed on what I've learned in my lifetime of lifetimes to someone younger, before dying. I am not human, though sometimes wish I were, if only to experience love and friendship and frosted cakes.

The joy I see from all three things seems worth experiencing.

Chapter 60

What's Next, Rose

"Rose, I'm here if you have any questions. We can talk, hug, or cry," February says.

"I'm not going. I'm staying."

February lays her hand on Rose's, covering it with her palm as if scooping up a fallen baby bird to warm.

"The Beyond is where you're supposed to go. You have a choice. Kamdyn didn't have a choice until you helped him. He wasn't scared."

"I don't want to go. Even *you* have no idea what it is. It was a vacuum of nothingness. I saw it. I don't want to be sucked into nothing."

"No one ever knows what comes next," Feeby says gently.

"The first time I opened the door—how come I saw darkness the first time, then a brick wall?"

"It might have reflected what you were feeling or what you are. Sounds like you might have glimpsed a bit of the Void element, from that book you read about elemental forms."

"Oh."

"The door's easier to open at certain times of day, like dawn and dusk. Otherwise, it likes to slam shut. When you're ready, it will provide the way. I won't force you to depart. I'm only here as your friend. A guide. I've never done this on my own before. I'm learning as I go."

"Good. You can guide someone else through."

"My grammy said there are three things a soul can do after your body dies. You can linger as a ghost, for a while. You can go Beyond, peacefully. You can turn into something wicked, indefinitely. Rose, you've seen the Scraythe. That's what you'll become. Your soul can't remain uncorrupted in the mortal realm without a body to inhabit," February explains.

Rose doesn't respond.

February goes on. "Eventually, you will feel so empty that you will have to tear at other souls to feed your loneliness. You sensed their desperation. You were feeling hollow and sad already, before you arrived at the Manor, right?"

"But you helped me, and I wasn't sad anymore."

"Rose, you'll be angry, and try to hurt your parents out of resentment. If you haunt and torture them long enough, they will end up like my dad. Even though you can't take their souls because they aren't dead, you can still hurt the ones you love."

Oh.

"When you eventually become a Scraythe, you'll peck and tear out Meat Bones' soul first, because it's easiest, because he trusts you." Her lips tremble as she speaks these harrowing words.

Ah. Shoot. What the hell? Rose winces. That one cuts bone deep.

"No one is in danger now. I'm not hurting anyone. I don't want to talk about this anymore," Rose says, taking her hand back. Is it possible to resist becoming a Scraythe? How far can willpower get you? She looks

331

away to disguise her alarm, down to Meat Bones lying on his belly by the doorway with his head between his paws.

He mopes a lot these days, ever since he watched Kamdyn enter the door to The Beyond. Every so often, Rose finds him sniffing around the door, checking. Rose wonders if he mourns Kamdyn, but February says he is ready to go—like Kamdyn was—and he's drawn by the pull of The Beyond now that he's seen it.

Her mind teeters wildly. She wrestles and resists and shoves back against the darkness closing in on the edges of her vision.

Keep it together, she tells herself. There's only one more week at the Manor before vacation is over. They aren't staying for all of August. She'll wait it out and return home safely with Meat Bones.

He will go anywhere with her. He understands the meaning of loyalty.

Chapter 61

Peacock Manor
Day 146,650

I think it's also my time to say goodbye. When I said there is always one who does not return at the end of the summer, I did not anticipate that it would be *me*. I thought my fate was set in stone. But I've figured out how to change it.

I've wondered if I can possess someone, as some of the spirits who come through my hallways do. But what I aim to do is more accurately a reverse-possession—I want to give all my thoughts and abilities to February. I'm afraid this will take all my remaining spirit and strength. But she is the right one, and it is the right time. I will have made a difference. I need to figure out how to do this, but I think it means I will no longer exist as the spirit of the Manor, or as anything at all.

I will cease to exist.

Chapter 62

The BoLS

Rose and February recline side by side in the sitting room, reading, while a few of Mr. Charbon's workmen repair the staircase and the walls Rose destroyed. She faces away from them, feeling guilty, even though she now knows they can't see her.

"All these people went through the door?" she asks, eyeing Kamdyn's small portrait.

"I think so. The portraits appear on their own. When I was little, the sitting room used to fascinate and frighten me at the same time. There's a different energy in here, you know?" February says.

"So the Manor is kinda magical?"

"More like, the Manor has a spirit, a soul, but I didn't know until this summer when it revealed itself to me. I always felt something here—that it was more than a house. It used all its powers to save us. I'm not sure where it is anymore."

"It's gone?"

"I can't sense it now; it's faded away," February says with an indecipherable look.

"Oh shoot, that's sad."

"It'd been around for a very long time, it told me."

"But it didn't know where *The Book of Lost Spirits* was either?" Rose presses.

"Nope. The book is lost for good, apparently."

Chapter 63

Sister

Over the next week, February continues to come over to keep Rose company. They are still best of friends, she says lovingly. And that she will miss Rose terribly when she returns home.

At the end of the week, she crushes Rose with a hug.

"I have exciting news. Your parents told me. They wanted you to know that they're having a baby! Congratulations, you're going to be a big sister!"

"Whoa. Sister, huh." *My parents, me, and a brother or sister.*

Sister. Guilt and regret over her own lies surge in Rose's chest, and she feels as if she might explode and collapse at the same time.

Sister. She's been searching for her sister this whole time to distract herself from pain and loneliness, instead of facing the truth. Now, she asks herself—what kind of big sister can she be? One who can help her sibling through the pain and loneliness of this world, or one who will only cause more of it?

Maybe she'll haunt the room and flicker the lights and perform pathetic water tricks for the baby. That's not a sibling anyone wants, is it? That isn't who she wants to be.

How can a brand-new soul start life haunted by a dead sister?

"What are you thinking?" February asks, her brows knitted together.

She barely hears Feeby. The new baby will get all the attention. Jealousy overwhelms her. She doesn't like her feelings. What if all these revolting feelings turn her into a hungry, resentful Scraythe?

If she accidentally hurts the baby—if anger overtakes her again, and if the walls fall like they did the other night—and she goes after her parents and Meat Bones?

She'll never forgive herself.

Not like she'd even be able to forgive herself, as a Scraythe.

Rose doesn't realize she is sobbing—convulsing—until February wraps her shaking body into a tight embrace.

She doesn't belong in this family anymore.

The new baby belongs.

She would be on the outside looking in, with only loneliness—the most cruel and unforgiving of companions—at her side, for eternity.

Chapter 64

Obsidian and Opaline

Rose clings onto February's hand as they face Rose's parents in the sitting room.

Mom clings to Dad's arm, and Dad appears older than she has ever seen him. She's never noticed the white hairs at the peaks of his forehead before.

"Can you tell Rose we love her?" he asks, his voice breaking.

"She's right here next to me. You can talk to her yourself, and I'll relay her reply," February explains.

"Is she really here?" Mom asks in a low voice. Her eyes shift around, not knowing where to look.

"Dearest, you feel her presence, right?" Dad says. Good ole Dad—he always believed in her.

"Yes. I do. I always did," Mom says.

"We love you, Rose. We miss you and wish we could have helped you sooner," Dad says.

"Mom, Dad, I love you too. I'm so sorry I scared you, Mom. I really am. I understand now. Dad, I hope you finish your book."

"I'm writing it about you, Rose. Your story, your life, your spirit."

"Writing…about me?" *I'm the ghost in his story?*

"Yes, Ambrose Green needs her story told—your life won't be forgotten. It will be written down, forever.

We'll send a copy to keep here at Peacock Manor's library."

"Rose, we wanted to tell you before you left—you're going to have a brother. We found out today that the baby is a boy."

"Wow, that's exciting, Mom," Rose replies, hot tears pouring down her cheeks. She's genuinely happy for her parents but also heart-wrenchingly sad that she will not have a chance to get to know her brother.

"Are you okay with that?" Dad asks.

"Of course." Rose sniffles.

"We wanted you to…if you want…will you name your brother for us?" Mom asks.

Rose swallows back the tightness in her throat. "I have the best name ever," she croaks.

She's been thinking of names ever since she found out she was going to be a big sister.

"Do I know what you're going to say?" February asks with a sly grin.

Rose shakes her head no.

"Valerian," she says. "Vale for short."

"Ah! That's perfect." February turns back to Rose's parents, relaying her answer.

"Vale Green?" her dad says aloud, testing it. He smiles, looking like the dad Rose remembers.

"I adore it." Her mother sobs, clutching the gold cross around her neck. She clasped it on the day Rose died and hasn't taken it off since.

It dawns on Rose that no amount of time will ever completely heal her parents. She sees it in their weary eyes and hears it in the tremble of their voices that echo their fractured hearts.

She wishes for one more hug.

But it's time to go.

They've already had a bit of extra time together, and after all, this is why they came to Peacock Manor.

Everyone is ready now.

"I love you, Mom and Dad. I'll be okay. Tell Vale about me. Leave out the part where I was sad and lost for a while. Tell him I was happy, in the end. Goodbye."

"We will always love you, Rose. Forever and beyond."

Chapter 65

And, In Parting from You Now

Rose and February tread up the West Wing stairway together for one last time, arms looped, leaving her teary parents at the bottom of the stairs.

February inserts the key into the door of The Beyond.

"Wait," Rose says. She grasps Kamdyn's book in one hand.

"What is it?"

"What's the deal with your pocketwatch? I'm not stalling. I need to know."

February lifts the gold watch off her chest. "It's my dad's, like I said, but it's been in the Peacock family forever. It's sensitive to spirit activity nearby. I believe it's been reflecting your state of mind. When we first met, you said ghosts are energy forms, and I think you might have a magnetic field affecting the mechanics. You know mechanical watches have kinetic energy, potential energy, all that."

Rose thumps her friend on the back. "Ah, okay. You're a science nerd too. Cool."

"I think it slows when you're calm, like when you were solving the first riddle, and speeds up when you're distressed. Look—it's telling the correct time now."

"Huh. Interesting. I guess I'm ready then."

The familiar doorframe glows and creaks open for February as she twists the key the rest of the way.

Glittering light and warmth spill out the door. Rose can't see into the brightness, but she feels its welcome.

The Beyond beckons her. It tugs at the core of her, and she wants to step into the glowing frame, no longer afraid. February is right: it's where she belongs. It scares Rose more to stay, realizing what she knows now, and she finally understands Kamdyn's quiet dignity.

Meat Bones squirms and wriggles, the same way he does when they are about to take a walk outside. He turns his nose over his shoulder at Rose, asking when they are going. His paws tread up and down in place. Rose kneels to give him a pat.

"Just a minute, sir, I have one more goodbye."

"I hope neither of you ever feel lonely or scared again. You're a very good boy, Meat Bones," February says, her sea-green eyes brimming with tears. "You're the best kind of friend."

Tears cascade down Rose's face, dripping down her chin, but she doesn't bother wiping them away. "*You* were the best kind of…You said we were best friends."

February weeps too. "I meant it. Look at me. We *are* best friends. You helped me—I was lonely too. And you got me and Robbie together after all these years. I'll miss you, Rose. Look how easily you found happiness in so many ways this summer."

"That was only because of you."

"There'll always be those who accept you as you are and love you exactly as you are. I think we learned that together, right? Sometimes it takes time to find the right people, but I'm glad we could be friends, even for just one summer. I love you. I'll never forget you."

Rose gives Feeby's hand one last squeeze before letting go and squares her shoulders toward the door.

"I'm ready. Meat Bones, buddy, let's go." His ears lift, and his tongue flaps out. He lifts his backside and bounds in. "I love you, too, Feebs. And, oh…thank you. For everything."

She focuses her sights ahead—forward—one foot slow and deliberate, then the other, but pauses, straightening up in the doorframe. She doesn't look back.

There is nothing left behind her anymore. She's said her last goodbyes.

She lifts her knees, pacing in place, mustering up her courage.

She ponders her last thoughts in the mortal realm.

If Rose Green can belong

to friends,

to love,

to herself,

all in one summer—

the possibilities are infinite.

She shuts her eyes to stop her head from spinning like a tilting planet and strides through the radiant doorway. She sifts through the thick fog of starlight and moon shadow—its cool luminous rays enveloping her, embracing her—and leaves behind all she's ever known.

Chapter 66

I Stand Amid the Roar of a Surf-Tormented Shore

Every step effervescent, every breath unnecessary. She and Meat Bones glow under the luminosity of a full moon. She glances at her hands. The lustrous sand glistens beneath them, glinting moonlight through her fingers. Part of her is that moonlight.

The effect of The Beyond is immediate. Her mind is free of worry and—for the first time in a year—her heart is free of pain. She feels buoyant.

They hike for a time along the midnight beach of an unknown coast flanked by foamy waves on her left. On her right, a row of gnarled cypress trees, like knobby old witches with wild hair, beckon them further down the beach.

The night sky shrouds their souls in a mantle of stars and galaxies. Meat Bones is usually a happy fellow, but Rose can sense the difference in him, in the air, in herself.

I love you, Meat Bones. Neither of us has to be alone ever again. They are complete and happy.

He howls with delight, as if celebrating a return home, unable to contain the joy within his small body. He slows to snuffle the air, detecting a scent from behind the trees.

A tall, dark-haired figure shifts elegantly in the

shadows, emerging from the ancient cypress trees.

"Hey, big fierce wolfie," a smooth, familiar voice calls out.

Kamdyn folds his long legs under him to kneel in the sand, greeting a pouncing Meat Bones with a full-body scratch. He steals a glance up at Rose with that solemn, penetrating glare. "What took you so long?" he asks, a half-smile curling his lips.

"Well, I was curious about the song you wrote about me, but at the same time, I wasn't sure if I could take hearing you sing again."

He tosses his head back and roars with laughter.

She's never heard him laugh like this. It occurs to her that his joy was always guarded before, suppressed by his knowledge that he had neither the choice nor the freedom to depart.

He scoops up Meat Bones for a cuddle, then rises to pace alongside her, clasping her hand in his as if it were the most natural thing in the world.

Side by side, their steps join together until, all at once, their bodies ignite into timeless starlight, burning swiftly like dried leaves ablaze in a forest of fire. A wisp of mild ocean breeze lifts the scanty bits of glittery stardust left of them
> up
> and up
> and up;
> spinning into the air,
> swirling them through the trees,
> over the moonlit waves,
> and silently, peacefully...
> Beyond.

Chapter 67

The Manor and February Peacock

February Peacock braces her hand on the black wall of the sitting room, her cheeks itching from her dried tears. She rubs her face and takes a ragged inhale.

She waits silently, wondering where Rose's portrait will appear.

On cue, a small portrait presses through the inky wall—high up, next to Kamdyn's.

It starts as a shadow before materializing into a serious and intelligent face with a natural frown, violet eyes and milk-tea-colored hair—set into a sturdy brass frame.

But the portrait hangs off-center.

"Well, we can't have that. Rose would never be able to rest knowing her painting was crooked," February says to herself.

She balances on a turquoise chaise to adjust the portrait.

It hangs loosely off its mount and detaches itself from the wall with the smallest press of a fingertip.

"Oh no! Now I know how Rose feels." February catches the falling painting with both hands but slips and tumbles backwards onto the chaise. Her fingers puncture the thin paper backing of the frame. "Oh! Shoot. Oops."

She flips it around to assess the damage, but notices symbols and words through the torn brown paper. As she peels away the backing, she discovers an old page of a book stuck behind it, inside the painting.

Her hand trembles as she stares in disbelief at the delicate, discolored page.

It can't be.

Based on the wording of the final paragraph and "The End" printed at the bottom, it is the final page of an old book, frayed on the left side where it was torn out of its binding.

Out of nowhere, the walls of the sitting room ripple and quake, and all the paintings slant, hanging askew.

She gasps, steadying herself against the chaise, as the letters D-E-A-D appear on the ceiling above her, written in smoky white wisps.

Shaking, February unhooks Kamdyn's painting and pulls away the backing. She discovers another page.

Painting by painting, page by page, February assembles the long-lost and hidden *Book of Lost Spirits*—all these years, concealed behind The Dead.

The riddle had been telling the truth, trying to point the way, this whole time.

She shields the frail pages from her tears—different from the ones she's wept often this summer—and whispers, "Thank you for your help, Peacock Manor. Thank you for trusting me. I'm grateful that you chose me."

Chapter 68

Peacock Manor
Day 146,660, or perhaps I shall call it Day 1

I didn't cease to exist!

February suspects I am the original spirit of The BoLS, but when the Peacocks built the Manor, they spirited away the pages for fear that the Scraythe might come to possess the book and control The Beyond. Since I had been torn apart, I possessed the Manor instead. Now, I am back in my true form. I am *The Book of Lost Spirits*. February takes me everywhere with her, and I no longer feel lonely and sad. She talks to me, and I can communicate with her through the pages anytime I want.

I am happy.

Epilogue

I Miss You, Robbie says. *This Blink 182 song came out the year I was born.* He spins the knob and the music grows louder, as his red car winds ever faster around the twisting mountain roads. The steep shadows of the twilight hour are violet and dusty rose.

Vintage, February replies. She sways to the melody. Her hair flies up and whips around her face. She stretches one arm up and out, over the windshield, grasping for the full moon.

Her face glows, and her jade eyes glisten in both relief and sorrow.

She's left her pocketwatch at home because she isn't working. She loves the warmth of the August night air swirling around her in Robbie's convertible and imagines this must be how hawks feel when they surf the thermal winds across the mountaintops every day. Free and wild.

Feebs, let's go to a beachy island next summer. Golden sand, turquoise water. We can learn to surf. I've never been to the ocean.

You know I'll have to work every summer. My family doesn't have the money. My dad can't do this anymore, and the Manor needs me. Other Lost Spirits need me. Peacock Manor can't ever be sold and has to stay in the family—so that we can continue to guide others.

She pats the book in her lap. The brittle pages have been stitched together into a binding.

What if you auctioned off more of the stuff you and Rose found in the attic? Some of it was valuable, right? Those coral candlesticks and the antique hourglass went for a lot. I'll help you rummage up there. Maybe that creepy doll collection can find a new home.

Maybe. She smiles to herself.

Feebs, do you think they're happy and at peace now? Kamdyn? Rose?

I believe it. I have to. The Book says they are. They belong to the stars now.

God, I miss Kam so much—more than I can stand. I wish I could've hugged him one last time. Remember how he used to make up songs about everything we were doing? He knows how much I care for him, right? You told him? Never forgotten? All that?

Yep, he knows. Never Forgotten, he said back. Forever. He was with you more than you know. He rode along on your deliveries sometimes. That first time you dropped off groceries for the Greens, Kam was in the passenger seat. Rose saw him.

I knew it! Things got moved around in my car. Mostly, he organized it—but once, I took off my shirt because it was too hot, and he must've hidden it. I had to make my next delivery shirtless. That jerk, ha-ha! I miss his idiotic pranks.

Yep, yep, that totally sounds like Kam. He said to tell you he haunted you as much as he could. Hah. He was there for a bit when you were swimming, and of course, Vale Green.

That was the best day anyone could ask for. We should go again, sunshine. And Rose…she went willingly in the end? Was she okay? I wish I could've seen or talked to her.

She was perfect. I'm so proud of her.

You were brave to go after her in the woods—it was so dangerous for you. Do you miss them?

Of course. I will, always. I'll carry memories of them with me forever. Rose's intellect and love of animals. Kamdyn's wit and directness. I became so close to Rose in such a short time, it broke my heart, Robbs—when I had to say goodbye. I didn't know this would be so hard.

I'm sorry. You do amazing work. I don't understand how you do it, but you're incredible, you know. I love you, Feebs. You're my everything.

He searches across the middle console for her small hand and twines his fingers in hers while he steers effortlessly. The curves are all too familiar—he knows these roads by heart. He was born on the mountain and will live on the mountain for the rest of his mortal life. His heart, however, has left his body and resides outside of him now, in February's hands.

I love you, too, Robbie.

When's the next one arrive?

Winter semester, my mom said.

She's shared all her secrets with him, and her world feels less lonely.

The truth has that effect.

She always knew what her fate would be as a Peacock, but now that she has The Book, she no longer carries the burden of that fate by herself. *There are always those who help you belong—you just have to find them and let them*, she reminds herself of her great-great grandmother's words. She clasps The Book

351

tighter into her chest. She will never have to go it alone again.

A word about the author…

When Yun isn't wishing she lived in a benevolently haunted mansion, she's working on her next book, napping, riding horses, reading, and eating snacks. It's always snack o'clock at her house in California, which she shares with her dogs, a talking parrot, and husband. She has degrees in International Relations and Economics from Stanford University, and has also lived in Texas, Taiwan, and Japan.

www.yunjohnson.com

Thank you for purchasing
this publication of The Wild Rose Press, Inc.
For questions or more information
contact us at
info@thewildrosepress.com.
The Wild Rose Press, Inc.
www.thewildrosepress.com